Mind Cloud

Mathew Bridle

The Reset

They wanted the war. *They* orchestrated the whole thing, down to the dust and the rain. The Unification War, the one to unite all nations and people under one authority.

Ninety years on, we live our lives in the Cloud, a world controlled by technology, trinkets, and toys. Do you remember all those conspiracies? Well, it turned out they were true.

Twitch

Quayside

Late '90, a dark day in the USA. Back again, collecting bodies and peering into dirty holes. A stack of three. I'm sure I've seen this one before: female, not too pretty, lips curve into a pout. I watch the rain wet them.

The weather is a furious deluge of grey needles. One glance to the heavens and I turn away from the sting in my eyes. That's when I spot him. Rickets, the bastard, has no respect for the dead, shoving his fingers in entry and exit wounds as though hooking meat in a slaughterhouse. He has his finger in the girl, scooping around in her eye socket.

'Rickets,' I keep a flat tone.

He replies, 'Twitch,' mimicking my palsy. 'What d'you reckon?' He stabs a finger at the girl, 'Hooker?'

'Don't think so.' I kneel beside the body, dragging it from the pile. Water pools around her in the soft mud.

Rickets insists, 'Hooker. Has that about her. Probably pissed off a client at a Halloween ball, got popped in the eye. May as well wrap her and send her to ReSyk.'

'She's mine. I'll decide when she goes for recycling and what she is or isn't.' I put myself between Rickets and the girl. 'Why don't you run along and fetch yourself some sparkle to shove up your nose.' He glares at me, thrusts his hands into his pockets. Kicks dirt over my shoes, then turns, taps the soles of the girl's boots with his foot and vanishes in the rain.

Datacorder in hand, I return my interest to the girl and set about the scene. 'Time is 19:20 on 1st

2

November '90. Victim is in her early twenties, blonde with a blue streak over the missing right eye. Whatever killed her, it wasn't a bullet to the head,' I say for the record.

I check her purple jacket for holes - nothing. Her shirt is clean too, well made, possibly tailored. Her skirt, above the knee, the kind I like, modest; still below seelevel. Then there are the boots, cowboy. Black toes on white shoes, embossed lace effect and purple side panels with white love-hearts. A real piece of craftsmanship. But no wounds, other than the eye. I cradle her chin in my hand and roll her head from side to side. She has a full set of white teeth. No hooker. I slip a finger under her tongue. 'What have we here?' A silver ring, dense, warm. Close up it appears to a be a stack of thinner rings, elegant.

I scan the area. The uniformed cops are keeping their distance, playing by the book. It's only me in the yellow wash of light from the warehouse wall. I take all the necessary pictures and upload them to the Cloud. Don't trust anyone. Too many quick fingers in too many places.

The other two bodies are Bangers covered in tattoos and piercings. Odd thing though, two rival gangs but neither from town. Gonna need to travel to sort this out.

I fish out my car control and press a button. The lights of the pickup swing around the corner, illuminating the cops: one, two, three. The car moves along, squelching through holes of filth in the potted road. I let it pass, stopping it close enough to pull out the sled. I drag the first body over and dump it in the

3

back; the second thug goes right on top. The girl I'm careful not to mark. I lay her out with her arms at her sides and close her eyelids.

Base is a twenty-minute drive across town. The rain is terrible, will it never end?

Three Stiffs

It's gone 20:00 when I get back. The shift isn't over yet. One torn up corpse after another. Now, this. Two gangbangers and a pretty young thing. Three for the slabs. Me and the Doc will cut them up and see what went down.

With a grunt I lift the body from the tailgate, holding her close though she feels nothing. The rain bounces into my face from her leather jacket. Another ten steps and I'll be at the door. My arms are killing me; perhaps I should use that gym membership. One kick and the door crashes against its stop. I struggle through without knocking her head.

The doors at the rear lead to the mortuary, where I drop her on a gurney, slumping over her body. She has a peculiar perfume; is it oil and dirt? My arms are pinned beneath her. I stand with a groan and slip my arms free. My back still hurts from yesterday, nothing eases it. Will the days ever be easier? I think back to my first day on the job, out on the wagon with Joel carting stiffs around before the era of the private morgues.

Right on cue, the cold smell of death breathes into the room. 'I was just thinking of you, Joel.' Leaning back against the gurney I draw on my vape.

Joel waits with a foot in the door. 'You want a hand getting the Bangers in, Twitch?'

'You're an angel, Joel.' I duck under his arm and go back outside into the deluge. 'Tall one, mind.'

Joel tuts, 'I'm not so tall. You're vertically challenged, is all.' He strides past me to the pickup, and peers inside. I rub my arms, everything aches. 'You okay? Was she too much?' Joel pouts through his grey beard.

'Grab the arms.' Yanking the feet of a Banger I fall on my arse clutching a pair of boots. Joel points at me, his deep laughter parting the downpour. 'You gonna help me up, or just laugh?' I force myself to sit and hold out my hand.

Joel thinks a while before saying, 'Just laugh, okay?' His black skin shines wet in the streetlight, his striped woollen hat sponging up the rain.

I struggle to my feet, muttering curses. Joel stands at my side, chewing the roach of a spliff. Grabbing the body by the jeans, I lean back and pull.

Joel waves a hand. 'Why not use the sled?' he says, pointing to the board strapped to the inside of the pickup.

'Sled?' More cursing, I'm piss-wet through and hungry.

Joel shakes his head, 'I'll do it. You'll only fall on your ass again.' Chuckling to himself he slips out the sled and lays the thin board flat. I climb up and roll the first Banger onto it. Joel presses the button on the board, and the sled lifts a couple of inches from the floor. I jump from the tailboard, taking care not to tread on the deceased.

'Let's get this guy inside. The sooner we get done, the sooner we eat.' I walk ahead of the sled, its soft hum a quiet thought at the back of my mind. All the while, I'm thinking about the dead girl: she's familiar but from where? I shoulder the door and wait as Joel slips through, then let it snick shut behind us. We take the body through to the slabs and go back for the last one. All three guests are inside. Now the dirty work begins.

Joel grins at me, 'Who's first?' He waves the cutting saw over each body in turn. 'The Spartan? Think they're some kind of ancient warrior race. He's come a long way to end up at the quayside.'

'He'll do. Then the Wretch, those sick bastards deserve to get cut up, even when cold. The girl can wait.' I make my way over to the side door where the Slop Wagon is pitched out on Harvesters. 'I'm getting some eats, you dining?'

Joel pushes the girl into the fridge. 'Sure. I'll have one of those offensive Jamaicans, and something cold to wash it down.' His voice stops at the door.

The Slop Wagon, as always, has a queue. Standing in the rain reminds me of the wife's funeral. What a day. Thought I'd never experience weather like it again. This is as shite as then. I don't regret watching her die.

The queue moves forward. Across the litter-strewn street, two guys are huddled together under the remains of the bus shelter sharing a sausage. Will I get used to seeing guys kiss? I shudder and shuffle up.

'Reece?' Tex, always formal when working, calls over the heads of the couple in front. 'Anything I need to put on?'

'Jamaican and a spinach patty.' I shrug at the brute and his bitch who turn to eyeball me. 'What?'

The lump eyes me up and down. 'How come the likes of you,' he pokes me in the chest, 'get preferential?'

I inspect the tattoos on his neck and face. The cover jobs can't hide the old gang stamps. The hooker I know;

she's been in for failing to keep her shots up to date and trading without a licence. The brute steps back when I pull out my datacorder, hands all apologetic. 'Hope your tags are in order.' I circle my thumb around the print reader.

The brute steps aside with a mock bow. 'Hey, just a simple misunderstanding, officer.'

The hooker squawks, 'Twitch, init?', waggling a finger.

The brute growls and moves back in front of me. 'You know 'im?'

I read the tattoos on his arms while I wait for him to finish snarling at his squeeze. 'You done?' I lean in.

The girl's eyes widen, and a river runs down her leg that ain't from the rain. The brute spins around. The knife in his hand cuts through my coat, nicking my skin. The datacorder emits a shrill whistle as I press down on the scanner. The brute drops the blade and backs up. I raise my hand, sliding my thumb forward. He screams and falls to the floor clutching his head.

'So, serious shit,' I say, kneeling in the gutter. I lift his chin on the end of the datacorder. The small screen flickers green, yellow, red. 'Says here I should terminate. What says you, John?'

'Terminate!' The girl freaks. She's yelling something so high-pitched I'll need a dog to translate.

'Hey! HEY! You're safe. He's done. He'll not move till I release him.' I try to remember her name. 'Trish? You work here and The Strip, yeah?' She nods, her eyes don't leave my hand.

'Yeah, that's right.' Trish reaches out a hand, no defence against the datacorder. 'Put that away.' The finger wags again. Her hair is slick against her head. The whites of her eyes shine with life. Water pours from her translucent jacket; beneath are just bra and shorts. 'I can't go in. I can't go in.' She shakes her head in tight jerks.

The brute groans and I turn to him. Trish bolts, her bare legs flashing white in the headlights of a passing truck.

Tex has a big gun trained on the brute. Always good to have a friend at hand.

I check the datacorder; the light's green. 'Any last thoughts?' My words catch in my throat. My thumb is over the print scanner loosening the mind clamps.

The brute spits, 'Don't pretend to care. Yours is coming. Only you don't know it yet.' He grins as I press the sentencing button. Nothing can stop it now. 'How's your wife?' He tries to laugh, but the tags explode in his brain.

Does he mean Jane?

Tex has my order in his hand. 'You ready to eat now?' Two cold ones and a coffee to go wait in a cardboard tray. Behind him is the gun he keeps primed.

'There you go,' I say, tossing a twenty on the counter.

Tex grins back, 'You earned it. On the house.' He swats the money aside.

I take it with gratitude; my pockets are near empty, and the cashpoints are all bust round here. A ReSyk wagon is on its way for the brute; the reward will come in handy.

Back inside, Joel is up to his elbows in a Banger. There's a chair by the table where I sit and unwrap the patty, a glorious mash of meat and spinach dotted with cheese, healthy enough to justify the grease. The spiced steam from Joel's Jamaican nasty burns my throat. You'd have to be born with fire in your blood to enjoy that shit. I finish up and wash my hands before pulling on some gloves.

Joel pulls his off and takes up the Jamaican nasty. 'What about y'coat?' he spits through a mouthful of chilli and lettuce. I shrug off my trench coat and kick it across the room, leaving a dirty stripe across the smooth, grey floor.

'Whoever shot 'im was trained. Nice cluster of holes, nothing left of the heart. One through the forehead and one through the groin. Anything in the BLT?' I nod towards the tag analyser. 'Bloods, legals, tags?'

Joel puffs, 'Should be by now.' He peels himself from the chair and walks over to the analyser with the greatest of ease. He never really walks, kinda floats like a ghost. I'm not convinced he leaves footprints either. 'Hm, uh-hu, I see.' Joel sucks at his teeth, an odd sound he uses to convey so many things.

'Well?' I pull off my gloves and walk over to Joel. The BLT is lit up with more coloured lights than Christmas.

'Blood says drugs. Legals are missing. Tissues don't make sense.' Joel's brow furrows at the screen.

'Why? Show me.' I step closer.

Joel pokes the screen, flicking through columns of data like they mean anything. 'This, this right here. The age: 42.'

'That can't be right. Dude ain't a day over thirty.' I glance at the dead Banger; all muscle and a yard wide, same as the brute outside.

Joel mumbles, 'I can repeat it, but it ain't wrong. Not since the Kid hacked it.' He peers down at me with a tilt to his head. 'Y'know. 'Tis nuttin'.' He shakes the thought loose.

'What? Come on, Joel, spit it out, no matter how crazy.' I put a hand on his shoulder and shake him.

Joel punches the upload button, sending the data to the cloud. 'Been stories comin' outa ReSyk. Some say they gettin' bodies back to life. Making new people and shit.' The BLT resets, ready for another slice of the action.

I close my eyes, thinking back to when the trouble started. I remember now: Jane had talked about the possibility of 'fixing' life, a kind of living stasis. Her team at ReGen, scientists playing God, were close to a breakthrough. It was the first time we'd argued.

I shove the Spartan in the cooler. 'You think there's any truth in it?' I say. The next one is ready for the knife, naked, smothered in tramp-stamps as I like to call them, more ink than skin. 'Here, Joel, look at this.' I walk to the other side as the old Jamaican lumbers over. 'There.' I point at the armpit.

Joel lifts the arm. 'Odd.' He rotates the arm around and around until satisfied. 'It's a code.'

'Code?' I lean across the stiff, inhaling as I do: oil and dirt. I examine the dark lines in the creases of the armpit. Joel rotates the arm. I don't see it at first, then... The front door bell rings and all thoughts wash out of my head like water down a gutter; sullied. 'Nail it all down and seal 'em up. There's something fishy about the quayside.'

Joel sucks his teeth. 'Tch. Fishy. Quayside.' His disapproval follows me to the front door.

The bell rings twice more. Someone's out there under the canopy, trying to keep out of the rain. I knock on the glass. The face staring back at me is the one on the slab.

'Can I come in?' She shapes the words with those lips; her eyes are bright and pleading. The rain runs from her hair sticking the blue streak above her eye to her skin. 'Can I come in?' She watches my hand as I reach for the latch. 'Please.' Her eyes hold the light, illuminating the depth of her soul for a moment. Stepping aside, I let her in. The girl darts inside, leans back against the door, shuddering the weather to the floor.

'Who … who are you?' The words stutter from my mouth.

She smiles, folds her arms across her chest, catching a shiver. 'Any chance of a hot drink?' The blue streak falls down her face covering her eye.

'Sure. Through here.' I show her to a seat in my office. I sense her gaze on my back as I pour her a drink from the filter.

'Thanks,' she sighs, holding the mug to those lips, allowing the steam to warm her face. 'I'm Talise. Good coffee, by the way.'

'I'm Reece, most people call me Twitch.' I wish I could stop the twitch in my eye. 'What brings you to my door? We don't have many callers here.' Leaning against a filing cabinet, I pour myself a drink.

Talise cocks an eye at me. 'You're a detective, right? I think someone stole my identity. Not in a digital sense, but for real.'

'What makes you think that?' I watch Joel on a monitor behind her, inspecting the second Banger; rotating the arms, checking between the fingers and toes.

Talise is outa her chair. 'Are you listening?' She puts the empty mug on the side and tries to pass me. 'Just like the cops. No one cares about the living, no money in it.' She sniffs and wipes the tears on her sleeve. 'Is there?'

Challenge accepted. 'Wait.' Gesturing her to calm down, I steer her back to the seat. 'You've been to a station, which one?'

Talise sucks in air, 'Fourth. The desk cop told me to come back with proof.' She holds her hands out, supplicant, waiting for God to give her the answers.

'Did they take your details?' I pour another coffee and sit beside her. Our fingers touch as I give her the mug. She's warm.

Talise sinks inside herself. 'Nothing, not even my name. I was no more than five minutes. Never took a seat or anything.' Talise goes through the motions with the coffee, breathing in the aroma. 'Really good.'

'What makes you think someone's stolen–'

Talise cuts me dead. 'Using. They are using my identity. Friends and customers say that I've been here,' she waves a hand loose in the air, rattling the bangles on her wrist, 'and there. Places I don't know or have heard of.' Her eyes are wet when she looks at me. I want to collect the tear. Test it, you understand?

13

'When was the last time anyone saw you somewhere you weren't?' I move forward, a little.

Talise glances up from her coffee. 'I dunno. Two, maybe three days. Why?' Her eyes are so deep, so blue, a summer sky flecked with gold. 'Are you listening to me?'

'Two or three days,' I breathe out the words. 'I believe you.' She stares at me, blinking the tears from her eyes. 'We need to run a couple of tests.' I raise a calming hand. 'Hear me out. We've something… someone. Makes no sense. We need to confirm you are who you say you are. Scan your tags. I can't help you if you're not in order.'

Talise nods, 'Okay. I get it.' She shuffles in her seat. 'Do what you have to.'

The datacorder is light in my hand. I press the scanner; a pale green light glows along the top edge. 'Just your birth tag.' I raise an eyebrow. Talise smiles. 'You look younger.' She shrugs, buries her face in the coffee. I squeeze the sides of the device, popping it open like a book. A picture of her appears on the screen, together with all known information. Not much to read. The girl's clean.

Talise leans back in the chair. 'Do you have tags?' She lets her shoulders drop a little, cradling the warm mug to her chest.

'Not as such. Goes with the job.' I finish going through her file and close the datacorder before shoving it into a pocket. Joel walks in.

Talise raises her cup to Joel. 'Hi. Black, three sugars, with a cherry cupcake, right?'

Joel's smile consumes his face in a mass of discoloured teeth. 'From the Coffee Grinder, Talise. What you doing here?'

'You two know each other?' I sit back, wondering if he'll notice?

Talise takes a quick sip of coffee. 'I make a note of every customer's taste.' She says it like it's what everyone does.

'Busy place, a lot of bodies go through there.' I stress the word 'bodies'. Still nothing, is Joel blind to her?

Joel jerks a thumb over his shoulder. 'How can you be…? How'd…'

'Yep. You finally see it.' I draw on my vape and blow a huge smoke ring.

'See what?' Talise snaps. 'Hey!' The tap on my knee gets my attention; I like the physicality.

I draw on my vape again. 'The reason I believe you is in the chiller. You got a strong stomach?' Grabbing the arms of the chair, I push myself to my feet. Joel presses his hand to my chest.

'You can't be serious?' he growls, crow's feet dancing in the corner of his eyes.

'The girl,' one glance at her and I correct myself, 'Talise, believes someone is using her identity. I say we show her what we know.'

Joel relaxes his hand, letting me through. 'What do we know?'

'Come on. Both of you,' I smile, heading through the back.

Talise is quick; she's through the door before Joel can object. 'So, what do you guys do here?'

'It's a morgue. We cut things up and have a look inside.' The next door scans my palm and I step aside. 'Ladies first.'

Joel grabs my shoulder and throws me through the door. 'Some gentleman you are.'

'Smells funny in here.' Talise holds a tissue to her nose as she wanders around the room looking at the surgical tools. Two bodies remain under wraps; one's a gangbanger.

'Once all the perfume's washed off bodies don't smell.' My boots clump on the concrete.

'You guys eat in here?' Her disapproval of the discarded food wrappers and cans is a picture. 'Slobs.'

'We do our best, ma'am,' I say. Joel and I lean back against the slab where her double lays.

Talise pokes at the shrouded thug. 'Is there a body there?'

'It's why we brought you in here.' My wedding ring taps against the slab behind me.

Joel clears his throat. 'You been to a quack lately? Clinic for anything?' He waits for the confession, peels himself from the slab peering down at Talise.

Talise puts a finger to those lips. 'Not for some while. About three years back I went to Central. Usual thing; check if I'm clean.' The way she said 'clean' it has at least three e's in it.

'And how long has this identity thing been going on?' I stand and roll my shoulders to ease my back. I hate the sound of grinding bones.

Talise's face falls as she thinks. 'Couple of years, I guess. Not sure when it started.' She throws her arms in the air, voice cracking. 'I make coffee in a coffee shop!'

'Makes no sense to me either.' I figure there is no use delaying it, so I pull the covers back. 'Found her tonight. Down at the quayside together with a couple of tattooed thugs.' Talise stares, her face the image of a miserable frog. 'Anything you can tell us? Anything at all?'

Talise takes time to examine the body. 'Those boots, cowboy, really? No.' Talise leans over the body, her face less than a foot above the dead girl's. 'I... she... looks peaceful. She's got money. All this,' she picks at the clothes, feeling each item between her finger and thumb, 'pricey stuff. Uptown. The jacket is JoJo, boots could be Black Tim, the skirt is Kwans. She doesn't make coffee, that's for sure.' I'll give Talise credit: she isn't afraid of the dead, even when it's her. 'She lost an eye?' Her finger quivers over the closed lid.

'Yeah,' Joel drawls, his tone soft and low. 'No idea what killed her yet. The eye was taken after.'

'No tags either, not even a birth one.' I replace the shroud. 'Nothing more to find without a knife.'

'She's untraceable.' Talise places her hand on the dead girl's chest. 'Never thought I'd envy the dead. Nobody can tell where you are, or where you're going.'

'I get dat.' When Joel is tired, his accent seeps into his conversation like a dirty secret. 'I need t' rest. I'm going to use the back room. 'Kay?'

'Do what you need. I'll take the lady home then I'll pitch up in the office.' The yawn gets out, deflating me. 'Sorry,' I try to stifle it but lose the will. Talise echoes my actions, shrinking into her chest as her yawn grows and grows.

'I appreciate the offer,' she yawns again, this time with a half-stagger.

I never let her finish objecting. I am on my way out before she can gather herself. 'Least I can do, after all this shit.'

There is no argument, just a casual nod before she shuffles out the front door to the pickup, where she melts into the passenger seat like the chocolate on the dashboard. She pulls the seatbelt around herself with deliberate ease. She knows I'm watching her, clocking details, the chip in her front tooth.

Pulling the datacorder out, I plug it into the dash. 'Talise, home address.' The pickup rolls out on the road, rain stabbing through the beam of the headlights obscuring the world, washing the dirt from the streets. Talise has her head against the window, drawing pictures in her breath on the glass. People run from the shops to their cars: scurrying rats caught in the downpour, hair ruined, life unchanged. Talise would never be the same. How could you be after seeing yourself dead?

Rickets

The Mesa

'You'll love it.' My passenger shoves my hand away, rejecting the sparkle on my knuckle. 'Best stuff around.'

With a quick snort the sparkle is up my nose and I'm on my way to party town.

'The view up here is spectacular.' I swing off the main road up the winding track leading to the viewpoint. The weather is not as pissy as yesterday but it's always wet out. 'Ooh, I like this one, murderous beat.'

I grin at my passenger who don't say much on account of the tape over her mouth. 'Lose Yourself, what a tune. That kid, Eminem, he's a genius, I tell ya.'

I crank up the radio, thumping the steering wheel in time to the beat. Inspired, I edit the lyrics. 'One shot. Straight to the head. Get the taste in your mouth, I don't shoot lead. Count those minutes, you gonna drop – dead.'

My guest is restless, in truth terrified. Took me a while to bind her bloody wrists and ankles. I'm a busy man with plans: places to go and people to do. Being a cop ain't all laughter and drugs. I've some serious shit to do or the bitch won't be happy.

We bounce and slide along the old track. Tyres spitting out rocks and mud at the wildlife. 'You hear that?' With a hand to my ear, I lean across and look into those green eyes. The bruising sets them off; emeralds in twilight. 'You have great eyes, lady.' She pushes herself back against the door, hands pulled tight against her chest. There are tears and snot running everywhere, streaking her makeup. 'Face is a mess though.' I swirl a finger in her mush as I gun the engine and handbraketurn around the next bend. The tail end hangs out over the quarry somewhere below.

Brompton sprawls across the valley, a dirty stain on the landscape. Most of the city is built outa bedrock from the earthworks. 'Can't say I love the place. I'm not Twitch, but the future's bright for yours truly.'

I encourage my date to look out the window. I doubt she can see much until we take the last bend and she's on the other side. 'I cut a deal with ReGen: every time I close a case I take the bodies to ReSyk and... what was it they said they do? Repurpose them! That's where you'll end up, once they fish your ass out of the lake.' If I had a smidge of care her stare would kill me.

'What?' I shrug. The whole thing makes me laugh. 'You, sweetheart, are my new ride; this old wreck is about done. I've ridden this old heap more times than you've been taken up a back alley.'

Pulling up her legs she spins in the seat and kicks my arm. The car swerves into a wall of rock. The window shatters, smothering me in glass diamonds. A second kick gets me in the side. I stamp on the brakes and slam her into the dash. She crumples into the footwell. I catch a glimpse of what guys pay for up her skirt. She'd be worth a few of my dollars for the distraction.

'You fuckin' deserved it!' Smacking her legs aside, I move on before too much time is lost.

Wind cuts across the hilltop, dragging the clouds toward the sea beyond the city and out through the glimmering mouth of the river where container ships stack up for the docks. I guess the redevelopment needs more cash; I'll fish around and find out who's behind with their voluntary contributions. The rain's gentle up here, but the town is stabbed with grey knives. Hard to tell if anything is moving.

A lake has formed overnight to the east, threatening to swallow up the lower reaches where drugs pass through peep-holes. Sunlight fingers its way through the clouds, lighting up the cathedral as though it were some holy shrine. Bishop Timms has more vices than the hardware store across the street.

Pulling up my collar, I shove my door with my foot and squelch it down in the mud until the sole grinds against the rock beneath. I turn toward the muffled screams from the footwell and smile.

'Ain't no-one coming to rescue you, my little songbird,' I say. Pushing the door shut I walk around to her side

'Pitiful!' I reach in and grab a leg. 'You've got spirit, girl, I'll give you that.' Bitch is kicking out like a mule on heat. With a sharp tug, she's outa the car. A swarm of muffled screams and blasphemies dribble out from under the tape. 'Tut tut. You won't get anywhere in life with a potty mouth like that. Shocking.'

She's writhing around, making the task of dragging her ass to the cliff edge harder. Takes me a whole minute to haul her over to the best view of Brompton she'll ever see. Pity about the rain. The sky is a dull blue-grey with ink splatters. Fumbling in my pocket I pull out my knife and extend the blade. She's got to her feet, weaving like a boxer.

'Going somewhere?'

She looks over the edge: one slip and she's in freefall. Thunder rolls over distant hills. Heavy rain is sweeping in.

She's watching me. Jacket pulled tight about her hunched shoulders. Shivering. A slick of mud drops from her calf. Her eyes follow the blade as I pass it from hand to hand. It dances with my fingers. My turn to watch now. She picks at the tape over her mouth. Her moustache comes away clean, smooth. I smile and take out a fat Havana. Roll it under my nose. The smell of wet earth and sweet rain tumbled in spring fields takes me back. Running through meadows, chasing a girl. Sunlight in her laughter. My fingers wrap around her hair and...

'Hey, stogie?' My guest has loosened her tongue. 'Mind cutting me free?' The Havana sits in a crescent at the base of the knife. I close the blade, snipping off the end of the cigar, and walk over to her. 'You won't get away with this. My father—'

'Is an idiot.' Her coughs shatter the billow of smoke I share with her. 'I care nothing for what you or your old man think. When they find you among the fishes, and they will, I'll get my reward.' I rub my forefinger and thumb together.

'I'm only a pay check!' Her diction is good. Probably cost more than I'm willing to pay for my pleasures.

'What else would you be?' The cigar is crazy good, a relaxing swirl of cedar, and cut grass.

'My father is head of Vetrurn.'

'Blah blah, who gives a shit?' I shrug. 'I got a job with your face on and a nasty habit to feed.'

Before I think what to do, it's done: I have her face in the dirt. Sometimes my own speed amazes me. A whiff of ozone in the wake of the lightning. Guttural thunder shakes the land. She has such an abusive mouth. I ain't got half the time I'd need to do all the stuff she's accusing me off. Besides, horse buggery ain't my bag.

Then she mutters something new to the wet earth. 'Say again?'

'What! All of it, or just the part where you molest children?' Funny how people can still laugh in death's embrace.

'No, I got that.' I'm spitting rain. My interest is gone so I cut the tape from her wrists and ankles. Nothing is dry. As I stand, water runs down my neck, soaking my back. My fingers knot in her hair. 'Up.' We're face to face. Her toes dangle over the mud. Lightning renders the heavens white and reflects in her eye. She's packing tech. Thunder silences her words. Something about James? Her brother?

Turning toward the car, I carry the patient to the operating table. She's screaming new blasphemies. Shit dark enough to make the devil blush. Wrapping her hair around her throat I pull so hard her forehead turns smooth. Clawing my face she screams, spluttering at the deluge. I've never seen rain like it. My finger slips behind an eyeball and pops out a souvenir. The blade flashes blue in the storm's anger as I hook it under the eye. The knife snags a wire running down the optic nerve.

Now the fight's gone out of her, she's easier to handle. I fetch the cutters from the trunk, being careful to protect the trophy. One snip and it's mine.

'You'll die for this.' The hair uncoils from her throat. 'They'll blow you to pieces.'

'Lady, they won't be the first to try.'

I grab her soft hand, pulling her from the hood. We walk real slow to the edge. Don't want to slip. The storm lashes the town into submission.

'Any last... ah fuck ya!' I cast her to oblivion. The thunder rolls out to sea where it goes to die, alone, in the dark.

Time of death: approximately 10:45 a.m.
November 3rd.

ReSyk

Another hazy morning. I squint at the intrusion of light; even this grey hurts my head. I tear a sachet open and watch the powder fizz. It swills around the glass louder than it should. I swallow it and let my gut deal with it. Mornings are tough on the mind. I'm already looking forward to the night. Might sleep the day off. If only.

The face in the mirror reflects the bad decisions in the bar. Scabbed cuts on my chin and cat claws down my cheeks. An angry bruise over one eye hangs heavy on the lid. I take a toothbrush but toss it straight back in the glass. The hairs on it ain't mine. The eyeballs in the glass watch me piss. There's blood in my water. I should get it checked. More shit to deal with. A quick shake. Time for food.

The fridge stinks. I've lost my appetite. Must get those samples to the lab before... Never mind. More evidence to trash. I answer the vibrator in my pocket. 'I'll be there.' Eventually. Jane Doe turned up in the quarry and the newsboys are vulturing.

The world tilts. I need some salts for my nose. I've no idea where I left my coat. Cushions scatter as I search sofas and chairs. The air fills with dust dancing in the daylight, but not the kind of twinkle to satisfy. I drag on clothes as I search. Musty trousers and a shirt that's more stains than fabric. The clock says seven; four hours to recoup. Why I do this job I'll never know.

Self-destruct is so much easier than living.

Hesitation. Every time I reach for the handle it calls to me. The datacorder on the hook: the right way.

Truth, justice and all the shit it drags behind. I pull the door until the soft click kisses me goodbye.

I shrug my coat onto my shoulders and head outside. It's not been the same since Pnu-90. Streets are quiet at this hour. Permit-holders only. Still time for the street rats to scurry back to the wells of despair they call home. A cough is a siren, scattering the fearful. Brompton is lucky, though. We got the lowest infection rate in the world. Only Atacama is lower; the whole fucking place is dead.

Somehow my car is parked straight. I guess the neighbours have learned to leave space. I pull the door open and shove the takeaway boxes to the passenger side. Some asshole used the broken window as a trash can. Stinks of meat and sweat in here. I hate this shit. Now I have to fish around in the trunk for plastic and tape to fix the window.

With a whine of electrics and angry gears I fishtail out into the main drag. Stray dogs chase inquisitive deer back into the wild. Strip lights fade in the rear-view mirror as gnarled bark and fevered stems finger the horizon. All around the desert, blooms are pinned to the earth by the rain. Months of searing heat, and now this pissant sky. What next, blizzards and hail? Hope not. I shudder.

Tyres hiss on the road like snakes on a mongoose. It's a straight line for ten miles then north to the quarry. Not far, but then trouble never is. The mesa rises from the earth, an eyebrow of suspicion. A winding causeway hacked into the western face scars the brow at the last incision. Nowhere quite like it for making a splash.

27

I drive on, half-listening to super-happy radio; the DJ swallows more uppers than a hooker. There's significant flooding in the lower reaches beyond the cathedral. Bishop Timms is worried about the junkies getting their stash wet and having nowhere to shoot up. Idiot. She ain't kidding no one. Perhaps I should pay her a visit, see what's itching her vestibule. Asshole.

I swing the car in a long, lazy arc, pulling up at the side of the diner. The alloy husk ripples in a neon bath of puke-inducing colours. Thunder rumbles over the mesa, trails through the air towards the harbour. The weight of it crushes my senses. Scary, if you're five. I rummage through the detritus on the back seat. My hat is there somewhere, under the mundungus fug.

I wedge the battered fedora on my head and step out into the shit-storm. Lightning rakes the hills around us. Seems I'm not the only one with a bad head this morning. I shut the car and turn up my collar. Rain spatters the sides of my face, clinging to my stubble. I wander over toward the cluster of uniforms. A meat wagon is waiting by the fishing shack to cart the departed to the morgue. I'll make sure she gets to the right place.

'What we got, jumper or junkie?' A cigarette sticks to my fingers as I shuffle the packet into my palm. I touch it to my lips and draw on it. Tastes mild.

'Too old to tell. Been in there a while.' His tone says he's seen it all before.

The vacant rear doors of the meat wagon spill light across the remains. A rotten grin stares back at me from a polythene wrap. Eyeless, fish-eaten sockets. 'Send it straight to ReSyk. We'll get all we need to know from there.' Piece of shit. Means I'll be back again for my girl.

John Doe is bagged, tagged and zipped up. Two guys drag him onto a sled and load the festering sack into the wagon. The doors bang shut and the locks snick tight. I drag my feet to the car. My forgotten cigarette is spotted with rain. I root around inside the car for a working lighter and intoxicate myself with nicotine and tar, watching the lights of the bone wagon drift out of range. Time I got moving. I grind my way across the gravel to the smooth tar. Now I realise I may have fucked up. Sobriety sucks.

Headlights intensify the rain. People are milling about and traffic is growing as the city reaches out to swallow me. Everything exposed to light gets cleansed. You can't see so much dirt when you're blind. Flashes, like memories, frozen moments of time. Hills, giant tombstones, between me and the mesa. Caught offguard in an unsuspecting storm. Am I being cornered in some cheesy horror flick?

The flood in Downtown is a festering mirror of the heavens above. Water pours from gargoyled mouths, spewing out their gospel onto the streets below. Bishop Timms' seat of power: a bastion of the authority of the unseen God. Wish I had faith to believe. The only provider I can trust is my pay check. An honest dollar for an honest day. With my record I should at least get a dime.

The city blurs by in a hungover haze. Glimpses of neon, pink and green light the secret corners of cutprice paradise. Cardboard lovers in paper-thin houses catching water in piss pots. I follow the main drag seaward to my date with the mystery corpse. My only hope is that it don't lead to some real police work. ReGen keeps me busy enough watching the harbour development. It's what comes with being the special liaison between the department and the tech boys. A perk of being the first fitted with the cloud rings. Not sure it's true, but hey, too late for regrets; the shit is in my brain for good. I turn off the drag and trundle up to the gate.

'Morning, sir,' the guard chirps.

I show the guard my ID and drive under the rising gate. Left at the junction and around the back of the clinical, white structure. Concrete and cladding with arrow-slit windows. White-washed kerbs and plastic grass verges. Into the maw we go. Meat wagons from every corner of the county. Bright yellow contagion symbols on every side: Pnu-90 is keeping ReSyk busy. One in, one out. Rules must be obeyed - even the dead have to wait in line.

I hang right and pull up in the police sector. Reception is quiet. More white walls. Lines on the floor mark out lanes. I sign in and follow the blue lane. Sanitising stations dot the walls, but the colour don't change. My lane slips through a heavy plastic curtain; the faint smell of bleach with a hint of lemon reminds me of an ex. Way too clean as dirty as she was. Gotta control the smile.

There's a counter, another reception, where I leave my coat and hat. I take the paper onesie and try not to shove my feet through it. Cigarette paper would be warmer. No chance of making a roach outa this. At the next door, it's goggles and face mask. By the time I'm done no one will know it's me.

One last door before the party. More sanitiser and temperature checks, then I'm good to go. I figure there's too much shit in my system to fit a virus in. I don the gloves and go through the door marked 'IN'. Got one thing right today.

The stench is incredible. Steel tables laid out in a banquet of flesh and bone. Still, more dignified than the public entrance. I check out the victims along the way. Some stabbed, shot, car smashes, and caved-in heads. Nothing new. Plague victims go straight to processing. Brompton has its space, like all the rest, colour-coded to match the patrol car livery. Ours is blue and gold.

As I unzip the bag, John Doe is still smiling. Nice to see a happy face at work.

'I'm Penny,' she says. No handshake. 'I'll be detailing it all, so spit it out and leave the tests to me.'

'You always like this?' I poke a finger in John Doe's eye sockets. Nothing but slime. I take a sample, putting it in the offered dish.

Penny pushes the dish into the BLT and presses buttons. I watch her. She's cute, even through the paper suit. Hers has a Vetrurn badge, a visitor?

'Can I you have your datacorder, please?' Penny stands poised. Finger on the panel, hand out ready. I shrug and make a sorry face. 'Not one for the rules, then.'

The absence of the device is recorded. Damn jobsworth!

I pull a tray from the side of the table and take a pair of heavy-bladed scissors. They cut through the body bag without a snag. John Doe is all exposed.

A tech boy arrives with a box and hands it to Penny. Opening it she takes out a datacorder. She strokes her thumb over it a couple of times as she approaches the table, leaves the device on John's forehead and returns to the BLT.

'Please leave it.' Penny raises a finger but doesn't turn around.

I retract my twitching hand. 'Looks different, is it new?'

'It is. This is a research unit. Not police issue. Though I believe they are sneaking into field trials.' Her tone is flat, disinterested.

'Can I take a look after?'

She looks over her shoulder. 'Sure.' I feel like a piece of meat in the alley markets. 'Okay... That's odd.' Penny walks over. Picks up the datacorder. Struts back, presses more buttons.

'What?' I round the table and read the screen. 'Can't be.'

'I know. I went to his funeral.' The printer goes into overdrive. Paper stacks up. Some of it I recognise, the rest is all chemistry and sums. 'This is for you.' She hands me a few sheets of double-sided jibber-jabber and hurries away. 'Leave the datacorder by the BLT when you're done.'

She's gone.

'It's you and me now.' There should be more meat on him than this. 'James Stapleton,' I mutter to myself.

Sometimes I only take it in if I hear it from a reliable source. Probably forget most of it by tomorrow.

The datacorder feels solid. There's a weight to it, purposeful. It's active too. Surprises me, given the secrecy an' all. No scanner. I press my thumb where the reader should be. It glows. 'Theo Rickets.' The voice is female, soft, fanciable.

I run a tag test. No surprises, he's clean. Dead - and buried. Three years in the earth without a box. He's bones. Then I see it on his finger. I stagger as I crash into the BLT. A quick glance around. No one cares. I dart forward and claim my prize. The ring feels heavy and warm. I finish up and leave.

I drop the gloves, mask and goggles into the recycling bin and quick-step to the locker room. I'm changed and almost skipping along the yellow lane when a voice calls me.

'Was there anything more?' Penny is blocking the reception door. Her green eyes light on me. I feel the measure of her gaze, taking me in.

'Nothing. Just bones. The real question is, who dug him up?'

'And why?' she says with a questioning tilt. Those eyes hold me.

'And why,' I nod, groping for the door.

'Do you have a card?' Her hand is out, waiting. She rattles the printouts in her hand. 'I'll let you know if I dig up anything.' I give her my card and bid her adieu.

The bar is calling me.

The Red Rooster

Music is thumping. Not loud. Thumping. My feet dance down the steps, drawn by the beat. The chimp on the door stops me.

'Ain't my first time,' I grunt, as he pats me down with those meaty paws.

'Rules.' The toothpick between his teeth twitches.

The boy has hands everywhere. He finds it all: gun, gadgets and stash. Damn. 'You should be a cop.'

'Pay's too low,' he grunts. 'You should work here.' His teeth glow in the UV, as do his tattoos: much better on black skin than the usual crap. This is art.

The door opens and a wall of sound assails my senses. The air is thick with cigarettes and arousal. It's buzz'n'. I see guys in a coven lighting fires in bongs while a girl on a pole slips into a stupor. They ain't seeing nothing. Their table's so full of beer and shots no one is walking home. In a booth a guy holds back as the girl in his lap grinds her ass a little deeper in. I have my eye on a slot at the back. A narrow space with an unrivalled view.

The bar is jiggling at the topless end. Young guys braying and bragging, they'll never score like that. Not here. Not anywhere. They're getting juiced for the real party later when the big guns come out. If you ain't spent enough by then you'll be invited to leave. They need to be seen now to be obscene later.

'Melissa!' I call the bargirl over. 'You're out early.' Smiling hurts my face; it ain't natural, not like her.

'You're late. Boss says to let you know.' The pink and purple lights play over her charms, catching the glitter in her valley. 'Here's your beer. And a shot. On the house.'

I take the shot and raise it to the camera over the bar. The liquor hits the back of my throat with an eager burn. Melissa leans forward. I'm drawn in by her momentum. 'You doing a row?' I could never say no to an invitation like that. She rolls a vial across to me and squeezes her babies together. I'm getting twitchy already. I empty the vial onto her chest and take the slowest snort in history. I nod. I skip to my table.

The booth is small. Good enough for two beefs, or a guy and a couple of dolls. It's just me in the neon abyss. I push myself back and stretch my legs. My muscles groan at the effort. A waitress in shorts teeters overs with a fresh beer and a list of eats. 'Steak, prime and juicy.' It's all I ever order. 'That, and a bucket of fries.' I eye the peaches under her shorts.

Then I spot him. The goon. A gorilla in a tux. Arms relaxed, hands clasped. Eyes on me. I act like I ain't noticed. There are better things to ogle in here.

'Mr Rickets.' This one came of out the air.

'Take a seat,' I say and sip from my glass. He watches me.

'You have been sloppy. Boss wants to talk.' He points toward the door in the velvet wall.

'Do I get to eat first? Or will it end up on the floor?' I put the glass on the table, turning it between my finger and thumb.

'I'm only messenger. Not muscle.' He was right about that, strongest thing on him is his accent.

Skinniest gangbanger ever. I look up at the nearest camera. Its eye blinks on and off. I mime eating and it nods in response. 'I wait.'

Skinny watches me watching the dancers spin in unison. Money is slipped into thongs. The air hangs with testosterone. There's a couple of girls at a table watching the dancers. Both slim. Both smiling. Pretty little things from what I can tell. One dark, one fair. No one is hitting on them. One rests her elbows on the table and bridges her hands over her drink. More eyes on me than I'm comfortable with.

My steak arrives with separate fries. No salad. No dressing. Nothing hidden. Juice runs from the meat as I cut it. Perfect sear. The man at my table is frozen in time. You have to watch close to see him blink. He refuses my offer of fries with a raised hand and checks his watch. The camera blinks. The gorilla is on the move. The girls have left their drinks on the table and are heading for the exit. The bar is filling up. Bare flesh is piling up everywhere. I'm waiting for something to kick off.

The velvet wall opens with a hiss. 'Mr Rickets.' Skinny stands, acting as a barrier between us and the bar. The gorilla flexes his fingers and slips a bronze pacifier over his knuckles. I need no more encouragement. A bell chimes as we pass through the doorway. There's a snick of electronic bolts, the door closes. Shut. 'Straight ahead. You know the way.'

For a small guy, he conveys a lot of menace. Best not piss him off. The cream walls are covered with pictures from the bar. Dancers in silhouette. Sparkling skin against glistening poles. Money raised in eager hands.

There's a door up ahead. Another camera. Another goon. He opens the door and we go through. It closes behind us with a rubber gasp and bolts slotting home. More pictures, up close, personal. Two doors staggered, eight feet apart. The corridor widens into a brandy glass. Plush red leather seats ooze from the wall. Two waiters stand behind cocktail bars. Three doors: one either side and the last a double leather prison door closing the mouth of the glass. Square windows make angry eyes into the room. I'm told to sit while my escort approaches the leather doors. He raps a knuckle on the glass. A face blinks in and out of view. The door cracks open and my man slips through.

I try to bait a waiter but they ain't biting. I sink back into the embrace of the seat. My heart wants to pound but the powder has blocked the rush. Should I be worried? I've done worse. Maybe. Not sure where this is going. I usually get a heads up when I need correctional guidance. This must be bad. I hope there's no plastic on the floor when I get in there.

My man is back. He nods in the direction of the world beyond. I pass him. My head is light and the walls ripple with colours. I sink into the floor with every step before bouncing back up. This is not the time to be high. Really, it's not. I don't remember the last door or the layout of the room.

My head swims. I see fishes and dolphins of ridiculous colours. Someone looks in my face. Beady eyes and blurred skin. Fur maybe? I'm stung. My neck throbs. I gulp in air tasting of sandalwood and honeysuckle. The taste sours into lavender and piss. The steak rising. Fries reforming in my throat. My head is thrust forward into a container. I vomit with fury. The acid in the spew burns my eyes and sobriety returns. I come up for air and smell the coffee steaming under my nose. There's a tissue too. I wipe my mouth and drink the coffee. My skull rings with tinnitus. I dry my eyes and look around. A door closes to the left of the desk and I'm alone with the boss.

'Wow. That sucks.' Reality is back.

She sits on the edge of the teak desk. Her legs are parted enough for me to see where her thighs touch in the pale shadows of her skirt. 'Up here,' she lifts my chin.

'You're a long way from home,' I say, and finish the coffee, looking around for more.

'Some things need my personal attention. How is it you get things so wrong?' She slides her legs around the corner of the desk and stands, smoothing her skirt over her ass. She continues around the table with my cup in her hand. 'First, you dump a girl in the wrong place. Then, as if that wasn't incompetent enough, you kill the wrong girl completely.' She pours a coffee from a jug and gives it to me straight. 'Twitch has the first girl, does he not?' I say nothing, nod and take the cup. 'And the second, has she turned up from her dive?'

'No?' I swallow the bitter liquid. 'Worse.'

She raises an eyebrow. Her blonde hair falls around her shoulders as she pinches the bridge of her nose. 'Go on. Enlighten me.'

'I got the call this morning. They fished a body out. I went over expecting it to be ...' I tap a finger to my temple, 'whoever she was. Some hooker,' I blurt.

'The woman you killed was Lois Stapleton. Does the name resonate with you at all?' Pursing her lips she blows across her coffee.

'No. Should it?' I shrug and finish my drink. The cup rattles in the saucer as I release it.

'Lois Stapleton is the daughter of Walter Stapleton.' I shrug again. 'Really,' she huffs. 'The Stapletons are the owners and founders of Vetrurn, our tech rivals. And you killed her.'

'Ah, fuck. Fuckiddy, fuck, fuck.' I rub my face with my hands. 'The bones they fished out this morning was James Stapleton.' The ring is a heavy burden in my pocket.

'He was buried. Here in town.' Dark lines peek over the neck of her pale-yellow sweater.

'I was there. I'm going to have to speak to the Bishop.' I can see the thoughts flickering in her eyes. 'I can go as part of the investigation. Case is open again,' I offer.

'I don't want her dead,' she snaps.

'Jane—' Her hand flashes up. Those lines thicken to cords.

'You're not to call me that here. It's Ms Clark. Understand?' A long red nail points right at me.

'Ms Clark,' I buzz back. 'Who was the other girl?'

'A researcher at Vetrurn. We need to locate another...' She waves a hand in loose circles. 'Someone to get deeper in the vaults.' Ms Clark levels her gaze on me. 'Can I trust you to find me a name? We'll do the rest.'

'Of course.' I relax into the chair, my hands shaking. 'I'm on it.'

'Here,' Ms Clark tosses a small ziplock bag to me. 'That'll keep you going for a while.'

'Appreciate it.' I pinch the bag between my fingers and salute my gratitude. 'I have a ... friend who works—'

'I don't need to know. Just a name. That is all.' She points a red-nailed claw at the door.

Time to leave and head to the bar. On the way, I check the side doors. All of them are locked. At the end of the corridor, a goon lets me back into the throbbing madness. My feet dance me over to my booth where Skinny is warming my seat. A meal is waiting with two beers and a shot. All is well again.

I can get wasted.

Talise

On The Town

'I hate him.'

'Who?' Cheryl wipes the drink from her chin.

'Over there, in the lonely booth.' I bridge my hands over my glass and rest my chin on them. My teeth ache from kissing the pole. 'I do hope I haven't chipped my tooth again. I'm looking more like a junkie than a scientist. Did I really study for years to end up in a titty bar?'

Cheryl snorts the drink over the counter and gives me a love tap on the arm.

'You are so funny,' Cheryl squeals, her eyes halfclosed in happiness.

The dick – Rickets they call him – has been escorted off the premises, as they say around here. Won't miss him. Thinks he can have a handful of whoever walks by. This is not the '70s. Mum used to say guys would often feel her up as she crossed the bar in her local pub. Things are better now, except for him. Wanker. Thinking of Rickets puts me in mind of the girl in the morgue. I shake off a chill. Should never have happened. A glitch in the system?

'We moving on?' I chirp.

Cheryl gulps down her spritzer and wipes the lipstick from her glass. Her lips are Morello, her skin ebony and her teeth so white. I love the girl, I really do, but she is nuts. She is up from her seat, bouncing on her toes, shaking that ass. It ain't big but it is very round, and I'm bound to smack it at least once tonight. If only my pancake tits and arse were more sculpted like those.

'Let's go, it's Saturday night.' Cheryl makes a grab for my bum to move me on. I hate it when she has a fella; I see less of her then. Tonight we have sworn a pact to stay away from the boys and party till we puke, which will be around 3 a.m.

We stop at the door to pick up our coats and hats before we step out into the rain. Mine is a pink, fulllength, wrap-around coat with sleeves over my hands. The buttons are a tight fit. My white pixie boots peek out from the hem. The hat, a bit of a woolly powder puff, turns into a drowned cat when the rain hits it. Cheryl is in a plastic mac, an opaque orange blur with the hood pulled up over her tight Afro.

It's warm for November. We walk along arm in arm, giggling at nothing in particular. Cheryl points across the street, her face all screwed up. A dog is taking the most enormous shit ever. Such a mountainous turd deserves a flag in it. The dog shakes off the rain and trots up an unlit alley. We hurry along, trying to put as much distance between us and the steaming pile.

I love nights. I don't mind the rain either. The neon lights reflect on the road and on cars, covering everything in new life. Pinks and yellows compete against vulgar greens, while cyan and magenta blend them all into a rainbow soup. Music seeps out onto the street from bars and clubs. You can feel the throb of rock coming up through the road from where the metal freaks bang their heads and share dandruff. Steam vents belch out the subway foods. There's a second life down there and it's calling us home.

An archway leads to Chinatown. Paper lanterns drenched in rain glow like the pumpkins left over from

Halloween. Christmas is coming. November will fly by, and the world will twinkle with a billion billion lights, bringing hope for a flash in time.

'Wong's!' Cheryl spins me about. We turn full circle and carry on in the same direction we started in. Cinnamon and sweet bread. Whoever put those together is a frickin' genius. We swing into Wong's, taking the huge stone steps one at a time, jumping up them in unison.

'Honey bun?' Mr Wong is always smiling, even when Pnu-90 took his wife. You see about the virus on the news but it's not until someone you know dies that it becomes real. Cheryl's mum is on a ventilator. She'll never be the same, but she'll pull through; tough cow.

'You know me so well. Pineapple ones and coconut splits, load me up with sugar!' I wipe the spit from my lips.

'Cheryl. You pork?' There's a glint in Mr Wong's eye.

'You wish, you saucy old man.' Cheryl does a wiggle as only she can.

'Shake that booty, girl,' I egg her on.

I take the paper bag from the counter with a soft squeeze. I can feel the sticky centre of those buns dancing on my taste buds. They're out of the bag and in my mouth before the change has finished rattling on the counter.

'You make me blush.' Mr Wong lowers his eyes; he's red all the way down his shirt. He fans his face with one hand while holding Cheryl's pork buns in the other. 'It's been good. Many pleasures to you. Thank you.' He makes a play of sweeping the spotless floor.

'Next time, Mr Wong.' I blow him a kiss as we pass the window on the way to Morgan's.

Cheryl has become a hamster; her face is so full of pork roll she has a job keeping it all in. She sighs as a morsel of bread evades her grasp and lands on the pavement. 'Dearly beloved, we are gathered here today—'

'Swallow it.' I yank her arm as she sputters her way through the funeral service for the lost crumbs. I take out my last munchie, the coconut bun. After a deep breath, I bite on the end, sending a jet of sweet cream over the pavement.

'Perhaps you should learn to swallow.' Cheryl splutters and coughs the last of her food out.

'Choke, you bitch.' I offer her my bottle of water.

'Ta,' she gasps, handing it back to me. I point at the swirling crumbs in the bottle. 'No charge.' Cheryl loops her arm through mine and waltzes me down the steps to the rhythm of blues.

Morgan's is no titty bar. Far from it. It's alive, the music is real. You can feel the slide of every dogleg riff as it chases around the room to come thumping its tail to the bone-hard bass. Blue as blues can be. Songs of prison and wanton women, broken marriages and old love, Morgan's has it all going on.

The air is thick, choking. Cigarette smoke melds into pillars in cigar heaven to swirl around the ceiling fans. Cards are dealt and beer is shared among strangers. Laughter fills every corner. Couples relax against each other as a saxophone sexes the air around them. The mood turns mellow and lips linger in silent song.

Freeman straightens up, drawing a swirl of steam from the dishwasher. He removes his glasses, rubs them with his blue-black tie and replaces them on the bridge of his broad, speckled nose. He sees me and smiles. His smile has a mind of its own. You can see it thinking as it curls his mouth upward at the ends, making the short bristles of his beard stick out.

'M'am.' Freeman is a baritone.

'Talise, stop gawking and answer the gentleman,' Cheryl barks, rousing me from my stupor. 'Lager please, my good man, and one for the pot.'

'M'am,' Freeman winks at her. Everyone winks at Cheryl, she's gorgeous. Freeman returns with a bottle and a short-stemmed glass.

'Nightcap for this one, please. Already gone to Lala land.' Cheryl half-slides half-walks to a table, but even then she manages to swing that booty. Older guys, black and white alike, salute and raise their glasses in tribute. I try not to. Wish I had half the arse she does. I squeeze in beside her.

'Show off,' I giggle into her ear. She's wearing the earrings I bought for her birthday last year. Gold monkeys hanging on big round hoops.

'Did you just tongue my ear?' Cheryl dabs her lobe with a napkin she nicked from the next table.

'No!' says I, feigning hurt.

'Didn't say you couldn't.' Cheryl takes a swift swig of lager. We both laugh at the same time until I snort. Cheryl stares at me. Those big brown eyes get wider and wider, then she explodes with laughter. She sounds common and dirty all at once. One or two fellas turn our way. One is huge, black and handsome.

I wave my hand in front of Cheryl. 'Oh dear,' a sigh escapes my lungs. She's acting like a rabbit in headlights. My phone chirps. A message. 'Cheryl?'

'Hmm, what?' She still has one eye on the beefcake at the bar. He's turned half-round, staring straight at us. Well, at Cheryl. 'I was listening.' The eyelids flutter despite the weight of the lashes.

'You weren't,' I raise a hand. 'Objection, your honour. But I wasn't talking.' I pinch her lips shut. 'You were getting all moist over Beefcake.' I nod toward the bar. There's something anxious about the chirp in my pocket.

'That your phone?' Cheryl deflects. Beefcake takes three steps and crosses the planet. He towers over us. Huge. Fuc-kin'-huge. I sense Cheryl at my ear. 'His face is up there.' She lifts my chin north. Cheryl warms her hands from the glow of my face.

'Evening, ladies.' Beefcake draws us into the depths of his soul with a voice made somewhere dark.

'Hi,' I squeak. Cheryl continues to stare.

'May I join you?' Conjuring up a chair, he sits at our table. There is no more room.

'I'm Talise, and this drooling slice of beauty with the booty is Cheryl,' I sigh. Now I know how the invisible man feels. 'She's available, for parties, weddings, funerals, and bar mitzvahs. She does take tips, but not at bar mitzvahs,' I witter on, if only to entertain myself. They're doing the silent shag-over-the-table thing. Sipping from their drinks all suggestive, Cheryl nearly swallows her glass and Beefcake is beyond standing.

The phone chirps again. Twice.

47

I reach into my pocket and slide the phone out. It's warm. Turning it over I read the text. 'Toilet.' My voice is infantile. I slide from the chair, phone hot in my hand, and head for the door, scything through the gyrating couples.

No one notices me leave, not even me.

Morning

Rain rattles on the skylight as I lie awake, listening. Thunder rolls around the sullen sky in search of children to scare. The crashes interrupt my thoughts, filling the blank spaces from last night. My phone chirps and rattles its way nearer to the edge of the dresser. Lightning, beautiful, splits the sky. I watch it rake the clouds, ploughing the atmosphere before the thunder slams the void shut.

'Death is no longer the end,' assures the seductive voice in the ReGen advert on the lounge TV. My covers heap on the floor as I drag them off. 'Save your most cherished memories to the Mind Cloud as a legacy for those you leave behind.'

Not my field of science. Biomechanics, life engineering, is what I study, and I make coffee. 'Never forget the wonderful coffee you make Talise,' I remind myself. Then I remember. Work! I'm out of bed and headed to the shower. 'Filthy peasant.' I shed yesterday's clothes into the laundry basket and jump into the shower.

The hot needles of water massage my skin. I stand with my arms raised to allow the circling jets to get everywhere. Soap falls into my waiting palm from the dispenser in the wall. The water pauses while I work myself into a lather.

My body is firm. Taut. My hips have a pronounced curve and my boobs have lost their droop. I must have slept really well, or forgotten what my body feels like to touch. No time for that now.

The normal routine is to let the shower work like a car wash, complete with a blow-dry. 'One too many sherbets at the club. That's what it will be.' I wonder how Cheryl got on with her fella. 'Stop,' I command the shower, and wait until the soft sucking of the wastewater being drawn into the recycler finishes. The thought puts me off having any hanky-panky in here.

The towel is waiting for me on the heated rail, seducing me with its fluffy desires. The floor is cold. I hotfoot it over to the towel. Wrapping myself in the broad sheet, I scoop up a smaller one, and twist my hair into a knot on my head. Padding through the apartment to the kitchen I dare a peek out of the window at the day.

'It's shit!' Neighbouring roofs are shallow lakes where ripples live out their short lives. Daylight is scant. 'Whatever happened to the sun?' News interrupts an advert for MyTown, some stupid mobile game. Pnu-90 has killed 400,000 people across the world and shows no sign of slowing. Images of funerals where only the undertakers mourn make up most of the headlines. A mother stares forlornly at the doctor who cannot save her son. Another widow laments her man. And war in the desert, still. I don't know which one, but the virus has got there too. They show a map of the world. Red

49

dots mark where the disease is spreading. Brompton is lucky: we have the lowest rate of infection on the planet. But we have the worst weather.

'The world has gone to shit.' I throw my arms in the air all theatrical and go in search of some coffee. The cupboard is crammed with samples acquired from the coffee shop. I must stop helping myself. Among them are Kenyan, Columbian, Icelandic Glass, and Geek. The bearded dude on the Geek coffee catches my eye and I'm smitten. Holding the pod to my nose I take a huge breath. Recycled straw does nothing for the senses. The water tank is full. The button clicks and I commence the coffee shuffle. Moonwalk, just bad. I will the thing to go faster. If the good half of my brain were in gear, I'd get the milk from the fridge, but I don't. I wait, snorting in the steam. 'Ping!' God, I'm loud. Excited. 'It's coffee time!' I scoop the mug up in one hand and twirl over to the fridge. Swing the door open, snatch the milk from the shelf, and splash it everywhere. 'Messy cow.' Slipping the milk back in the fridge I bump it shut with my bum.

The last few steps to the sofa wear me out and I collapse into its leather embrace. News, news, news. Every channel the same. Virus and war. Even the local one is stuffed full of everyone else's problems. Then, Rickets. 'What's that fucker doing on the TV? Ugly bastard wants a twatting.' Where'd that come from? I barely know the guy. Though he has tried to get to know me through his wandering hands. He's grinning like a loon.

'You're a detective, right?' The newsgirl, all tits and heels, waves a mic at Rickets.

Rickets thrusts his hands into his jacket pockets, cocks his head and says, 'Technical Liaison Officer, in this jurisdiction.'

Newsgirl swings the mic back to herself. 'How so? This is ReGen, isn't it?' She waves a batwing-arm at the battered dockland and the container ships stacked with stuff.

Rickets adjusts his stance, stepping forward like a chicken pecking seed. 'They asked the department to monitor security. And the department—'

'Chose you, Detective Rickets?' She's as stunned as we are.

Rickets nods. 'My relationship with ReGen goes back a long way. I was the first to be fitted with the memory tech. I have a good rapport with the guys over there. This is part of the developing relationship between the divided tech boys and the money men.'

The screen goes dark. When it comes back on my coffee is cold and there's dried spit on my lip. The sun has poked its nose through the clouds, a tad. There's pale blue beyond the grey, if only for a while. The phone chirps: I feel it buzz beneath me. I fish around, lifting one cheek. The phone gets hotter as I stare at it. I blink. My right eye hurts. 'Bloody eyelashes. Why do we have them? Just so they can get into our eyes!' I pull the towel from my hair and screw it into my eye. The phone chirps twice more. 'Sod off!' I launch it across the room. The battery and the case go in different directions.

The phone chirps.

The towel drops off me in the middle of the lounge as I dive into the bedroom. The chirp of the phone pecks at my bare bum. My heart pounds. Sweat beads all over: waste of time having a bloody shower. Knickers fly through the air, chased by socks, jeans, jumper and hat. Can't go out in the wet without a hat. 'Stupid.' My foot catches in the gusset of my knickers. I crash into the dressing table parked beside the bed. Tears sting my face, it hurts so much. Going to leave a bruise too. 'Slow down.' I turn into a street mime, trying to get my senses in order. The canary is still chirping in the lounge.

'Breathe girl, breathe.'

Better. Turning, I lower my bum to the bed and sit. Yesterday's bra, which I didn't wear for long, smells ok. It's on, tight, but on. They're bigger by a whole cup size. I give my boobs a squeeze: quite firm for the age. Something's up. I get the knickers from the floor and pull them up. My reflection in the dresser mirror has more curves. The knickers are snug. Socks are still okay, so at least my feet haven't gained any weight. Jeans, however. 'Breathe in, Talise,' I gasp as the button slips through the hole. I pluck the jumper from the bed, pink thing with a dopey-eyed cat on the front, and yank it down over my head. Dressed at last. I can go strangle the chirping sparrow.

Why don't I want to look at it? Last night? I think back to Cheryl and the bloke at our table. The phone chirped then, I remember now! I read the text and ... It chirps again, twice. I'm staring at it. The battery is over on the carpet. How is it still working? My trainers are right next to the phone. Shoving my feet into them I scuttle off to the kitchen and retrieve the sugar tongs. 'Stop it!' Bloody thing is getting impatient. I pick it up and march it over to my printer. Lifting the lid I dump it face down on the glass and press the copy button. While it prints, I pincer the phone and take it to the bathroom. It clanks against the white porcelain and slips to the vacuum plate. 'Any last words?' I stamp on the flush button and it is gone. My trainers squeak as I spin around on my heel and march out, triumphant.

Must've been in a rush, my coat is on the floor. I pick it up and slip it on. Something flits by the window. Dark, buzzy bird. Glancing at the printer, I see the image of the phone: the screen is blurry, except for the time. I walk around the back of the sofa and retrieve the battery, stuffing it into my pocket. A dozen or so steps and I'm through the door, heading for the street.

It's quiet out here. Sunday quiet. Everyone's gone to church to throw money in the plate in the hope it will appease the big guy upstairs. Sure it don't work that way. I'm going in another direction. First I have to try and remember where I parked. I reach for my phone, and sigh. Flushed it. 'Stupid cow.'

The apartment block is exactly one hundred yards square, so the car won't be far away. I like it here. The factories at the river mouth are out of view. The streets are wide and pavements well-maintained. It ain't the rich bit; no way could I afford to even take a piss there. Here the shops are good and everything works. There's even a phone booth, full of cards advertising personal services. Someone from Downtown has taken the trouble to come all this way.

'Hi.' I wave at the girl in the walk-in test clinic. She has a customer by the hand, their head is down. Must be bad news, hope it's not the virus.

The car, a squat collection of curves, is parked up ahead, beneath a streetlamp. My ear is drawn by a buzzing sound, like an angry wasp chasing a fart round a tin. I see it, sitting on the streetlamp, its beady black eyes daring me to look away. The car starts as I approach. The door pops open, allowing me to take the seat behind the wheel. Check the mirrors and press the throttle, zipping out into the empty traffic lane. The bird flies ahead into the shadows of the high-rise living quarters.

I turn down toward the main strip, slipping between two trucks from the quarry, dirt clinging to the undersides where the rain and splatter can't reach. One turns off toward the main highway, giving me a clear view of the road ahead. The other rumbles down the long slope to Quayside.

The dull thud of the wipers beats into my skull, compacting my hangover. How much did I drink? I've had a boob job and a bum lift but no memory of either. Neon signs wink on and off indicating the slip road to Route 6. Traffic is a bit heavier here, busy for a Sunday. Driverless buses surge past, pulled by the magnet rail in the road. Faces peer out into the gloom. The world has forgotten how to smile.

Slipping across to the far lane I join the hiss of traffic. I hit the cruise control, and the steering wheel folds into the dashboard. The miles flit by until, at last, the clouds end and the sun is there to greet me.

Sunlight warms my eyelids as I let the car take me to my destination. 'Siri, play something soothing.' I melt into the gentle melodies floating around me.

'You have a message,' Siri interrupts. 'Would you like to hear it?'

'Go on then.'

'Would you like to hear the message, yes or no?' Siri has a lot more patience than I do.

'Yes,' I hiss.

'Hi Talise, it's Mo at the coffee shop. You comin' in today, only it's a bit late and we're kinda busy. Would be good to know. Ciao.'

'It's Sunday! Hell, no!' The sun is high, almost full. This place ain't seen rain in months. The plants are withered and brown. I frown. 'Siri, what's the time?'

'The time is now 1:35 p.m. on Monday 6th November.'

'Monday!' The car comes to an abrupt halt. Vehicles flash by, their horns blasting. 'Monday! How?' I facepalm sweat into my forehead. 'Siri, take me to work.'

'Which work will it be?'

'The Coffee Grinder. I have an apology to make.' I take a calming breath. 'Phone Mo.' The car takes the next junction and heads back into the storm.

Coffee Grinder

'I know. I'm sorry.' Head down I charge through to the back of the shop, already half out of my coat. A clean uniform of brown shirt and black trousers waits in a tidy pile with my name badge on top. I strip to my underwear and toss my gear into a locker. It's a squeeze but I get it all in, even the raincoat. There are one or two staff members with light fingers. The trousers are a tight fit. I have a quick feel for camel toe. I'm good to go. The shirt's a challenge: one cough and someone gets a button in the eye.

'You got new tits?'

'Pervert.' I try not to laugh at Bren, who has Down's. Says what he sees from under an unruly mop of red hair.

Bren taps his busted watch. 'You're late.' He points to the serving area. 'Mo's not happy.'

'Aren't you meant to be clearing tables?' I wink at Bren.

Bren scuttles off for his cloth and special tray. We all clubbed together for his birthday and raided the Disney store. We came out with a load of princess tat and the tray, also a princess one. Bren's used it every day since. You've got to like him; not a bad bone in the fella. Keeps himself fit too, often does a few push-ups to entertain the customers. Anything is better than his singing.

'You made it!' Mo nods to the queue. 'All yours.'

Mo's a funny bugger. One minute he's raging about nothing, the next he's handing out chocolate apologies. Love those chocolates. The place is pretty full with the usual lunchtime crowd. Odd thing though: the streets are near-empty but we're always busy for lunch. Mostly with ReGen employees having an extended business meeting. They do like to gas on about their projects and how they're going to reshape the world with their genius plans. Most of them don't even look at each other. Faces glued to screens like flies on shit, most of them trawling the streets in MyTown.

'Yes sir, how can I help?' The old boy comes in at two every day. 'Is that with milk? No, sure? Three-sixty then, please.' One of the few still using cash. Most have taken to touch payments, or use it as another opportunity to fondle their phones. 'Take a table, Cyril, we'll bring it over.'

Cyril holds out a gnarled hand. 'That a Union Jack on your badge, girl?' The coins jingle in his palm.

'It is.' I inspect my name badge.

Cyril doffs his tattered cap, revealing the grey nest of hair beneath. 'Your Majesty.' He swirls the hat with a flourish before plonking it back on his head, and shuffles to his seat singing 'God Save the Queen'.

'Coffee, black with two sugars.' The voice is a massage to the ears.

'Cherry cupcake?' No need to look up.

Joel stands tall at the counter. 'Miss.' A smile is poised on his lips.

'Take a seat, sir, I'll bring it over.' The events of this morning project on the walls of my mind. I serve a couple more regulars and dive out to my locker. 'Just a sec,' I say, slinking along the narrow space behind the counter. I open the locker, take out my coat, fish around for the printout. It's wet but still readable.

'Oi,' Bren calls. 'Come on, lazybones.' He beckons me out. I skip along and pass him, knocking his cap forward. 'Hey!' His hand springs to his head. 'Bully!' The spittle of his rasp speckles my neck.

'Bren.' I can't chide him; little sod has the grin of the Cheshire Cat. I grab Joel's order and scoot across to the window seats. He sits in the same cubicle whenever he can. A people watcher.

Joel takes the plated cake and coffee. 'That for me too?' He points at the paper.

'Oh, yeah.' My face is hot. I can feel the heat sinking down to my chest. 'It was from my phone this morning. After I removed the battery.'

Joel inspects the paper. 'Okay. I'll add it to the file of weird shit.' Teasing it between his finger and thumb.

''Preciate it.' I skip back to the counter before Mo hollers.

People come and go in a steady stream, traipsing wet footprints across the ridged carpet to the white strip along the counter. Bren whisks a mop across the floor at every opportunity. 'I'm singing in the rain,' he warbles.

'Go on Bren, murder another classic.'

He blows another wet raspberry and shoves his glasses back up his nose with meaning. The singing gets louder, a caterwaul. Right now I envy the deaf.

Bren rushes over to the door, mop in hand. 'Wait!' He pulls the door open and waves the customers goodbye. His anti-bac is out, the door handle clean once more. Next, he'll wipe it over his hands and the mop handle.

It's been busy, time for a break.

I take a coffee and iced bun over to the back table where I can watch the world go by. 'Bren, chair.' I stab a finger at the crumbs on the varnished wood. It's all so old school. Mo still thinks digital watches are 'pretty neat'. The chairs always feel cold through the thin fabric of my trousers. I wait for my bum to warm, then press my back against the chair. It, too, is cold: wooden fingers pressing into your fat areas, if you have them.

The jabbering couple at the table in front are loud. Their mouths move with clarity. Lips in sync with each other: question, answer, question, answer. Billy and Johnny, known them a while. Constantly playing the MyTown game. This one looks as dull as Brompton, even the avatars match. Their volume tells me they want someone to hear. They want someone to know how clever they've been. They want to spill the beans. I'm listening, the scientist part of my brain fully engaged. ReGen has been naughty. There's no surprise there. The mind-clamps have hidden functions. I want to join in but can't as I'm a barista today. But they can't help themselves, bleating on. Something about instability in Patient Zero. 'They', whoever they are, are coming apart. Their boss is hiding something, they're sure of it. Just as it gets interesting a phone beeps. I glimpse a QR code, and they leave. Bren serenades them to the door and I'm alone with my thoughts. I need to see someone about this.

I know just the man.

Twitch

Walk and Talk

'Sorry. My bad.' The lady passes me, her face full of thunder. What would I get for tripping her up? If I had not stuck out my arm she'd be face down in the gutter. Some people, eh. Whatever.

The sun is out somewhere, I'm sure of it. The weather girl is prancing about on a screen in the tech store. Her dress cut for a slimmer build. A small stack of tyres roll over her waistband but she carries it well. Her smile is broad, and her every move flowing together in a writhe of snakes. I never get the weather. The news girl is speaking now with a rhythmic nod. Bishop Timms is the news again. She's become quite a regular. She's cool. The last honest person in town? The news feed shows the extensive flooding Downtown. The new river wall is trapping the water on the wrong side. Houses are thigh-deep in filth. Debris - someone's life goes splat in the pan. Bodies are piling up at the wall: cats, dogs, people. All kinds of detritus. The bishop is fuming, don't think I've seen the girl quite so animated. Compassion tugs at my chest. I don't wanna go. A fight I can't win. Not since ...

My pocket vibrates against my chest. It persists until I cave in and answer. 'Yeah. Sure. I'm about ten minutes away. Get me one to go. Anything brown and steaming that ain't from a pavement.' A new objective. Bishop Timms will wait: she's solid, she'll understand.

This ain't my part of town no more. The streets are wider, cleaner. Less blood. Dogs are on leads. People are keeping their distance. Some wear medical masks. I don't, no need, not here. The rest of the world is dying from the plague but not Brompton: Brompton is near disease-free.

If not for the rain it would be a pleasant November day. A cold bite left over from last night. I miss those rude mornings when the sun is cold. A sharp intake of iced air shrinking your lungs. You know you are alive on days like those.

I crawl by Electric Wonderland. If it plugs in, they sell it. The news feed on the window tracks me until I turn and face it. Pretty Michelle, the news girl, is smiling despite the carnage around her. A bulldozer has been crashed into the river wall in Lower Brompton, releasing all the floodwater. People are cheering. Helping hands are sifting through the shit and silt. Knee-deep mud blankets the world. Bishop may be in trouble. Only she would have done something as crazy as driving a digger through the river wall. I expect she'll be in Precinct Four, again, getting herself more bracelets.

The camera follows Michelle as she squelches into the filth. The ruin of life is all around: plastic bags and bottles, dolls and pushchairs, furniture. A stool points an accusing leg at the towers of ReGen. Cheap chairs black with slime are washed with the tears of God. The camera pans. Left is the monolith: Brompton Cathedral with its drooling gargoyles. A yellow bulldozer is wedged in a gap no one will be coming to fix. Good. Right out west is the sea where a spot of sunlight cheers the water.

'Hello?' My voice sounds loud in my ears. An old lady shuffles by in jelly sandals. Her grey hair sticks to her liver-spotted scalp. The ginger cat in her bag mewls; he don't like the rain either. The old lady spits on the pavement, nodding at me as though I should clean it up.

I've missed the news story. But the fading image of the black towers beyond ReSyk has piqued my interest. A column of red and blue lights. ReGen has some interesting stuff going up and down to the clouds. I'm guessing drones. Time to move. My coffee will be getting cold.

I cross the road, weaving through the meagre traffic, a skater chasing a puck. The streets shine with water. I turn down Canal Street, crammed full of gay bars and clubs. Some comedian has scrubbed out the 'C' from the road sign. I chuckle. Been like it for years, funny how they never fixed it.

'Hi, Twitch.' A guy in a bright orange suit filled with muscle straightens in a doorway.

'I know you?' I slow up.

'Saw you put that brute down over Harvesters.' He holds the high ground.

'Bus stop? Slumming it, weren't ya?'

'My friend likes Tex's.' He flips a lighter in his hand. Smooth.

'He's solid, Tex. You can trust him.' I'm moving again. 'Have to go. Stay safe.'

'You too. Leon,' he shrugs. 'I'm Leon.' He points up at the rainbow sign over the door.

'Cool unicorns.'

I stride out of Canal Street. Dodge a fat Mary hooker touting for 'bizniz'. I cross another road and dart over the corner of Chinatown. Wong sweetness teases my tongue. My gut growls. No time for treats.

Cars hiss by. The rain picks up and the hiss garners splatter. Gutters swirl with dark eddies down the everthirsty drains. A mother tugs a child into a shoe shop. He's squalling louder than gulls chasing fishing boats.

He ain't happy. That's when I spot Joel. No amount of steamy windows can disguise the dude. I rap on the glass. Wait.

Leaning back against the window I see nothing, observe everything. My mind is on the pretty lights going out of ReGen. My thoughts are broken by a paper cup thrust under my nose. Talise was right. The coffee is something.

'You comin'?' Joel heads round back where his car is parked in a tiny lot home to three vehicles and a dumpster vomiting trash. An old rug lolls from it, lapping up the rain. Joel opens the car and we both get in.

'We have to clear the fridges back at the morgue.' I flick the loose fabric trim hanging over the door.

Joel tuts. 'Meant to fix that.'

'Bangers can't tell us anything new. And Talise, well…'

Joel pats my knee. 'She's all done. Nothing more to learn from her now. Oh, reminds me.' He tugs a folded page from his pocket.

'What's this, love letter?' I unfold the paper with one hand, sipping the cappuccino.

Joel sucks his teeth, 'You wish. Cute thing like her. No.'

'Hey, Jane was a looker.' I go blank. The paper is my world.

Joel snatches the paper from my hand. 'Twitch.'

'What, what?' The world rushes in. Streets blur by, greyed by the rain. Lights. Red, blue, green and white. They ain't real, just in my head. They exist all the same.

Joel's old brow knots up, his dark eyes boring right through my pretence. 'Where'd you go?' He checks the printout. 'I'll take this to Kid, he'll work it out.'

'Yeah.' The world's woozy. Head spinning, coming loose. Cracks forming in my brain. Tiny splinters of light opening windows to my soul. 'Not sure. Kid. Yeah, he's smart.'

Joel has the eyes of a chameleon. One on me, one on the road. 'You up to this right now?' The lines around his eyes deepen.

'Sure, why not?' The seat folds around me. Familiar hands holding me tight. Next thing we're pulling up at the office and I'm fumbling with the door handle. Joel strolls over to the roll-up door, twirling his key and playing air guitar. The car door swings open and I kiss the tar. Legs ain't working right. Picked up the wrong knees, walking like a flamingo.

Joel stands over me. 'We making a habit of this?' I'm weightless. The ground is two feet beneath my face. Blood and spit dribble from my mouth. 'In you go, Fido.' Joel folds me into the car and shuts the door. He swings the vehicle around and backs into a loading bay. The place is huge. Two of us rattling around in an old warehouse. Serviceable. Cheap.

I'm moving. Feet catching on trollies. Hosepipe arms and sausage fingers. 'Something ain't right. You gone all mushy and not a titty in sight.' Joel drops me on the office couch. He floats over to the filing cabinet. Pours a coffee and turns. I remember the cup in my hand. It's dark when I wake.

The lights are off inside. A green eye glows on the coffee filter. The exit light is white through a green, running man. Blue and red flashes strobe the windows. Feedback. Squealing in my head. One second, no more. Memories. One intense memory. Jane's death.

'In here.' She sounds happy.

'What's cooking?' I toss my coat over a chair.

'Steak pie, chips and those green things you like.'

'Peas!' I slide an arm around her waist.

Jane twists from my slender grasp and opens the oven. 'What do you think?' A golden-brown pie, so meaty I can taste it.

'It'll hold the gravy just fine.' I peer through the little window on the fryer: bubbling chips.

Jane smiles at me over her shoulder. 'Cherry ice cream too.' She's full of promise and pleasure. I'm almost falling for it.

'What have I done to deserve all this?' The table is laid, and there's beer in the bucket, the right kind.

She peeks at me over her glasses. 'Nothing.' She reminds me of my teacher, Kissy McGee. 'Have you been naughty?'

'No more than normal. You?' I lean back against the counter and watch her cook. She's wearing something different. 'Been shopping?' Always a bad guess. Then I spot something that don't belong here.

'Won't be long. Why don't you get yourself a beer?' She nods toward the table. Her hair falls from its pin, hangs loose about her shoulders.

'You bring work home?' I fish a beer from the bucket and crack it open. The hiss chills the air between us.

'No.' She catches a breath. 'Why?'

'By the toaster - the case.'

'Oh. That. That's just... a something.'

'A something? Steroids, amphetamines.' Slurping from the can, 'Magic potion.'

'My work is not potions.' The oven door drops with a bang.

'So it is one.' I walk back to her. The case is open; a needle on the side and another in the case.

'It will change the world.' She swallows. 'Give me that shot in five minutes.'

'Or?' I put the empty bottle on the side. She smacks my hand down as I reach for the case.

'I don't know... it's not exact.'

'You took the shit without knowing what it'll do?'

'Shut your mouth. What are you, a damn fish?' She grinds out the words. I can hear the muscles in her jaw locking.

'I'm not helping you play God.' I let her stagger back, her legs stiff.

She falls back against the table. 'The shot!' She tumbles to the floor.

Grabbing the case and needles I go over to her. 'N. O.'

'Bastard!' Her hands claw at the rug, tugging tufts of shag.

I read the label on the needle. 'XG12. What does it do?'

'THE SHOT.' Convulsions rip through her.

'Still no.'

'Reanimates.' Her face reddens for a moment. Her jaw slackens, skin pales.

'And the one you took?'

'Give me the shot, asshole.'

'You don't look so good.' Her skin is turning grey, breath shortening. I open another beer and sit at the table. 'What does it do?' Veins are swelling in her neck and face, turning black. I check the needle and put it away.

'Stasis ...' she hisses.

Dinner is excellent. The pie is all meat with a thin crust. The chips are golden and the peas perfect. I make the gravy thick, smother everything in a rich brown river. Best thing she ever did.

Darkness again.

On a Limb

I get a coffee. Joel must be around somewhere since the jug is full. The door to the morgue is open, a fire extinguisher stands guard. The Bangers are floating on sleds, their tattoos dark on their grey flesh. Dead Talise is under a sheet, a small dignity. Everyone goes to ReSyk naked. Joel waves a languid hand as only Jamaicans can. He floats over, meets me at the bottom of the three stairs.

Joel stares at me. 'You OK?' His knuckles pale around the handrail.

'I'm good. Good as I'll ever be.' The smile is forced but I mean it.

'Hm.' Joel steps aside with a sweep of his simian arms. 'All ready to load. Did what you asked. We are clear to follow through.' He tuts at me.

'What!'

'You're like a kid. You think toilets are funny.'

'Toilets are funny. Farts are funny. Follow through is only funny to an observer.' I pat myself down.

Joel hands me what I'm looking for. 'Lost it. Again.'

'You're a saint. A big black saint.' The vape swirls in my mouth. Cherry and cinnamon, sweet and exotic.

Joel slaps me hard on the back. 'And you're a short white ass whose memory is shot to shit.' The vape clatters over the floor.

'Thanks,' I stroll over to get it. Talise is all quiet when I lift the sheet. 'We learn anything about her yet?' I pick the vape off the floor.

'Nutt'n'.'

"What about the ring?' I brush the blue streak of hair over her missing eye and lower the covers.

Joel walks the first Banger to the wagon. 'Kid has it, and the printout.'

I grab the next sled and go after Joel. 'What printout? Am I missing something?' Leaving the Banger aside I fetch the keys to the wagon and open the rear doors.

Joel slides the Banger into a groove and locks it down. He turns, the whites of his eyes alight. 'You don't remember? You go all stupid for days and don't remember?'

'Days! What are you talking about?' I lock my Banger in the other side of the van and we both go back for dead Talise.

Joel's got big-eye. 'The coffee shop? Talise gave me a printout of her phone. Said, some shit came on the screen after the battery came out. She made a print of it. I showed it to you. You went stupid. You've been out of it nearly two days.'

'Fuck! What!' There's a whistle in my head.

Joel prods me with a pudding finger.

'Precisely.' 'You hear a whistle?' I let my breath out, slow.

'Whistle. Like a payday one, when I'm waiting for my check?'

'Funny boy.' My head feels loose when I shake it. There's a beep.

Joel takes out a taped-up block from his pocket. 'Kid's done.' He taps away at the worn silver buttons.

'You ever gonna get an update?' I snatch the phone from his hand. More duct tape than I thought possible.

Joel plucks the phone from my fingers. 'Latest thing in tape. Only the right signals getting in. Nutt'n' frying my brains.' He taps a finger to his temple.

'Nope, weed's done that already.' We grab either side of Talise's sled and walk, heads bowed.

Joel starts, 'There's all kinds shit going on. I tell ya, Twitch. This Pnu-90 ain't no bug, sure as this rain ain't truth.'

'Joel.'

He stares at my raised hand. 'What?'

'D'you mind?' I jab a finger at the rear of the wagon.

'Oh, sure.' We slide Talise in and lock her down. We take a door each and lock the dead inside.

I start the truck and roll out through the open door. I wait for Joel to shut up shop. He lumbers back and drops into his seat. We're on our way to ReSyk.

'Y'know.' Joel cracks the window down, 'As I was saying.' He rests an elbow on the door pocket and turns sideways in his seat. 'How come it only rains here? How come no one here gets sick? Sure we have a few. Half a million out there.' He waves a hand at the steamed-up window. 'Brompton, a city of 120,000? Two cases, no deaths. No masks, no lockdown, no nutt'n'.'

'I get you, I do.' I shoot the lights, taking the corner with a slip of tyres. I catch the back end before it slides right out. 'You see that?'

Joel jerks a thumb over his shoulder. 'You trying to add us to the passenger list?'

'The bird.' I lean over the wheel, trying to catch another glimpse. 'There.'

Joel follows the line of my finger. 'Ain't no bird.' He shakes his head, dreadlocks peek from under his hat. 'No bird round here flies backward.'

'Get a picture. Camera. Glove box.' I ease off the gas. The bird circles, hovers, flits and darts. Joel snaps away, keeping the camera close to his chest.

Joel taps at the screen on the rear of the camera. 'Got it. Ain't no bird. It's a drone.'

'Sure? I mean, it has wings but it don't fly like a bird.' The drone shoots straight up, vanishing into the brooding sky.

Joel holds the camera for me to see. 'The eyes.'

'Cameras.' Nodding I make a left, heading for the old route.

This part of town is rough. Dark alleys lead into darker alleys. Pits of oblivion where no cop goes without backup. A sightless place to while away the hours and speculate. Depravity rules this slice of life.

Litter scatters behind us. Fast food bags and styrene boxes exchange homes in the gutters. Stray dogs stalk filthy rats. Hookers light every other window, flesh for sale. Behind every letterbox is a peepshow of carnality. Real people doing real things for cash. No credit. An untraceable world. Another corner and the backstreets become memory.

The maw of ReSyk stretches before us. The front yard is quiet. I select a vacant bay and slide in. This is going to get ugly. A guy in a bio-suit glows in the corner, hosing down the concrete. Bits of something slip through the grating in a wash of ooze. He signals us to wait until he's done.

73

The detergent gun foams the grey concrete into a frenzy with its bleached kiss. Bioman twists the nozzle in his fat-hand gloves. A blade of water slashes through the foam. The world is safe again. The jet stops. The windscreen is stippled with droplets. With a flick, I set the wipers going until the smears are gone from view.

Bioman waddles over. 'What ya got?' Joel hands him the slip. 'Three on follow through! Busy afternoon, guys?'

Joel does the teeth thing, 'Yup.'

'Wanna make sure it all goes down the right tubes.' I fake a laugh.

Bioman yanks off his glove and stabs a button on the wall. The wall opens. We have our own way into Hell's Kitchen. Time to get stewing.

Inside the place is spotless. Bodies on gurneys, bodies on tracks. Conveyor is full too. Bioman wanders in, his yellow suit glistening in the blue-white light. 'Here's ya codes.' He gives me three red strips from a book of tickets. Looks like I entered a tombola. Don't fancy the prizes much.

As we step back through the wall opening three trucks roll by in silence. Electric haulage lugging containers outback. Delivery? Something new going up? Joel takes the codes from my hand. 'I see 'em too. Loads coming through Quayside. Docks are full. Ships queued up for miles.' He slips a coded tag over a toe of each Banger. Takes a breath and gives dead Talise her ticket to ride. We get our delivery onto gurneys, fixing them together in a train. I take out my datacorder and scan the tickets. The train makes its way to the last stop. We walk in slow.

A brunette slinks over to us. Average height, about 160, 112 pounds. Ice-blue eyes, a tiger in red heels, lips to match. 'Penny.' I shake her hand. Her skin is soft and warm despite the chilled air.

'Twitch, this is Joel.' Those eyes carry me to exotic places. 'Fancy shoes for the work.' Words tumble out. 'I'm a visitor. I work for Vetrurn. We're looking for some missing tech.' There's gravel to her voice, dry but not hoarse. She stands straight, military.

'You're welcome to examine these three. Don't expect to find much, Bangers aren't heavy on implants.' We pass through the vast hall where cops from across the county are poking around in corpses. They ain't like us with our private facilities. Most of what they do is done right here in view of everyone else. Sometimes someone from another district knows the deceased. Most time they cut, swab and go. Too few hours in a day to process them all.

Penny guides us away from the auto stripper. 'Not there, try this,' She has something bright and shiny, like her nails.

'What is it?' A peek down the sides reveals nothing.

Penny unhitches the first Banger and slots the gurney into runners in the floor. She beckons. 'Watch.' A touch screen materialises in the side panel. Banger number one goes under the microscope.

The whole unit lights up. Lights are partying; all I need is music and I'll sweep the girl across the floor. It's a hologram. Detailed. Better than any TV, almost solid. 'This is our latest scanner. Molecular lasers. Think of it as an MRI with light. We are turning the patient into a data stream, before reforming them. We will be able to examine them right down to the last molecule.'

Joel runs his finger over the readouts, transfixed. 'How are you able to read so much data so fast? We have a modded BLT but it ain't nutt'n' like this.'

Penny draws a breath, and purrs, 'I doubt you have the financial resources.' Joel nods.

'What can you tell us about the deceased?' I lean in close to the image.

Penny reaches for my hand. 'Touch it.' She lifts my hand toward the hologram.

'Joel,' I grab his sleeve. 'Try it.'

Joel shoves his big mitts right in, stirring them around. 'I can feel it all. All the bones and guts.' He steps back. Scans the readouts. Dives right back up to his elbows. 'Incredible.'

Penny presses the eject button and loads the next Banger. 'Hmm.' She taps the screen. 'Hmm,' lifts an eyebrow, pouts. Presses more buttons.

Joel retracts his arms from the hologram and stands next to Penny. 'Both the same, huh. Two bodies in one. As though someone stuck a whole load of muscle on a mouse. Mixed DNA too. Conflicting ages?'

Penny turns her head. Biting her bottom lip, she stares right into Joel's dark eyes. 'Uh-huh. Well-made too. Some ingenious tech. I would love to see how this was done. We have muscle grafting and rejuvenation at Vetrurn, but this is designer. This is incredible.'

'And they make thugs with it,' I remark. Penny turns to face me. 'I put another down, same as these.' I take out my datacorder and flip it open. 'Show me the last sentencing.' The datacorder beeps once. The screen flickers into life. 'There's the meat-sack.' The body structure is unmistakable.

Penny's glance lingers longer on Joel. 'Who's doing this?'

Joel growls, 'Only one place sells body sculpting.'

Penny breathes the name. 'ReGen.'

'ReGen.' I eject the body and load our dead friend.

We watch in silence as the hologram of Talise forms before us. Penny sniffs. A tear flows down her pale skin. 'Not Talise,' she croaks.

'You know her?'

Penny touches the image. 'Knew her.'

Joel touches a screen, starts scrolling through the data. 'Talise is alive. Who or what this is we don't know.'

Penny takes a tissue from her sleeve. 'Alive?' She wipes her nose and dabs her eyes. 'I don't understand.' She presses on the side of the scanner, opening a small compartment. The tissue floats into a bin.

She takes out a silver block about three by six inches. Penny grips the top and bottom edges. With a sharp tug the block doubles in size. 'This is mark three. Our latest datacorder. I'll register them to you both.' She takes another from the opening and repeats the process. We both get one. Better than Christmas. 'Place your hand on the screen, fingers apart. Wait for the buzz.'

'What does that do?' A mild pulse of electricity excites my hand.

Penny takes her own datacorder from her pocket. Opens it. Two dots appear on her screen. 'I can locate your datacorders through my own. You can use them to communicate directly with me. You can also use it to make secure calls and searches.'

Joel turns the device over in his hands. 'We can go dark!'

'Too late for you, brother,' I quip but wilt under Penny's death stare.

Joel rests his hand on her shoulder. 'Don't mind him. He's an ass.' Penny shrugs and turns away. 'Am I reading this right?' Joel jabs at the data. 'Talise has an empty mind?'

Penny scrolls the data up and down. Runs some numbers. Presses a few more buttons and twinkling lights. 'Yes.' One more check. 'Talise has been wiped. Died because her brain stopped functioning. She ceased to be.'

'Wiped! How? Is that even possible?' The hologram shimmers. I eject the body.

Penny purses her lips. Places the datacorder to her mouth. 'Data sync. Subject Talise Jones. Initiate DNA trace.' She spins on her heels. 'I'm going to arrange for you to come up to Vetrurn. There are things you need to know. I'm also going to see if I can arrange a visit to ReGen, peruse their operation. This kind of... surgery is illegal.'

Joel closes his datacorder with a click. 'I need a drink before we go down the river. Let's secure these three and come back in a while.'

We follow Penny along a corridor to the steady clip of her heels. Joel swings in step to the sway of her hips. Going to have to hose him down before he mounts something. The white walls are interspersed with smoked windows masking the office workers trapped within. The one spot of colour is the rest room sign, and that's grey. We file in. A couple of cops glance our way, sniggering like kids comparing their dicks.

Penny is quiet. Her face gets masked in swirl of steam every time she draws from her cup. Chocolate. Thick enough to stand a spoon in. The coffee tastes burnt but I ain't drinking vended tea. Joel has water. He sips it as though he has a mouth ulcer. He's watching Penny. I watch them both.

'Hey.' A cop from Fourth. I've seen him here before. Dick by name and nature. Spends more time here than the streets. Not many want to come here. The cutting's OK but the next step ain't so cool. Disposing of physical evidence.

'Hey, Dick.' Joel flashes me a frown.

Dick chases a plastic stirrer around the box. 'Got much on?' Coffee draws a line down the plastic cup. Non-recyclable, which is odd considering the location.

'Old case. Going cold.' Trust no one. Penny winks through a pall of steam.

'I've a fistful of Bangers. Downtown boys, thin as your dick.' He laughs, flicking coffee from the stirrer before he tosses it at the bin. The stirrer joins the others on the thin corporate carpet.

'That so? Ain't no one got no meat on 'em down there.' My coffee is done. I drop the cup in the bin. 'Easy.' I tap Dick's shoulder and head for the door.

Dick inclines his head toward me. 'See you around, Twitch.' They all want me to bite. Until I do.

'Hope not, Dick.' I'm out the door with my posse close on my tail.

Penny scoots up alongside me. 'You know him? He's not from your precinct?'

'No one is. We don't exactly fit in anywhere. We were assigned to Eighth. I pop in sometimes, register my cases the old way. Get out as quick as I can.' I draw on my vape. The whistling in my head eases.

Joel strides ahead. He has his new datacorder in his hand. 'This do the doors?'

Penny smiles. 'Anything your old one did, and more.'

Joel holds the datacorder up to the door panel. 'Hm.' The lock snicks. 'Welcome to hell.' Joel holds the door.

Penny steps through. I'm on her heels. Joel waits for the door to clunk shut. We're in for the journey.

We gear up with rubber gauntlets and overshoes, paper hats, goggles and coats. Penny has a locker where she stashes her heels, switching them out for trainers. We inspect each other. Don't want any of our clothes exposed to the shit in here. Joel flashes the door with his datacorder and we are all enveloped in a chemical haze.

Citrus. The air is lemon. Yellow lights in the floor blink to guide us. No bath tonight, I've not been this clean in years. We file through and the lemon glow sours to purple UV. We splash across the boot wash and we're in. Bioman is back in a new suit. Gone are the fat hands and hippo thighs. A few grey strands of hair refuse to comply with regulations. Bioman is a beast under the violet. The pale walls absorb all the ambient light. Death rules here.

Penny steps around Joel as he slides his datacorder under a scanner. A green light strobes the open screen. A wall hisses open. Banger number one rolls into view, his naked skin bathed in UV. Bright spots, alien eyes, glow around his groin. Penny taps the screen of her datacorder. She writes with her finger on the screen - shapes not letters. Red lines criss-cross the corpse forming a grid of shrinking squares.

Penny draws another shape. 'They have a 3D scanner!'

'Why would you scan the dead?' I whip out my datacorder, flick the screen open and snap a photo.

Joel makes the sucking sound.

'What?' I move over to the side.

Joel jabs at a screen. 'It's more than skin deep.'

Penny squeezes between us, not an unwelcome thing. 'So I see. It has ultrasound. Very detailed, right down to the bone.'

The gurney drops to the floor, collapsing into a flat bed. The Banger is supported on a rippling wave of energy. A second scan captures his underside. The wave moves the body on through a door in the end wall. The second Banger comes in and is subjected to the ritual. He too passes out of the room. Talise rolls in, her body small enough to fit inside a Banger. The scanning begins.

Her body is clean, no fluids, confirming our own investigation. No tattoos. No markings at all. Not a single scar or stretch mark. 'What a horrible waste of life.' The others nod in agreement.

Penny snaps a few shots. She inserts her datacorder into the scanner. 'Record and upload.' Coloured lights bounce along the top edge of her datacorder. Both mine and Joel's ping at the same time. 'I'm sharing the data with you. All three. I want to make sure we do not miss anything. Talise was… a colleague. I would like to know what happened to her, how she ended up like this.' She nods at the departing corpse.

The floor lights up. A strip of yellow lights leads to the next room. We follow the yellow brick road.

The lighting is better. Near normal. But the process is anything but. The bodies float up in turn. I smile at the snake tattooed on a Banger's arse; it goes right up his crack. That's one nest of vipers I don't want to investigate. There they all are, hanging by their ankles. My heart is racing, thumping on my ribs. Then. Zip.

The ceiling opens. Two irises twisting out. Stainless steel poles descend, telescopic. I want to see something else. I focus on the back wall behind the Bangers, I don't want to see Talise but my mind wanders. Where a man's thoughts go, so his heart will follow. Red light floods the room disguising the cutting tool. The telescopic rods slide down the sides of the bodies, stopping at the hips. They ascend. The bodies descend. The floor opens, the floor closes. The bodies resurface, skinless. We move to the next room.

We don't hang around in here. Meat stripper picks the muscles off, snipping ligaments. Real neat. Our clients are lowered face down over a trench and disembowelled. Just bones with brains. One last saw. Separation, they no longer resemble anything. Fit only for dogs.

We leave in silence, in respect, for our lunch.

After stripping off all the hazmat and safety shit we head back to the car. Penny has other places to be. She waves her datacorder. 'I'll be in touch. I can promise the visit to Vetrurn will be more enjoyable.'

Joel shrugs. 'Could be worse.'

'How? It's already raining.' I shove Joel toward the car. 'Sorry about him. He's an arse.' Penny just smiles and walks away. The rain wets her hair. She don't care though, you can see it in her walk. There's no rush in her step. She eases herself into her green sports car, rolls out of the car park and drives back through town.

'Let's go see what these new toys can do.' I slide into the driver's seat and fire up the motor.

Joel is nodding like a toy dog. 'Cool. Tasty. Ooh.' We weave across town. He continues his monosyllabic commentary. The central route is shorter but the back route is faster, with fewer lights and junctions. Just a whole lot easier, more thinking time.

Rickets

The Bishop

The streets are filthier than ever. Would never have thought it possible for life to sink any lower. The air hangs with the stench of corpse and sewage. Time to go, don't want any shit on my new shoes. Supposed to have had a new car, but the screamer on the Mesa blew my paycheck. Now I have to go to the one place I hate.

Most of the places along here are busted in. Doors hang from their hinges like the bruised eyes of a boxer. Squint enough and you can catch the light inside. A shithole full of shit. The whole place needs flushin'. An old broad scuttles by with a bag of cats. She hawks up a fur ball all knotted in phlegm. She ain't well. There's blood in her spit.

The hag stares me down, 'You want it?'

'Get outa here.' I flash my badge and she's a dirty memory. Not the kind I like to keep. At her age tits are in the waistband. Makes my flesh crawl. Perhaps I should follow her stench and extend mercy.

There are patches in the sky. Not blue. Grey, a smeared windscreen. The streets are mute in this miserable half-light. A shopping trolley rattles over a grating. Can't be sure what's pushing it. Junk is stacked so high all you can see are shuffling feet beneath a polythene sheet. Dangerous part of town if you're on the wrong side. Gangs with no name cut and run. Anyone dying here goes straight to ReSyk.

The west door of the cathedral is a vulvic arch of stone. The red stone lips curve out into a wall engraved with history. Names no one cares about. Gargoyles drool from above. Their glistening eyes disapprove of the neighbourhood. Limp flowers lament over urns. Grass grows through the cracks in the pavement. Moss clings to the corners. Ain't no life worth saving here.

An iron gate sits ajar. A notice on the front declares a welcome to all. The gate yields to my foot and groans aside. I stand between two benches cut into the inner entrance wall. There are two dips worn by centuries of fat asses. The iron ring on the door rocks to and fro. There's no wind, but it moves. Water pools around me as I think. The metal is cold in my hand. Rust textures my skin through layers of black paint. The door sighs open.

Yellow incandescent bulbs glow like lame suns. Warm light reaches out to touch me. I shudder. Is it cold in here? Leaflets, a whole rainbow of goodness. Information no one wants. But I do. I take a red one, paling toward pink. Rummaging through my pockets I find an unlucky coin. It clatters in the empty dish. Guess the Bishop will have to eat at the soup kitchen.

The vaulted ceiling stretches beyond sight, a golden haze above the silence. Wooden pews herringbone down the nave to the lectern. People have been busy; the back of the pews are smothered with names scored into the old wood. Incense burns on a pitiful shelf nailed to a smooth pillar. They say the prayers of the saints rise as incense to heaven. Smells like dope to me.

A babbling pensioner mutters nothing. It's all for nothing, so why waste the words. His head is bowed. His knees knobble on the heartless floor. A fruitless homage. Rags, not clothes, hang from his frame. His skin is greyed with age, wrinkled perfection.

My footsteps chant my approach to the mercy seat.

'Rickets.' She slides out from behind the lectern.

'Bish.' Shadows fill the corners. Frayed rags afraid of the light.

The Bishop shrinks with every step she takes down from the transept Dias. 'Now I'll have to disinfect the place.' She checks me out. 'To what do I owe the honour.' She holds out her arms; her wrists reflect the gnaw of handcuffs. 'You come to take me away too?'

'Just want some information. 'Bout a body I found.' I scrape my hand across my face.

Bishop Timms scoops up a Bible, clutches it to her chest. 'Uh-huh. We got plenty of those laying around.'

'This one got resurrected. Went for a swim at the quarry.'

Timms waves beyond me to a sycophant vagrant saying goodbye. 'Sounds to me you got it all in hand.'

'This one was dead when he got there. Any of yours go for a walk on the water?' I don't want to but I return her smile. Disarming.

Her dark eyes brighten to copper halos, windows to her soul. 'Same two as always.' I lean in, inclining an ear. Timms tippy-toes up, her breath warm on my skin. 'Just Peter and my Lord.' Shrinking back she winks, 'Unless you know any different?' She half-turns, halfstays. Picks at the fading chrysanths scavenged from a grave. The congregation has more life in it.

'I want to know about James Stapleton.' The words catch in my throat. I scratch my nose. The itch moves to my cheek, I chase it to my ear.

Timms turns. Finger raised. 'I held the funeral. Pretty girl gave the eulogy. His wife, I believe. Now, what was her name?' She shakes her head, loosening memories.

'Any idea how he got outa his box?' Mouth is dry.

Timms turns on the spot like a dog preparing to settle. 'He was never in it.' She clutches her face in her thin hands. 'What was her name? Ugh, I'll get it, don't rush me.'

'What do you mean, he wasn't in it?' I slip a hand inside my jacket to secure the plastic pouch between my fingers.

Timms stares through me. Those deep eyes latch on my hand. 'You keep your shit in your pocket. This ain't your crack house. It's mine.'

'Stapleton?' The word sticks to my palate. 'Funeral.'

The Bishop straightens her robe. 'Service. We provided a service. You know nothing of the family?' She heads off to the choir space. I follow.

'No need. Everyone does.' There's an altar at the back beneath the curve of stained glass. She waits, hands rested on the purple cloth.

Timms examines everything with a keen eye. Stays put. 'Ignorance is not a virtue. In this case, considering your occupation, it's outright laziness.'

'What do I know?' The shrug is for show. 'The Stapletons are rich control freaks. Got a finger in every pie. Clean as sewage water.'

Timms lifts an eyebrow, those copper headlights gleam. 'You mistake them for your employer. Jane Clark. Twitch's wife.' She faces me, all the humour flushed from her eyes. 'The Stapletons are good people. Walter is an acquaintance.'

'What, you play golf?' The smirk soon leaves my face.

Timms bares her teeth. 'Not since the rain. You could learn much from people like them. Walter worked hard to build the company. His son, James, fought for this country. His daddy fixed him up when he came home on a stretcher. Lois, the sister, she's smart. Got more brains in her right eye than you'll ever know. James's wife, Penny, that's the name.'

'Penny. Brunette? Works over ReSyk?' My mind reels. The whistling is still soft. I need to blow my nose.

The Bishop ain't happy. 'ReSyk! It's a shithole. She's a scientist not a butcher, you ass.' Her finger stabs my chest. 'James was murdered. By a cop gun. Sick bastard took his eye and left him floating in the quarry.' The finger stabs and stabs, bulleting my chest. My head swims. The pillars of the church loom down, arches warping into accusing mouths. I gotta go. 'Run Forrest Run,' she shouts at my heels. 'You might want to keep an eye out for Lois because she's gone missing too.'

The pouch calls my name. Hot in my palm. My foot snags in the pile of supplicant bones: I never saw the guy in the shadows. The pouch spins open in the air. The floor comes up to catch me. I reach out. My fingers snap against the stone. Head ringing I scramble forward to Snow White's ashes. The taste is off, mud, cold, but the fizz is clean. My tongue wants more.

I'm a dog lapping at its own vomit.

Something taps my thigh. The praying bones kick me. 'I'm a cop. You want a ride uptown?' He stops. Blood on his lip. He limps off to the shadows clutching a twisted wrist. The Bishop is bearing down. Her robes flutter. One last lick and I'm up on my feet. Stumbling from pew to pew I reach the leaflet table and confetti the floor with the message of hope. The Bishop is on me. I don't touch the ground until rain spits in my face. Daylight.

'Hey!' she calls. I turn round in tentative steps. We lock eyes. I follow her path. I see only the pouch in her hand. She stops at a crypt, the white stone bright. She empties the pouch. Her offering, my sacrifice. 'Come back when you're a real cop.' Timms slips through the maw of God.

My powder is dead before I get to the grave. 'Bitch.' My fingers trace the name at the top of the list. James Stapleton. 'Shit.'

The sky splits. Heaven rages down. God or Thor, it's thunder either way. Someone ain't happy, besides me. Sweat pours from my flesh turning my clothes into a second skin. I raise a foot. Slap it down on the wet step. Heart pounding. Eyes roll in their sockets, swivelling. I need a hit of something. The right stuff is back home. But I need something *now*. Snot salts my lips. Breath comes heavy as my feet pound toward the dark pit where cops won't go.

Cat woman is pulling rats from a hole in the wall. She snaps their necks, ignoring the yellow teeth gnawing at her knuckles. The clowder in her bag slash at her, hungry for meat. The rat suffices for now. When she dies in some filthy hole they'll feast on her.

The alleys grow dim. Daylight fears this place. It sucks the light from everything and spits out slag on the streets. It's a dirty place. A second home. I knock. Bolts grind back on dirty rails. A hatch inches open. A bag of powder dangles in the void. Digging deep inside the lining of my pocket, I pull out some old notes. Real cash. Cash that's been inserted places. Dirty money, paid for things, snorted stuff, rubbed on skin, but still worth the same. Cash is king here. No credit. I snatch the pouch from the void. The joy is mine.

I pull open the zip seal and tip the contents into my mouth. The fizz is wild. Effervescent sex erupting in my mouth. The streets fill with light and colour. The whistle in my head subsides. I zip the remnant of powder and stash it inside my coat.

I'm Gene Kelly dancing in the rain. Scooting puddles at cat woman. Her spit mixes with the rain on my face. I take her in my arms and dance her up and down the alley. Man, how those cats can sing. She's screaming, I'm singing, it's a caterwaul. Everyone is happy. We swing around. Her feet are off the ground when she snaps around the lamppost. She's saying something, I don't care what. Her spit is red, her breath rattles, I can't understand her gargling snort. I move along. Places to go, people to do.

Morning After Pill

Acid. Old Chinese and gut acid. I pick the crispy bits from my shirt. The room spins slow. I think it's stopping. Coloured lights blink and fade in dirty pools on the back of my eyes. It's colourful but it ain't helping. A strong taste of piss offends my tongue. Not the first time I've slept in the bathroom.

'Shit!' The radiator is hot. I lose my grip. Back among the piss and crispy noodles, I get a flash of yesterday. The drug den, dancing in the rain, The Rooster. Some chick with a blue streak in her hair spins around a pole. A party? Dunno, my head ain't on right. I try to sit again. My arms hurt with the effort; the quaking stops when I sit.

A phone chirps. Instinct says it's mine. I pat my chest, dislodging more crispy noodles. Another chirp. It's not in my trousers. I climb up the porcelain bowl to my feet, pausing at the cistern to catch my breath. A mistake. The smell of the toilet scatter is ripe. Noodles and blood clots bobbing around in a sea of booze and... I've no idea what that is. I cough and add another charm to the mix. I hit the button and watch my recent history swirl into the depths of the apartment block. My shins hurt.

Memories fragment into splinters of thought. I can't tell them apart. Voices. My voice. A recording of a meeting on a twisted tape. Taped-off buildings, furnishings - bloodied. Bloodied hands, blue gloves and a scalpel. Face down on the operating table. I pass out.

Dark. The lights are off. I must have sat here for over ten minutes without moving. The blue-white LED blinks on. Pain shoots through my eyes. I see nothing but white spots fusing together. With a hand on the wall, I get to my feet. My pants are around my ankles and the floor is clean. When? How?

There's a small glass shelf over the sink where I keep my recent collection. Only three. An eye is missing. The broad from the Mesa. It was my favourite eye, I'll not get another of those. I pull up my pants and stagger out into the hall. Daylight is fading across the floor, highlighting the tattered rugs and toppled cups.

Left. Bedroom, fresh clothes after a shower. I thrust the dirty laundry into the hamper and step into the cubicle. Water runs over me. Jets of hot water prickle my scalp, heat seeps through my skin awakening my soul. Jane. I rub myself with soap and rinse off.

Stepping out, I wrap myself with an old towel and walk back to the kitchen for coffee. The phone chirps twice. It ain't the time. I flip through the cupboards. Biscuits, broken and crumbed, soften in a glass jar. I take one together with the pill pot. I take a yellow tab with a mouthful of biscuit. The milk smells but I drink it all the same.

One, two, three. Got to count. I switch on the coffee. It gurgles in rhythm to my gut. Five, six, seven. I open the fridge, taking out breakfast. Pizza curls over my fingers. Eight. I close the door and put a ringed mug under the coffee spout. Steam sputters into the mug flecking the inside with old grouts. Nine. I take the black coffee over to the couch with my breakfast and fall into the seat. The TV senses me. I switch from the titty channel to the news.

'Last night's carnage is all around us, as you can see.' Newsgirl jiggles around to show us the stench-hole Downtown. Timms is a dark angel hovering over the debris. She's pulling something from the wreckage. 'Bishop Timms?' Newsgirl teeters as close as she dares.

Timms peers over the piles of crap. Stays where she is, wiping slime from a child's limp arm. You can almost hear the mud sucking as she pulls the body out. The old demon falls to her knees. The camera zooms in, catching the tear as it kisses the child's filth-streaked cheek. Now she's coming over.

Newsgirl is in a flap. Backing up faster than a runaway car. Timms is dripping mud. Slicks of it dropping from her gown. A right papal mess. 'Hey,' Timms calls the fleeing crew. God speaks. They halt. 'Can't wait to get away from the real news? Don't come down here looking for development. You have Rickets for that.'

'Bitch.' Twelve. Lost count. I finish the pizza and shake another tab into my palm. Tossing it into my mouth, I wash the half-chewed pepperoni down with a slug of coffee. My mind settles. No more racing thoughts. I sit here, not out of choice. I stare at the TV. Will the phone ever stop?

Someone in my head is speaking to me, I think. I need to recover the body of Lois Stapleton. Someone has filed a report down at the Fourth. JD901103. Someone gives me an order. Get it done. I get up and follow the canary chirps. I check the phone. I dress and leave.

Brompton is busy. No one cares about the weather no more, we all got rain hats and coats. I follow my feet across the street. Down an alley to Quayside. The phone chirps again, buzzing in my screwed-up fingers. It rolls onto its back as I open my hand. It's a picture, a kind of code. The ones you scan for tracing. I'm staring at it. Still staring. I flick it off and toss the thing into a pocket. The tabs are working now, full sail to the wind.

What am I doing in this alley? Fourth precinct is the other way. I turn and head back through the spilt trash cans and old boxes. Leaflets float by in the gutter, damming the drain along with all the drink cans and candy wrappers. They don't sweep the streets down here anymore, ain't no one to care. There's a drugstore up ahead, its window lit by a glowing green cross. Light spills over the window display discolouring the condoms and diapers. Everything is sick, and not in a good way.

Some kind of bird flits around overhead. Rancid thing spreading disease, perhaps I should shoot it? As if we didn't have enough with Pnu-90. My car sits with one wheel perched on the sidewalk, turned toward the traffic. The door sits ajar, water dripping from the bottom. I shrug and swing it out. There's a smell. Not the usual one, this is bad. The bag on my seat is stained. Old blood. The raffia handle is shredded. Torn. I've seen it before somewhere. The old cat woman from Downtown.

Yanking the bag out I toss it across the street. It lands with a squelch, and broken cats spew across the sidewalk. I get in and press the start button. Listen to the engine purr. Images of the old woman seep into my head. A body twisted around a pole. The sharp mewlsnap of the bag beneath my feet. Not my best night.

Pulling out, I roll to the end of the street. Two eighteen-wheelers hauling containers marked with foreign flags go by on the soft whine of electric motors. Not seen them before. Traffic slides in close with a blare of horns and abuse. There's a delay as I mess up the gears; the engine grinds. I wave the complainant adios with my middle finger. The day is getting better.

The trucks follow each other, waiting at junctions, pulling out around parked cars in sync. I follow them. Fourth precinct is on the right. The report can wait. Two more minutes and the mudflats of Downtown flash by. We pass over the river, heading south to the county line. The road winds on. The bends broaden and straighten out. Just desert from here. At least the rain has stopped. The trucks peel off. One right, one left.

There's nothing out there but dust and cacti. The heatwave had no impact here. The car bounces over the hardened earth as I swing back around toward the city. A monotone world greys by the window. All colour is lost to the rain. There's a red light up ahead and the longest queue of cars in a month. Six. I punch the radio on and mouth the words to some old Fleetwood Mac song, something about chains.

Across the street, people are raging. One car is up on the pavement parked on a streetlight. The other is crumpled up its rear. The drivers are waving their arms, crazies in a Mexican standoff. Some cheer before the lights blink green. The old engine growls as I ease the pedal toward the worn-out mats, steel shows through in places. I like to grind things under my heel. Another pair of those white trucks head out of town toward the Mesa. Ain't nothing on any manifest about those trucks. More work.

Some bum pushing his life in a shopping cart trundles across where I want to go. He ain't bothered by the horn; life left his sorry ass along with hope. 'Don't pick it up!' I catch my thumb on the dash as I vent my frustration. The filth stops to collect more filth. Now he's adjusting his stack of shitty treasures to fit more shit in without spilling it all. Heaven forbid any of it's useful. 'Move along!' I honk three times. Nothing, not even a shrug.

I can see the buzz of red and blue lights heading out to ReGen. Something must have kicked the hornet's nest. The old shopping shit-shack pulls the covers back over his stash and meanders in front of the wailing sirens. Black and whites flit in all directions: someone's getting hounded. The station will be easier to negotiate now the pack has fled.

Precinct Four

The back streets are lined with cars. I nudge a couple of fenders getting parked, not in the compound, can't risk getting boxed in. In case things go south. Been a while since I stalked around here. There are faces I don't want to see. Memories best left in the trash.

There's a camera watching over the gate; its red eye blinks. Iron stretches twenty feet on either side of me. Eight feet high lipped with razor wire. Who breaks into a police station? There's a small recess in the middle where the two gates meet. I insert my new datacorder. There's a moment of doubt, but I'm in ok. The gate rolls back on its shit-filled tracks, shoving the crap aside. I slip through and the gate grinds shut behind me.

It's a short walk up steps filled with memories. My hand closes around the cold galvanised rail. I wait for a couple of chick cops to mince out into the grey daylight. The skies are darkening, streaks of light flicker in from the sea. The grumbling sky spills its guts. I shove by, not wanting to get any wetter than I have to.

'Ass hole!' the chicks cluck. They must know me.

Same old, same old. Nothing changes. The Fourth is all drab grey walls, scuffed floors and torn seats. Desks piled with beige folders spewing paper no one reads. A door sits ajar. The captain shines a seat with his fat ass, crams another donut down his pie-hole. His beady eye follows me around the room. A chair scrapes behind me.

'Rickets, in here.'

'Cap'n.' I doff my cap like the gent I am.

Captain Coulson holds the door open for me. 'In here.' He shoves the donuts across the table to me. 'Have one.'

'Yesterday's?'

The chair creaks under Coulson's ass. Spare flesh is pinned into submission by the chair arms. 'Says a man who eats from bins.' The whites of his eyes gleam against his black skin. 'What do you want here?'

'Following up a case.' I pour a coffee from a filter on the side. There's a note stuck to the wall with a name on: 'T. Jones'. He's been up to Vetrurn? I ease myself into a seat. Have to resist putting my feet on the desk.

Coulson takes my coffee. 'That so. Help yourself to one.'

'Thought I had.' I repeat the process. Something about the name on the note is all too familiar. It'll come to me. 'Anyhow. Perhaps you can help me. Save me poking around.'

Coulson sighs. 'Poking around! You've been locked out of the system, Rickets. You got in because I let you in.' There's a quiet rattle to his voice. A dust-crusted screen over the door shows the iron gate. 'Should learn to park too.'

'Yeah, perhaps.' The coffee tastes bitter. 'JD901103, what can you tell me about it?'

Coulson jabs at the keyboard, one chameleon eye cocked at me. 'Stapleton, James. Came in on four of eleven. Died three years ago, gunshot to the heart. Remains have been claimed from ReSyk by the family. Who are not interested in pursuing the case. Case closed.' He fat-fingers the keyboard. The printer spews pages into a tray. 'Now get out of my precinct.'

'What, no hugs?' I gather up the pages, wedging them into my inside pockets.

Coulson grins, 'No kisses neither. Next time wait for an invite.'

'Why all the hostility?' Lights flash in my eyes and I'm in the past. I'm at the station, only standing by the door. I'm watching a tight skirt wrestle across the front lot. I'll be seeing more of her. If she's lucky, all of her.

'Rickets! You shithead, you listening to me?' Coulson is in my face, his jowls gibbering like chocolate jelly. 'Something funny?' He cocks his head to one side.

'I was distracted. You were here when ReGen came.' A quick glance around the room reveals all the desks are locked down. Every screen is a black-eyed caution.

'I was. You got yourself all signed up, sealed the fate of us all.' Coulson backs up a step. 'You'd only been here a couple of months. Leapt at that skirt like there was a sale at the brothel. You always were a sexist pig. Now look at you. Lone dick. How come you don't have a private space like Twitch and Joel? Shit, whatever happened to that partner of yours? Wilson, that was him.' The last donut goes into his gibbering cave; a sugar moustache sits in the shade of his fat nose.

'Wilson had to leave. Difference of professional opinion. No idea where he slithered to.' Of course I know.

'I heard he was one of ReSyk's first. Rumour has it he never got buried. Got lost in the system.' Coulson reads a memo on a desk. 'Must get some flowers for her wife. Can't make up for her loss. She was a good officer. Gonna miss her.'

'Brompton's full of stories. You musta seen those nutters protesting the weather?' I shake my head at the thought.

Coulson shrugs those walrus shoulders. 'Maybe there's something in it. This is the only town in the whole damn country with endless rain. Odd, don't you think?'

'Nah. Morons. How can anyone control the weather?' A patrol car crushes a loose can in the parking lot.

'Even I've seen the drones going up and down outa ReGen. Hey, perhaps you can tell me something.' Coulson smiles, hippo style.

"What, lay it on me. If I know, I'll tell ya the truth.' I've learnt a lot from my time with ReGen.

'What's with all the white trucks? Two by two, wherever they go. Never see 'em return.' Coulson edges toward the window, coffee cup in hand. 'You're the man in the know.'

'First I saw of them was this morning. Followed a couple south outa town.' It was out before I could filter it. Shit, told the truth: at least I won't need to cover my tracks with half-truths.

Coulson nods with a pout. 'I don't believe what I see. Not a flicker of doubt on your face. You had a meeting with God or something?'

The lot is filling. The sound of cops bringing in perps is closing in. 'Just a representative.' I clam shut. Something don't feel right. 'I'd best be going. Sound's like the chase is over.'

'I'll see you out. Keep an eye on those light fingers of yours.' Coulson shuffles me to the back door. A guide I don't need.

'I know the way. I can do this, I'm a big boy now.' I grab my crotch at the old Captain. There were laughs, sometimes.

Coulson winks, pointing at my gesture. 'They give you one in man-size? Was it a matching set with a ring? Or did you get down on your knees and pray, cock sucker.'

'You've lost none of your charm, Cap'n. I might just apply for the job as your assistant.'

'You can assist my shoe up your ass. Now get out of here before I call the cops.' Coulson squeezes by to get the door. He wasn't lying, my prints don't work here anymore.

The rain is brutal. Cap is shouting. 'What?' I make a sign that I can't hear. He pushes me to the stairs. The door clunks shut.

Grey. The whole world is uniform grey. I cross the lot and slip through the waiting gate. A dripping ticket on my window tells me what everyone knows. So I'm an asshole for parking where I shouldn't and damaging old vehicles. The ticket spirals along the gutter until it's sucked down into the underworld. I dent the protester's car one more time and head home across town to read through the info. I don't expect to learn anything. I never do.

Traffic moves slow. Water is everywhere, except Downtown. Timms, the old bitch, done good there. Crossing lanes early, I touch the brakes and side-slam the barrier. Pedestrians pass by with their shopping dragging their arms to the sidewalk. One of those blackbirds flits by the window and vanishes in the squall. This time I ease out to my lane and wait for the lights to go septic. I should be more alert than this. Perhaps the pills were too many, the count too long. I've not snorted today, yet… The lights change. Traffic splashes by, drumming on the side of my car. Two more turns and I bump a wheel up the sidewalk. An old man shakes a fist at me, says I was too close. The engine judders to a halt. I listen to the weather beating on the tin roof. The old guy is still glaring at me. His mouth moves but I don't care what he's saying, I just raise a hand and go inside.

Water trails behind me, but at least the floor will be clean. The elevator reeks of piss and dirty sex. I take the stairs. Two flights later I've seen enough painted cement for one day. The door opens on command. How did anyone get past the voice lock?

Time for real coffee.

The kitchen is a mess. I surpass myself, a new record in heaped shit. Reaching for a mug, I knock the radio on. Crockery slides from the wash pile, protesting at the cramped conditions, no doubt. My coat, heavy with the weather, clunks against the dining chair. Relief flows through my shoulders. A hiss of mountain pine freshens the room, needling the coffee with a hint of nature. I grab the coat. The image of a rippling lakeshore cleanses my mind. Damp forest, autumn gold, framed by canvas. She's with me. I turn toward her smile and all I see is the mocking grave.

Papers, old wrappers, pouches of stuff, it all goes on the table. No wonder the coat was so damned heavy, there's enough crap here to start a recycling shop. Then I find it. Four inches of cold, black metal A faded smell of cordite is burned into its soul. There's a number engraved in a crude hand along the barrel. I don't need to read it. I put it there.

Talise

Meeting Someone

'No!' I don't believe my ears. Cheryl, between mouthfuls of cake and tea, is spilling the beans on the hunk she met at the club. 'No! He didn't' She does the nodding dog impression.

Cheryl smooths her shirt down her sides. 'Hands. My God. I swear.' She raises a hand; a gold ring twinkles on her finger.

'Let's see.' I summon the trinket to me. 'Fancy.' No gem but attractive, a set of gold bands fused together. I'd prefer it narrower, but who's complaining. Not Cheryl.

'Keeps my finger warm.' Cheryl plants a red-lippy kiss right on it. For a moment, it glows. I say nothing, not one to spoil a magic moment. The last twat who bought her a ring tried to turn her into a drug mule. Not this one, though. I think he's real. Not met him much, only down Morgan's, probably two, no more than three times max. Don't see my mate now.

Cheryl, from what she tells me, spends most of her time skewered at the groin. Lucky cow. Makes me think of my last fella. I miss him. He used to work for Rickets, whom I hate. I'm sure the bastard had something to do with Wilson's leaving town. Wilson was good to me.

Cheryl busts into my dreams with 'Anyway, why are you in here on your day off? You got something going on with him? He's been ogling you since we sat down.'

'Thanks. That - is Bren. He's either mopping the floor or looking at my tits. You're not funny!' Snorting is not lady-like, but I can't help it, the cow has me in fits.

Cheryl sits back in her chair. 'But you could though, eh! Shall I call him over?' She nods at Bren. Bren is knuckle-deep in his nose. Not brought his lunch again. 'Start the ball rolling. We'll get you laid before the day is out.'

'Stop fucking waving,' I swat her hands. 'I have enough of him when I'm here. He was the first to comment on my boob job.' Cheryl snorts tea through her nose. 'You're not going to drink it now?' My face tightens as she swallows the last of the tea. A clock pings on the wall.

Cheryl springs into life. 'I gotta go. I only have an hour.'

'Sucks to be you.' I flash my teeth in a smile.

'You not coming? Or are you wanking later?'

'Cheryl! For fuck's sake! Not here. No,' I bury my chin in my top. The heat of my chest is tremendous. I'll be red for hours. 'I'm meeting someone.'

She's across the table in flash. 'Is he fit? Can I meet him? Does he have a friend?'

'No. No. And no.' I tap her nose with a spoon.

Her tongue flicks out and licks the cappuccino froth from my spoon. 'So,' her breath is warm on my face. 'You're down for a bit of rug tonight. Scissor sisters, dirty bitch.' She gives me a shove in the shoulder.

'She's from my other job. Wants to talk about something at work.' Bren scoots over to the door. A figure is waiting in the doorway for him to finish smearing dirt around the floor. 'She's here. Now sod off.'

Cheryl scutters to the till. 'Not a chance.' Her words hang in the air. She interrupts my guest, sending her straight over to me.

'She's nice, your friend.' Penny sits in a vacant chair. 'Are you almost done? I've ordered something to go.'

'Have I done something wrong? Am I in trouble?' I ask.

Cheryl drops into another seat. 'Lovely to meet you, Penny.' She offers her hand across the table.

Penny's eyes catch the glint of gold. 'I like the design of your ring, where did you get it?' Her words are woven through with intrigue.

'Me fella. We met a couple of weeks back.' Cheryl recoils her hand. 'Not an engagement ring. He's just me fella.' She checks the clock. 'Uh-oh, I'm for it when I get back to work.'

'Shouldn't be so nosey.' I can't contain the smugness.

Penny's eyes flick between me and Cheryl. 'Been lovely meeting you. If you do discover where he obtained the ring, please do inform Talise. She can update me. Unless there's a problem with that?'

Cheryl flaps a hand. 'No worries. If I can get him to squeal, I will.'

'Should know by tomorrow then,' I bite my lip. Cheryl flings her coat on, plants a wet kiss on my cheek. 'Caio bitch!' And she's gone.

Penny lifts her takeaway to her chest. 'She's quite a character. Cheryl, is it?'

The chair grinds across the floor. I slip my coat around my shoulders and zip up. 'Yeah. Been a mate all my life. Helped me through some tough times.'

Penny is first to the door, after Bren. 'Bye-bye baby, baby goodbye.'

'Kill another classic, Bren. Now I'll have to sell all my tartan. The Bay City Rollers are ruined forever.' Penny has a car around the corner. She has one of the devices the cops use. The parking meter registers the payment and the clamps sink back into the road. 'I don't trust those. What if you forget and pull away? You'll rip your wheels off.'

Penny smiles at me, 'Not quite.' She holds a door open for me, and I sink into the plush, cream leather interior. I admire how she walks without a care in the world, elegant, back always straight. She gets in and the car comes to life. The steering wheel folds out of the dashboard.

'Where to?' A voice of silk and satin, more seductive even than Penny's.

Penny raises her arms for the seatbelt to fasten her in. 'Work.' I do the same; the belt snakes like a pervert around my midriff. A map ghosts on the windscreen. We move out into the lane and flow with the traffic.

'So what's the deal?' We pass a man searching through a waste bin, tins and plastic pile up in his shopping trolley.

Penny lifts a finger from the wheel. 'Not while that's there.' A black bird hovers over the road, turning on the spot. 'Are you aware of how many birds can hover that long?'

'Kestrels,' I start counting on my fingers, 'hummingbirds…'

'None,' Penny tracks the bird, 'to be precise. Kestrels can hover for short periods. Hummingbirds

111

flit, hover and flit away. Nothing hovers, rotates ninety degrees and continues to hover. They also do not ascend into the clouds immediately afterwards. There is no such creature in the animal kingdom. That is a drone.' 'A fast one.'

'Also true. It has maintained the same distance from us ever since we left the Coffee Grinder. Now, what could be so fascinating? Siri, take control.' Penny lifts a hand from the wheel, opens the centre consul between us and takes out her gadget.

'You have a thingy too? Twitch has one. Is it a police thing?'

Penny flips the device over in her hand. 'This is a datacorder. We make them at Vetrurn.' The drone appears on the small screen, next to a scrolling column of code. 'We do more than repair humans. We improve them.' Turning to face me her left eye changes colour, flashes, then returns to normal. A screen slides out of the dashboard with a picture of me sitting where I am and my info listed next to it.

'All a bit scary,' I remark, though I don't sound scared, even to me.

The drone falls from the sky, bouncing beneath us. I check the mirror: there is no debris.

'Talise.' Penny releases the wheel and turns to face me. 'You've worked for us for eight years. Never moved on, never changed jobs. How many others do you think have done the same?'

'Loads! Vetrurn is huge.'

'No one sits in the same post for more than two years. Not a policy we enforce, we want people to be the best version of themselves. You are something...

special.' My screen expands, taking up most of the dashboard.

'What's this? Is it an MRI?'

'Not exactly. We have some equipment installed at ReSyk. We assist the police with their investigations. This scan was taken a few days ago. This is you. Or at least, the old you.' Penny swipes a slender finger over the screen, zooming in on the brain. A second brain image appears. 'Do you remember the scan you had in the spring?'

'I had a scan? I don't remember it.' My mouth is dry. I will my heart to slow down but it isn't listening.

'You went for your annual compulsory check-up. When you returned to work the next day, you complained of whistling in your head. This was,' she taps the second brain image, 'your scan.'

'What's all the lightning flashing around?'

'Brain activity. This is mine.' The first image is swapped for a new one. This one has a gentle pulse. 'My brain, as you can see, is within normal parameters. Yours was off the charts, yet you remained calm. Your respiratory, pulmonary and lymphatic systems were all normal.'

I study the figures. This is stuff I know about because I coded the analytical systems. 'So what's the panic?'

The city blurs by in parallax grey.

'The dead you came in for ReSyk.'

'You know about her?'

'As I said, we provide technology to the police, and the military too. We want to move you up in the company. We think you're in danger and want to

protect you. But first, we have to find out how this occurred.' Penny lets it all sink in. 'This is the brain of a normal deceased person. Our new molecular scanner can recall the memories in the brain. They don't last long, but they
do leave a trace, a pattern.'

'Like data on a hard drive?'

'Yes, a good simile.' Penny draws a long breath, her eyes fixed to the screen. 'Yours was blank. Wiped clean.'

Litter twirls in the gutter looking for somewhere dark to hide.

'Wiped?' My brow ripples like sand washed by the tide. 'How, why, who by?'

Penny turns back to look out the window. 'We're here. This is my private space. No one sees us come or go here. Except for Mavis. Let's get inside.'

I follow Penny into the building. We are somewhere on the complex outside the city where no rain falls. A house, from a forgotten time. Wood beams and dark iron-studded doors. The door opens on our approach. Warm light fills the space between the walls. The light flows around us everywhere we go. We hang our coats on an old stand; proud umbrellas stand to attention round the base in a hoop of wood.

I follow Penny's figure through the house. Deep carpet hugs my feet, begging me to stay and enjoy the writhing fire in the hearth.

'Don't be fooled. The house is more than it appears.' Penny turns a corner, shrinking from sight down a staircase lined with family photos. Smiling, happy people playing in the surf, sharing lives. I have no such memories.

Penny steps aside. 'Welcome to my lair.' She sweeps her arm across Techno Wonderland.

'Wow.' Next to a sofa the size of my lounge are three computer desks, each one with three screens. There are no wires anywhere. 'Do I smell cinnamon cookies?'

Penny chuckles. 'Christmas is my favourite time of year. Cinnamon cookies and milk, a childhood memory of my mother. Detectors sense mood and stress, triggering olfactory systems. This is the default response. As you spend more time in here the systems learns you, part of our personalised welfare at work.'

'You're assuming I'm going along with whatever it is you're proposing?' I am though. I want this. I have to string it out and see what other buns are under the counter. Would I serve coffee again? 'You call it a lair. This where you do all the top-secret stuff?' 'Where there are fewer eyes. Yes.'

'Except Mavis?' One last question.

'Yes. Mavis has full access.'

'She's the AI.'

'Smart girl.'

One long stride and I am in my new office chair. My fun is cut short. 'It's alive!' I leap out of the chair, stabbing it with a finger.

Penny laughs. 'The chair is moulding itself to your shape.'

No need for a second invite. 'Ooh.'

'The gel in the seat responds to the electrical activity in your body.' Penny sweeps an open hand around the room. 'It all has sensors. It won't allow you to work if your brain functions are low. You have to take a break.'

115

'What's over there?' A ring of blue-white light cuts a perfect circle in the wall.

'Penny approaches the halo. 'This is the scanner I mentioned earlier. This is the next generation. We hope to be able to recreate memories. Repair damaged brains. ReGen uploads a lot of information to Mind Cloud. That's what they call the metal rings they imbed in people's brains. Crude, but effective. I suspect you have been processed by ReGen without your knowing.'

'Are you serious?' Her face is soft; gentle creases fold in around her eyes. 'You are serious.'

'After Twitch and Joel left ReSyk a few days back, I studied the data from the three bodies, including yours. None of you had legal tags. The UK does not enforce birth tags. The dead you had none, yet the living you does. The Bangers had birth tags but no legal tags. Their anatomical structures were identical, as though they had been cast in the same mould.'

'You think someone is making gangsters? Cosmetic surgery for thugs?' A ridiculous idea. What Banger could afford… 'Oh.'

Penny reaches out a hand. 'What is it?'

'I lost a day. The night Cheryl got off with her new fella. I left Morgan's and ...' My head is ringing.

Penny shakes me by the shoulder, 'And what?' Like a mother.

'I woke up with these,' I say, grasping my boobs. 'And a new arse. I joked with Cheryl 'bout it. We were eating Wong's buns. We'd been to Wong's. It's a bakery. You so need to go there.'

Penny comes over to my chair 'Slow down. Stay there.'

116

'My head.' Squeezing hard. The noise. 'Ringing. Hurts.'

One more breath.

Hacked

'Talise?' I recognise the velvet voice. The soft hand on my skin, the fuzz of peach musk. Penny.

'Where am I?' The light is gentle, the cup in my hand is warm, not hot. Fans, small, purring whispers, dispelling heat behind me. Computers?

'I reclined your chair for your comfort. You fainted for twenty-two seconds. If you are OK with the idea, I would like to scan you and run a comparison?' Penny slides her hand along the arm of my chair. The chair folds in around me, returning me to a sitting position. I press my feet into the floor and breathe.

'Do I have a choice?' I take a sip from the cup. I turn to face her.

Penny smiles a perfect smile. 'We always give you the choice. Only the dead lose the choice.'

'All very reassuring.' I finish the drink and follow Penny to the halo in the wall. 'Where do you want me?'

Penny waits. Draws a breath, then confesses, 'This is an experimental scan. While it completes a full molecular breakdown it also traces the electronic signals within the body.'

'Will it hurt? I don't fancy being sliced, diced and my vitals transmitted to all the perverts.'

117

Penny taps the wall beside the halo. A line draws itself from the ceiling to the floor. 'Because you are conscious, there is no need for the halo.' The line broadens into a slit. A block two inches deep, eighteen inches square slides out from the slit. The block unfolds into a floor panel. Slender arms, black and smooth, assemble themselves into a frame. My first thoughts are a medieval torture cage.

'You want me on there?' I point to the floor panel where two pale-blue footprints glow on the black.

Penny taps the wall again. 'Only if you want to.' A second cage forms next to the first. 'I will join you.'

She slips out of her shoes and steps on the plate. Screens descend from the ceiling. I copy Penny, wishing I could change my socks. Despite her perfect appearance she does not mind my toes poking out through the iridescent orange.

'Sorry.' Now my actions ensure she sees my spuds.

Penny smiles at my feet. 'You can remove your socks. The scanner works best against bare skin.'

'Should I strip?' She raises a hand, laughing. 'Phew, cos I can't remember if I have pants on.'

Penny's eyebrows lift a half inch 'They are right there.'

'Oh! No. I mean knickers, panties. What you call pants we call trousers back home. Oh, whatever.' I want to pull my jumper over my face. 'Can we start?'

'Press the button on the left screen.'

I reach out, my finger quavering over the pulsing green graphic. 'Bugger it.' I jab the button.

The thin arms of my torture booth glow amber; a cooing warmth strokes my body. Beginning from my feet, a model of my body forms on the right display. First the bones and the tissues keeping them together. A network of veins and arteries spiral over a web of muscle. I glance over at Penny's screen. A red light pulses next to her head. When I check mine I have one too.

The amber switches to blue. Globs of light drift across my retina. Now it's red, purple, yellow, a flash of white, and I'm gaping like a fish. When my vision clears Penny is at my side and the cage has returned to its den. Only the footplate remains, warming my feet.

Penny takes my hand. 'All done. You can step down now.' I stumble from the plate, glad of her firm support. She summons a chair with the click of her fingers. I sit and wait while it adjusts to my body. 'Now for the clever bit.' Her tone is higher than normal. Her movements are quicker, more animated. There is a datacorder in her hand.

'When did you pick the thing up?' The upholstery squishes around me as I press myself deeper.

Penny spins around. 'Ah,' she shrugs, 'there is no simple explanation.'

'You're a frickin' robot. I knew it.' Proper genius, me.

Penny smiles. She'd be a great mum, not old enough to be mine, but who's counting? 'Not quite. I was a soldier. We were ambushed by insurgents. Our vehicle was destroyed.' She continues preparing the next part of the science show. 'I was pulled out, but the private who saved me was shot by a sniper. The support group arrived as he bled out. I came home and got a job. Went to pay my respects to his family.'

Another of those cages forms in front of us, big one this time. 'Vetrurn reconstructed me.' She points to her arm and eye. 'Along with new skin: I suffered a lot of burns.'

'So, it is a robot arm!'

'And the eye.' Penny presses a button on the screen in her palm. 'You, my new friend,' the pause is agony, 'are astounding.' The cage lights up like a perfect night sky - hundreds of minuscule lights forming into holograms of me and Penny.

'I'm naked!' I bury my face in my hands. 'First my socks and now this.' The cry of my woe fills my ears.

Penny walks behind me, and rests a hand on my shoulder. 'Me too. Here, see this.' She strolls over to the hologram and detaches her left arm from it. She puts her hands over the image of her face and spreads them out. The skin derezzes. 'These holograms are charged particle arrays. The light particles are excited. Try yours.'

I zing over to my image, with all the goods on display. 'Feels fizzy.'

'Think of it as a touch tablet. Pinch your fingers to zoom in. Grip and swipe to move objects. A quick spread of both hands will break the image into separate parts, the reverse will bring it all together.' Penny goes through the motions, opening up her hologram. There are a lot of wires and computer chips. She must have been hurt real bad.

'Why does it say I'm forty-two? I'm only twentyeight! Stupid thing needs a serious reprogramming.' The skull comes apart in my hand. 'What the fuck is that? Was that the red dot on the screen?'

120

Penny slides an arm around my shoulders. 'The red dot shows the presence of embedded tech. You've seen mine. Yours is Mind Cloud.'

'Bastards.' I swing my fist through the hologram. My brain goes massive. 'I'll sue the fuckers.' Intoxicating lavender fills my nose. I gulp in the fragranced air. 'Fuckers.' Spittle drips from my lip. 'Why does it make me think of Cheryl?' I bury my face again. 'The ring!' 'We will send someone to find her,' Penny's soft tones soothe my rage.

'Is it working now?' I probe the back of my neck; can't feel anything, not even a scar. 'How'd they put it in?'

'You are manufactured. Your brain structure is different, at a guess.' Penny turns the hologram brain in her hands, separating the hemispheres. 'Now I can show you. Your brain is constructed of three sections. The outer hemispheres are a shell. This is not a single unit.'

'Are they dead people?' Wrapping my arms across my chest I take two paces and turn around. 'Why would they do it?'

'They are not from people at all. They are constructs. One-third normal size, inside a shell to keep them together. The Mind Cloud is acting as a clamp, controlling the memory storage. I wonder…'

I follow Penny to the scanner. She taps the wall and takes something out of a long, shallow drawer.

'What are they?' I ask, craning my neck to glimpse the jewellery. She steps back before motioning me forward. The drawer is full of Cloud Rings. 'Where did you find them all?'

Penny's eyes bore right into me. 'ReSyk.'

'These are all from dead people?' My hand goes to my mouth to steady my trembling lip.

'Yes. We signed an arrangement to retrieve any of our augments from the deceased. We enhance people but stipulate that the components must be returned to us on death. We keep finding these. The police, most of the military and now the emergency services are all equipped with them.'

'Wasn't that on the news, a few years back? Some precinct or other.' My fingers hover over the trinkets. 'Can I touch them?' Have to maintain ignorance.

Penny pulls the drawer right out and says, 'Help yourself.' Over a hundred of them in rows of coarse sponge. 'I want to find out if your Cloud Ring can connect with any of these. They are near-field transmitters, one-way communication.'

'Can you read them?'

Penny takes a ring from the drawer. 'Come with me.' We walk beside each other to the computer desk. 'We can access the data, but it is meaningless without a decoder.' A translucent box lights up as she inserts the ring. We sit down and wait for the computer to finish downloading.

'I can hear a whistle. It's quiet. Like a hangover.'

'Been a while since I had one of those - hangover, that is.' The click of acrylic nails on plastic keys amplifies inside my head.

'You got any quieter fingers?' I scan the room for a water fountain. 'Where can I find a drink?'

'Oh, I'm sorry,' Penny swivels in her seat. 'The dispenser is over there.'

'The cabinet.' I am halfway when I realise I've left my shoes by the scanner. Shaking the despair from my thoughts, I open the tall, white cabinet. 'How do I work it?' There is enough space for a big mug and the fingers to lift it. I jab at it and wave my hands in vain.

'Stand in front of it and speak clearly. Tell it what you want and it will attempt to make it for you.' Penny's heels clip across the room. She eases me aside. 'Here, allow me.'

'User, Penny detected,' the dispenser enunciates in perfect HAL 9000.

'Why?' I have to laugh.

Penny feigns hurt, 'He's a classic.' She turns to HAL. 'Earl Grey, hot.' More of those twinkling holographic lights solidify into a cup of steaming tea.

'Picard, really?

'Sexiest Captain of the *Enterprise*.'

'Baldest. Shiniest scalp award.' I hip-nudge the pouting Penny out of the way.

A red-eye irises open. 'New user detected. State your name for system access.'

Creepy, but I resist saying so. 'Talise.'

'How can I assist you, Talise?'

'Coffee.' Simple enough. The twinkling lights solidify into a cup of brown ooze. 'No. Coffee, like at a coffee shop.' More lights. Better but not coffee yet.

'Americano, cappuccino, latte. Brazilian. Kenyan, Columbian. Any combination of these will give more pleasing results,' HAL advises.

Penny blows across her cup and sips her Earl Grey with more noise than necessary.

'Right.' Adjusting my stance I assert, 'Cappuccino, Columbian, easy on the froth.' Lights again. The pervading pleasure of the Coffee Grinder floods my senses. Snatching the cup I take a sip. Tastebud seduction. I am home. 'Perfect. HAL, you're a wonder.'

'Thank you, Talise. Profile updated.'

Penny escorts me back to the desk before coiling into her chair. I hold my cup to my lips, cleanse my nostrils in the bitter steam. Several things happen at once. The translucent box goes dull. The screens flood with data. The rings all expand and my head whistles the national anthem. I stumble into the table, splashing coffee over the keyboard. Penny springs from her chair and whisks it under my arse. I fall into it.

'Ow,' is all my tiny brain can muster.

'Are you alright, Talise?' Penny turns my chair to face her.

'The rings. I don't think I'm meant to see this.' I ball my fists into my eyes. Two cops and a soldier. All dead.

'You can read the data?' Penny puts her hands on mine, lowering them into my lap. Her eyes fill with questions weighed with compassion.

'No. I can see what they saw, how they died. The whistling is the upload. Did you ever do computer history at school?' Penny never stops enquiring with her eyes. She gives a nod. 'The noise of the old modems is what I hear. I understand now. What else did the scanner do?'

Penny recoils. 'Nothing, it builds an image by analysing all the electrical bridges...' She straightens. Turns to the computer and clacks away. I look at mine swimming in coffee and think better of it. 'I have a theory. If true, you got born again.'

'What are you on?' She blitzes through code on the screen. My three-part brain spins around like a bloody Rubik cube, sparking with every turn.

Penny is wired. 'If this is correct, then as the scanner went through your system, new synapses were activated in each of your brains. Signals are crossing over. Perhaps... I'm not familiar with the workings of Mind Cloud, but -' Her nails click against the screen. 'No signals can penetrate this laboratory unless I want them to. ReGen are blind here.'

I poke myself in the chest. 'I'm part of the Cloud?'

'I think so.'

'You need to run tests.'

'Yes.' A single nod. An "I can't make you do it" kind of nod. 'In the field.'

'Will it involve cake?' Pressing my tongue to my teeth. 'Right now, I need cake.'

'Cake is good. Chocolate better.' A jewel leaks from her eye. I reach out and collect it. 'You're very brave.'

I tap a finger to my forehead. 'Can we make a backup?'

'Yes, we can. We should.' Penny pushes my chair from her, spins me around and scoots me over to the scanner.

I go to the wall and prep the Iron Maiden. With a bow, Penny steps back and lets me do it all. I bathe in the amber light. Delight in the union of red, green and blue. My mind is alive. The squeal of the modem subsides. I read every life in the ring collection nestled in the drawer. One hundred and twenty-five more memories are added to the collective. I know their faces, I know their fates. I know the secret things - how the ring in my head works. I, Talise Jones, have been awarded the keys to the kingdom.

Field Trip

Sunlight and rainbows. We're a long way from town. Brompton is somewhere beneath the filth-laden sky, out of view. We choose a car, an older one, an uninspired matt blue. The interior is grey fabric, soft. The springs adjust to comfort me. Penny jumps in beside me, no slinky dress and heels. A simple yellow jersey, dark jeans, all loose fit, and blue trainers, still stunning. She would make potato sacks cool.

Penny drives west to where the ocean rolls against the container ships waiting for a tug to the harbour. Their numbers are dwindling. I count four. Stacked with Lego: red, blue, green and a spot or two of white. Memories of the playroom floor littered with tiny bricks and my bare feet. My younger brother would kick the stuff everywhere. Twat would piss himself with laughter as I danced around, picking bits of plastic from my feet. Prick.

'Oh, I'm sorry, Penny, I was miles away. Thinking about Lego.'

She nods. 'We're going to ReSyk. I have some theories I would like to like to explore. If you're willing?' Penny disarms me with a smile.

She hands me a datacorder. 'How does this work?' Pink one. Think I'll add some cute stickers on the outside, make it mine.

Penny makes a kissy face, wrinkles her nose and sneezes. 'Excuse me.'

'Well-controlled.' I open the datacorder, although in truth it opened itself. 'What's this? Am I supposed to know what this means?' Numbers flow down the screen.

Something clicks in my head, a soft pop. Patterns form in the numbers.

'Siri, drive me to ReSyk.' Penny swivels in her seat. 'You've gone quiet. Are you alright?'

'What do you see?' I flash the screen at her.

'Transmit data. Or at least, it appears to be.' Penny takes my toy and compares it to hers. 'Yes. Transmit data. A new signal. No, a boosted one.'

Vegetation rolls by the window as we sink from the hill toward the harbour. Vetrurn's central unit is up ahead, a huge structure of marble and glass, glittering like a frosted cake. 'Aren't we getting cake?'

'The best bakery is not far from ReSyk, so I thought we'd do a raid on there on the way back.'

'We can go by Wong's, Chinatown?' I wipe the saliva from my lip.

'That good, huh?' Penny returns my gadget. 'What do you see?'

'At first I saw a load of numbers. Then I thought "what is this stuff?" and patterns started to form. The screen is full. Blocks of colour, hundreds of them. I think about sorting them into shapes, Tetris-like.' Love a game of Tetris, me.

Penny cranes over. 'How are you doing that?'

'The signal is coming from the edge of the rain, over there.' The scent of the sea comes up to meet us. Bird drones flock around a blue light: must be a tower of some sort, can't make it out through the haze. 'Some sort of timetable. Numbers and times. The other stuff I've no idea about.'

Penny takes the wheel; this one doesn't fold away. Buttons litter the central spokes, and she hovers her thumb over one. 'Walter, I've some data for your tech team. I have tagged it under "Talise".'

We bump off the road onto a stone-studded dirt track. Sliding my seat back, I reach around for my raincoat. Penny stops the car and fishes about behind us for her coat while I wrestle mine around my back, punching the window in the process. Penny opens her door and steps out, slips her slender arms into her coat sleeves, so ergonomic she sickens me.

'There is no rain here,' Penny holds out her hands. 'See.'

'Oh!' Peering out of the window I notice the wet ground twenty feet away. The door opens with a click and I tumble out in a tangle of sleeves and zips. Penny moves around the car toward the drones. I huff my coat on and scurry along behind her.

The drones' sound is more air current than noise. Penny taps at her datacorder. I do the same: gotta appear knowledgeable. The data is changing. More streams of numbers overlap into one collective thought. They share some of the numbers from the core transmissions. Once assigned, the drones slip into the grey sky and sleep. 'Odd behaviour.'

'What is?' I ask. Penny follows the data source. Time to get wet again. 'The drones received data and went to sleep. Think they might be recharging.' The rain is gentle, refreshing. 'This isn't rain, it's mist. I know a guy who grows weird plants, keeps them under a mist. This ain't natural.'

'No, here we are.' Penny scans the tower. A grey stone base, a nine-foot cube. Green wires trace the edges to the gunmetal legs, piercing the mist, all the way to the blue light. Drones are clustered on all four sides of the tower. Must be hundreds of them. Eight-inch pipes loop out above into some brown tussock grass. Gushing water babbles over stones. We walk toward the sea, still a way off.

My hand drags through the bowed grass. 'It's fake!'

Penny lets the grass slip across her palm. 'A clever fake.' The water gets louder until I almost fall into the gutter stream. A vent clanks underground, spewing out its waste. Penny crouches by the water. 'This is all artificial, some kind of resin, like a garden fountain. She scans everything: stones, grass, soil, pipes and water.

'What do you think it all is?' The stream widens. More pipes gush. The stream deepens into a pool of clear water.

'It's clean, with minute traces of silver.' Penny stares out to sea, checks her palm and turns to me. 'There's a sequence here that I'm not seeing. Frustrating, to say the least. The need for chocolate grows.' We scythe through the grass tugging at our feet. The car has turned itself around. 'We are being surveilled.' We head back and get in the car.

'Drone?'

'Drone.' Penny eases the pedal to the floor.

'One's coming.' A red dot pulses on my screen, trailing digits. 'Are they armed?'

'No idea.' Penny thumps the centre of the steering wheel. 'Shield.' The car shimmers pink.

The drone circles around us. Another dot pulses. 'HUD.' Side windows turn black and the windscreen becomes a combat display.

Red dots appear on the windows. 'Are they targeting us?'

Penny smiles, 'No, we're targeting them. Can you still read their signal data?'

'Yes. We're about to have a lot more company.' Rain pelts the shield but not the car, the view is perfect. 'This is nice. A bit cotton candy. I like it.'

Penny swings the wheel; a drone slips behind us. 'I'm so glad you approve.'

'Someone kicked the hive.' Lots of dots, the whole display goes red. 'Data merging.' I concentrate on the data. Streams combine. The dots vanish, exposing their four-character codes. 'Hex.'

'I forgot that you code.' Penny gives an appreciative nod. 'Incoming.' The view turns black - drones. 'Fortunately for us, I don't need to see the road.'

'They're shooting at us!' Ducking forward to escape the fireworks on the window, I drop my datacorder. 'Bollocks!'

'A true Brit.' Penny eases back.

'Why are you slowing?' Retrieving my new favourite toy, I sit up.

'Small calibre fire, insufficient to penetrate the shield.' Penny's confidence is not as reassuring as she may think.

'Thirty-two drones. All in sequence 00 to 20 hex. Tower has one hundred and eight more.'

Penny stops the car. 'Can you tell if they have any protection?' The drones fire away at the screen. 'Don't panic. I've analysed their ordinance. In numbers they can kill, but alone they are unable to penetrate the armour on the vehicle.'

'Reassuring,' I lie. 'They have no protection at all. Polycarb shell, tiny weapon. Could be Rickets.' Heat races to my face. 'Sorry, thinking out loud.'

Penny drops the shield. The drones close in. She counts, 'One, two, three.' The shield flares out from the car. The attack is over. 'EMP.' Opening the door, she turns to me. 'Come on, let's see what kind of birds we have in the net.'

I'm not keen on the idea. Penny has had all kinds of military training I'm a trained barista with a science degree. This scares me. Penny tears one apart. 'Clipped together. Not expecting anyone to mess with them. Almost a toy.'

'Smart way of hiding what you're up to.' I yank one apart too. 'What's this?' Buried in the heart of the drone is a small hopper of yellow-grey grain. We break a few more. Some have the grain while others have small highenergy cells.

'We'd best take these to Walter's team.' Penny searches the skies. Grey over Brompton, bright sun everywhere else.

We gather everything into the boot of the car and head to Vetrurn's principal office. We were close enough to spit at the perimeter when the drones attacked. Minutes later we park at a loading bay. A squad of guys pick over the car. The drones are whisked away to a secure area and we get a new vehicle, the same as the last one right down to the reg plate. Am I part of a small militia?

Is the cake a lie?

We drive out of the old industrial gate into Brompton. People go about their lives as though rain is all they know. A ten-mile drive in any direction will land you in the desert. Heat is what we know. Heat is why I came. Rain I have back in Blighty.

Penny takes a breath, the kind when something has to be said, the elephant-in-the-room kind. 'Earlier, you mentioned Rickets. Do you know him?'

'Know of him.' The neon signs are dull today. Brompton scrolls by in a cartoon parallax, the same five houses on an endless loop.

'You want to talk or -'

'I hate him. He goes to the Rooster bar, where I dance.'

'Really!'

'Yeah, I dance. Pole, not lap.' Penny's catching flies, mouth open and everything. I want to string her along so bad. 'Rickets is in with the owner, Ms Clark.'

Penny whispers a name, 'Jane. Oh, oh I'm sorry, do continue.'

'You know Jane?' We turn at the crossroads on the border of Downtown. The cathedral spire flips a finger at the world and we turn west. 'She's a weird one. Suits

Rickets, he's an arsehole too.'

'Jane is the liaison between Vetrurn and ReGen. She worked out the tech share. They keep a lot from us.' Penny slows for the entrance to the mausoleum of ReSyk.

'And you tell them everything, yeah?' I pick at the seal around the window.

'No. They're, how did you put it, assholes.'

'Arseholes. We put an "r" in it rather than our fist.' We both laugh and get out of the car.

'Your datacorder grants you full security clearance here and over at our ReGen research laboratory. I'll take you there another day, once we have the breakdown on those drones and we know what to search for.' Penny palms her way into the building. With a buzz, my datacorder opens the door. I pass through unmolested. She leads me to the locker room where we kit up and head over to her scanner.

So many dead people here. The ones at Twitch's were different somehow. One was me: weird, I know. The other two - I don't remember their faces, they're slabs of meat to me now. There are more like them going through the process. We wiggle on and bypass all the gooey stuff. But there's a surprise waiting for us on the scanner.

'What's it say?'A note has been stuck on the scanner, a body lies on a sled.

'It's from your friend, Twitch. He wants us to check the "stiff" out and let him know what we find.'

'Can't he do the scan himself? And how long has this dude been here?' I peek under the cloth. 'I mean, has *she* been here. Damn, one manly woman.'

'Let's load her up.' Penny takes the sled and loads the woman into the scanner. Fascinating as it is, I prefer my scanner back at the office. 'She has a Cloud Ring.'

'How? The scan is incomplete.' Penny puts a hand on one hip and taps a toe.

'The upload. I was trying to resist, but I thought what the heck,' I shrug. 'Lynne Cooper. Security on West Quay. Odd thing, though.'

'What?' Penny summons the hologram and sends the body for recycling.

'There's more in her Cloud Ring than a few minutes of near death. All her personal data. Bank stuff, all sorts. Can you cancel the recycling?' 'Why?'

Penny blinks.

'She ain't quite dead.'

Twitch

Kid

'You called?' Kid's basement is dark. Reeks of body odour and pizza. Coke cans wrangle for dominance on every available surface with crisp packets and chocolate bar wrappers.

Kid has his hand out. 'Decoded.' I take a wedge from my pocket and flick him a twenty. He makes a face like somebody farted.

'Gimme a clue,' I prep another twenty.

'Coordinates.' He waves Talise's printout like a pair of panties. The twenty edges his way. 'And override code. Bit like those idiots trapped in MyTown.'

'Makes no sense. Override what?' We swap notes. Unfolding the paper I go blank. I'm aware, just not aware, not there anymore. Kid snatches the paper from my hand and the world swims back in.

'Where'd you go, man?' Kid shoves the paper in my face. I go again. 'This is hilarious.' We spend some time playing peekaboo with the printout before the penny drops. 'Oh, shit. You have it too. Only different.'

'I have what?'

'I suggest you lose that.' Kid points to the paper. 'Stop looking at it!' He feeds it to the shredder. 'I'll mail Joel a copy.'

'Might be best.' A yawn stretches my face. 'You have any luck with the ring?'

'I so did,' Kid scratches at his mop of ginger hair. 'The ring is a data store. This one is from a soldier. First Lieutenant Sutcliffe. Served three years in the field, science geek. Discharged through injury.'

'Same shit the cops have?' The ring feels heavy in my hand. 'Ain't these clamped around the brain stem?'

'Yep, to it all.' Kid slurps coke from a can.

'If she's alive then how'd that ring end up in a dead girl's mouth?' I grasp my head between my hands.

'You OK, Twitch.' Kid plucks the ring from my hand. 'How the hell did you open it?'

'Open what?'

He catches me before I hit the floor and flops me into a tatty, black leather chair. The high back curves around me.

'The ring. Dude, look at it.' He holds it out on his palm. The stack has separated, split open. He takes the ring over to his trash-heap desk. Between the screens sits a black box in an eruption of wires and clips. He puts the ring in a yellow foam donut and attaches a couple of small clamps. Kid's fingers blur over the keyboard, thrashing out code. A second screen erupts with windows, stacking them like a game of patience. 'I should not be seeing this.'

'Seeing what?' I scoot the chair over to his side and lean in. 'I know her. The chick from ReSyk.'

'ReSyk? Says here Vetrurn.' Kid expands a window on the screen. 'See, Vetrurn.'

'Penelope Sutcliffe. Research Specialist at Vetrurn, second in command to Walter Stapleton.' I sit back. 'She gave nothing away. Came across a bit stuck up.'

'There's a name here you should see.' Kid opens another window.

A young girl with a blue streak in her hair over her right eye turns from the camera. 'Talise. What's she got to do Vetrurn and Penny?'

138

'Notice anything?'

'Nothing obvious,' I lean back in. 'Who's that nerd?'

'Not him, Quayside.' Kids points a finger. 'Some group, huh?'

'Well I'll be…' A bell chimes. Kid stares up at a security monitor. Joel's ugly face peers back. 'Make him wait. No, let him in, he's got food.' Joel lumbers down the stairs, an oak of a man. Never still, scared of taking root.

"S'up?' Joel dispenses the goods. The bag has weight, two maybe three items. 'You're like a kid. It ain't Christmas. Santa ain't coming down no chimney.'

'We don't have one,' Kid laughs, lifting a slice of pizza from a box. He sticks the rest down on the side and takes a second slice. He bites from each one in turn.

Joel pulls a chilli burger the size of his head from a paper sack. The smell is inviting, but I know the taste will send me straight to the crapper. The conversation is reduced to caveman grunts and primitive gestures. Man-talk is the order of the moment, interspersed by coke-fuelled belches and anal venting.

'How's town?' Kid belches his ABCs.

'Wet.' Joel tosses his coat over a heap of clothes.

'Careful.' Kid pounces on the offending coat. 'Can't ruin the disguise.' He separates a brown shirt and black combats from the heap, tossing them across the room to fester in solitude.

'Where'd you get the family photo?' Joels stalks across to the computer desk.

'Courtesy of Penny.' I mimic her soft tones. Still needs work, but it gets Joel in the right spot.

'Hey, she's a good girl. Ain't one of yours.' Joel winks back. 'S'who are they are all?'

'We've got Talise. Rickets, old man Timms, and Ms Clark. Plus Penny of course.' The chair rolls back as I stand. Kid moves toward me. 'I'm OK.'

'He have one of his turns? You try and make him work?' Joel swings an arm around my shoulders and coils me in. 'He's kinda delicate, soft - weak.'

'I love you too. Not in the sausage way.' Joel slides his hand down my back and tweaks my arse. 'Don't.' I jab a finger at his joint-laden lips.

'Sweet-cheeks.' Joel rolls the joint to the other side of his mouth.

'You guys all loved up? I have a question.' Kid tugs the ring from its cradle. 'What are we going to do with this? I mean, it's evidence but it's impossible evidence, right?'

'Right.' The ring snicks shut in my hand.

Joel hands Kid a thumb drive. 'The only questions we need to answer are simple. Who put the ring in the girl's mouth, and why? We have a line-up of suspects right there.' He waves at the screen.

'What matters is when was that? Talise is younger, and Timms, well, not seen him in a while. Jane had nothing to do with Rickets until after the announcement of the Cloud thing.' I ponder, staring down into the coffee Joel has thrust into my hand.

'Unless she did.' Kid passes the thumb drive back to Joel.

'Unless she did what?' The coffee is sweet and strong.

'Unless Jane knew Rickets all along. What if Rickets is ReGen?' Kid opens another coke and glugs it down. 'Could be.' The spliff waggles back across the plump Caribbean mouth. 'Didn't he just come outa nowhere. Somewhere downstate?'

'Yeah.' My hand feels greasy as I run it through my thinning hair. 'So did I. Half the force are new. People have been leaving the lower precincts for years. Most of them are new guys.'

'All got those rings?' Kid points at my pocket.

'Yeah,' I shrug. 'It's the rule. No thanks to Rickets volunteering his brain.'

'Rickets was first!' Kid laughs. 'This photo looks all too convenient. Someone wants you to see this. You were meant to get this shit cracked. I've told you all along this rain ain't real.'

'Don't start the conspiracy shit.' Somewhere in a corner of this dungeon is a bed. 'What would anyone gain from making it piss down all the time?'

'Plenty.' Joel's about to dispense his fortune-cookie wisdom. 'No one is looking up. We all go round with our heads down. But I think someone has overstepped. We got warehouses of containers. Electric trucks driving themselves all over the city.'

Kid nods along like a toy dog, 'And the drones. Hundreds of fuckin' drones everywhere.' His eyes snap to me. 'ReGen has a tower spitting them into the sky.' His eyes brighten. 'Those containers. Full of bodies, from all over. Pnu-90 - they made the virus. Four thousand a day dying out there, in this country alone. More than a million all told, and this shit's only gettin' started.' He wipes the spit from his mouth on his

141

stained sleeve. 'Except in Brompton. What we got? Two or three cases in the hospital. We got the only hospital with empty beds! ReGen fund the city. No one asks questions. Well, they should.' He lashes at the air, his face red and sweaty.

'There must be more than three people sick in Brompton.' I shake my head.

Kid stabs at the keyboard. 'Here.' Admission details, he's got the hospital records! 'See. Two. Minor infections, both from Downtown. I'm telling you, this shit is man-made and controlled by ReGen. They got shit down there can raise the dead.'

Jane stares at me from the screen. 'That image is less than five years old.'

Joel squints at it. 'How so?'

'The blue crane, zoom in on it.' The desk presses against my leg. 'Closer. There.'

'Well I'll be ...' Joel catches the falling spliff. 'Same warehouse where we found Talise and those Bangers. Construction started in '85. Jane came to the precinct in '85, three months after Rickets.'

Kid is jacking code. 'Bet he already had the ring.' More data pops up on the screens than any normal brain can fathom. 'There.' He waggles a finger. 'Birthdate. That's the real one, and there's the inception date. Eight years difference.'

'You're pulling my dick.' The whistle returns. 'My head.' Joel catches me in those simian arms.

Joel has big brown eyes with milky whites. 'What's up?'

His hands are warm on my skin. 'I feel... odd. Head whistling, getting stronger.'

'This happened earlier.' Kid searches the desk, scattering trash. Tins rattle on the floor, rolling away to the underworld beneath the desk. 'I'll get help.' 'No hospitals.' I want to puke.

'You know this one.' Kid snatches up a bundle of duct tape with buttons. He jabs a couple and waits. 'It's on speaker.'

A single ring and it's picked up. 'Hello, Kid?' I know the voice.

'Got a friend in need, down here in the cave. You need to see this.' Kid hangs up.

'Now what?' I force the lump in my throat down.

'We wait.' A map pops up on the screen. It's local. A dot leaves Chinatown.

'How are you doing that?' My head shakes. Hands wave in the ether, not all are mine. 'Don't bother to answer. You'll hurt my head with science.'

In Two Minds

Bells ring, crowding thought space. Faces swirl in and out. Everyone is talking in tin cans, metallic facades of reality. Thunder of feet on stairs beating my eardrums into submission. Lips move, words cascade into water. New voices enter the maelstrom, dopplering across the void in my head. 'Focus.' Colours, girly shades of yellow, blue, and pink in perfumed clouds break the atmospheric fug. A pleasing miasma of summer. Summer, what is summer? People break in, or is it out? Faces from a present past. A soft hand caresses me. Glossed lips brush love against my own.

'Twitch!' The whistle ceases. 'You in there?' Weight leaves my pocket and mind simultaneously. Blue hair flops down, striping an eye. Pink fuzz covers a torso perched on blue.

Talise? The name drags its way out. 'Penny?' Wow, a head-turner in plain clothes. 'What happened? Why are you here?'

'Kid called for help. When he calls, we come. We take care of our own.' Penny clears a chair, commands the seat. 'Any chance of a safe drink? You really do need to clean up, Kid.' Kid hides his blushes and carves a trail to the kitchen.

Joel moves to a spare computer and fires it into life. The datacorder comes out: he's up to something or avoiding something. He does something.

'Perhaps you can fill in some blanks.' My brain slops around in my head. Slapping to one side it melts into a soup at the bottom. 'Can you explain this?' The chair rolls back and I stagger into the table. Legs feel strong but loose at the knee. 'This picture here. I put it about '85.'

She don't bat an eye, 'You'd be right. I was there with Talise.' Talise turns to the screen. 'Rickets, his assistant Wilson, old man Timms, and Jane. Your ex-wife, I believe.' Perfect, emotionless report.

Stubble rasps my palms as I try to make sense of it all. 'Current wife. Never divorced. She looks well. Should be dead.' Next time I'll make sure of it. Stick a knife deep in her gut and tear her stone heart right out. 'Tell me, Rickets.'

'I don't remember being there. Is that the dead me?' Talise runs a finger over the face of the nerd in glasses.

'It's the dead you. You've been created since then. If you have no memories, perhaps we should try to unlock them. They did, after all, empty your old mind. As for Rickets,' Penny blows out her cheeks, 'well, we believe Rickets is patient zero.'

'Patient zero?' My mind jangles.

Joel presses keys and chases the mouse around the table. 'The first one.'

'First one what?' Something moves in my head.

'To have a Cloud Ring. You have one too.' Talise taps the back of my head. 'I can feel it.' She looks at Penny. 'He's a construct. Just like me, only older.'

'A... what!' I turn Talise around to face me. 'I'm a what?' My hands shake, the world shrinks. Parts of my mind are going dark.

'We were both made in a lab somewhere. I'm guessing ReGen. It's possible Rickets was too. We all need to get to safety.'

145

'I knew it!' Kid spills drinks everywhere. 'I told you all!'

Talise looks to Penny. 'The House. Has it enough rooms?'

Without hesitation, Penny is herding us out the door. 'It would help us all.'

'I, I can't go. I have work - in town.' Kid darts across the room for his uniform.

'You kidding me?' Talise in on him. Poor Kid. 'But how?'

Kid fumbles beneath his matt of hair, above the nape of his neck. His face falls, eyes round out. 'Hello, Talise.'

Bren.

'Why?' Talise's shoulders sag. 'You watched me change!'

Kid goes jazz hands. 'Can explain.'

'Fucking right you will.' Talise marches him out by the nipple.

We file out in turn. Penny pulls out a datacorder. 'Kid is coming in. Clear the place.'

Outside the weather is grim. Everything is washed out. Talise shoves Kid into the back of Penny's car; thought she might have something with a bit more swank. I jump in the pickup with Joel and follow Penny out of town. She don't hang around. Straight to the speed limits, never misses a gap, no pause. She's good.

'What is it, Joel? I can see questions all over that face of yours.' He sucks his teeth.

'You OK?' He watches from the corner of his eye. He opens the glove compartment and takes a match from a box, holds the stick in his lips.

'I'm OK.' A thousand thoughts jangle my mind.

'OK.' The matchstick disappears at one side of his mouth then reappears at the other, then rolls across his lip.

'OK. I'm OK.' I drum the wheel as we leave the rain behind.

'You ever reach out to those gangs?' He's watching every crease in my face. I sense him, scrutinising me.

'Yup, they say they don't come to Brompton. Nothing here worth fighting over.' Which is true: a simple text to a snitch and we get all we need. They don't want a piece of this town. Some bitch sets herself up as queen of the snort. Ain't enough worth dying for.

Joel fiddles with his datacorder. 'What do you make of these rings?'

'Something stinks. To be honest, I can't recall a single perp coming in for cop killing. In truth, I don't recall much at all. Memories are all pretty recent.'

Joel tuts, 'Serious? You don' remember being out on the wagon? None of the stuff on site? Nutt'n' I taught ya!' He shakes his head with an elephantine weight.

'Nothing. I've been trying to remember life before Jane. I don't even know when we met. There's a few bits, broken memories. Take just now. I was having that moment when the girls arrived. I remembered a kiss. Glossy lips on a summer day. Jane never wore gloss.' Purple or red, deep colours, matching nails.

'You don' remember fishin'?' Joel sinks inches into his seat. 'I taught you to cast, down on the beach. Watching the sunset, smoking pot and getting wasted.'

'Nothing.'

Joel wipes his eyes for effect. 'I'm so hurt right now.

You done gone tossed away my friendship.'

'If you say so. But I don't remember that either.' A gate bars our way. Nothing more than you'd expect at a posh house. The gate slides open, gives me a sense of hidden security. I watch the sky for drones. There's nothing out here but sun and blue sky. I should move out here; the brown earth and cactus invite solitude.

'Well, here we are.' Joel is out before the handbrake is engaged.

I follow on. Eyes everywhere. Brompton is not a safe place. The weather sits over town in a fungal cap. A weeping mushroom smothering the city with its viral spore. The sea is there, rolling west into the spangled horizon. Penny's car has to be the most boring vehicle possible to own. Nothing to make me want it. A dull interior encased in a duller box of flat lines. I punt the rear bumper to let it experience my disdain. Solid. One good thing.

'Hey!' Joel waves.

Penny is waiting. 'I would check my watch if I owned one.'

'Wouldn't make me hurry.' The place is impressive. Simple furnishing. So much space. So much light. Windows along most walls pulling in light. A fire burns in a hearth beneath a black timber mantle. I breathe in the scent of smoking wood though no smoke escapes the hearth.

'Follow the stairs down. You can search the place later.' Most women would annoy me with a comment like that. Not this one. I want to dislike her, get under her skin, but I can't.

148

Taking the stairs two at a time I spring into the room. Kid acquaints himself with a computer; he's never so happy, even without the brain clamp. Talise has Joel in some sci-fi gadget, probably end up with a part on *Planet of The Apes*. Penny wanders by, gestures for me to join the party with Joel.

'You probably have questions for me too.' Talise pulls at a hologram of Joel. 'As human as he can be.'

'So it's bust?' They stare at me. 'It sees him as human, with those arms!'

Joel two-finger salutes, 'Funny boy.' He points to the frame he stepped from. 'Shoes and socks off.'

'You can't be serious.' A big ape hand sweeps me across the floor. 'If you insist.' I kick my shoes at the oaf and peel off my socks. Feet are a bit black, maybe I should hunt down a shower. Maybe.

Talise has a serious face on. 'This won't hurt.'

Joel sucks his teeth. 'Damn.'

Amber? Should I get ready to run? Two screens fill with data. One has a flashing light. Is that ever a good thing? The scanner whirs and flashes but it all ends well. We're still friends.

'Penny,' Talise's tone is soft, cautious.

Penny steps up to the hologram and yanks out the brain. Boom, it's in pieces. 'Two parts.'

Joel pokes at the image with his gorilla mitts. 'Always knew you was a half-brain.'

Talise twists out the core of my brain. 'The Cloud Ring is different too. Not standard, and not like yours, but something in between.'

'You had one? How'd you get it out?' I sidle around behind them, don't want to damage my fragile mind.

Penny pouts and sighs, 'I had similar problems to you. The whistle. It all began after the bomb. At first, I believed it to be an after-effect of the blast. PTSD or something. When I came here, for augmentation, the whistle ceased. I discussed it with James, head of research back then. Before his death.'

'Nice guy.' Joel glares over at Kid, who's whooping like he's won the lottery. 'I'll go see.'

'Talise worked with him. You won't remember. The inhibitors in your ring are blocking signals all over your brains.'

'Brains, plural?' Here comes the science shit. I pull up a chair.

'You have a dual brain, two coupled together. Talise has three. Her Cloud Ring is different from all the others. To answer your next question, we get them from ReSyk when we reclaim our tech. You're both a kind of sleeper cell. I am not convinced you are supposed to know. The scanner activated synapses in Talise's brains and she has learned to communicate with other rings.'

Talise drops into a chair at my side, 'Not always willingly. The woman you asked us to scan at ReSyk -'

'I'd forgotten her.' A small detail.

'She wasn't dead, not quite. Not in a coma either. You know those science films when they whoosh off into deep space in a sleep pod?'

'Stasis chambers.' Why does that worry me?

'She, Lyne Cooper, is in stasis. The scanner couldn't detect it. The ring in her head activated when I got near and dumped its data in me. This scanner has done the same to you. You will experience memory bleed between your brains. I'm guessing, more hoping, they'll settle down at some point, become one.'

'Kinda makes sense. I had a flash earlier when you came for us. A memory, not mine. More a sensation.'
'And?' Penny leans across, stares right into me.

The words catch in my throat, 'A kiss. It wasn't Jane.'

'An ex?' Talise grins.

'More - current. Only...'

Joel lumbers up. 'He don't have no ladies. To be true, he don't do hookers neither.'

'Thanks, Joel. Why don't you tell everyone how sad I am.?' The shit.

'They can already see that!' Joel ruffles my hair.' He's a good boy. Makes his momma happy.'

'You're an arse.' I join in the laughter, with everyone but Kid. He's having a party all his own, punching the air like he won the Super Bowl.

Penny and Joel stroll side by side over to Kid.

Talise glances my way more than once. 'I get it, Twitch. Since Wilson vanished I've got no one. I might act all free-spirited but I run a mile when it gets physical.' I ain't listening much. Those lips do more than talk. 'One day, Talise,' I get up, place a hand on her shoulder, 'we'll find where he went. Get some peace for your heart.'

'Thanks.' Talise shuts the scanner down and joins the rest of the gang at the computers.

'This gear is unreal!' Kid's grin is a maniacal charade of yellow teeth. 'I've got all my files from backup. Killed my systems back home and –' He spins a full circle in his chair. 'ReSyk. Couldn't get in before. Always, always shut me down and booted me out. Bastards even slipped a worm up my ass.'

'So what are we looking at?' A screen full of numbers.

'Production stats. They see it as a factory. These figures are the bodies coming in. This is the throughput of each stage. This is weird.' Kid bounces around in his seat, opening windows and probing data.

'Well, that's litres and units.' Nothing unusual there. Loads of places use those measures.' I don't get it either.' Not sure how it'll help me.

'They process bodies into a liquid and,' Kid rattles the keys, 'stripped units. Skeletons.'

New Day

Today is the first time I've awoken with a clear head. Could it be the sun? Sunlight, I almost forgot you. My room or suite is stunning. How can one person live alone in a place this size? Talise had warned me about the shock of waking up in such palatial surroundings, she wasn't wrong. The whole place creates a sense of wellbeing. I even had shower and shave without a second thought. Didn't need to get into an argument with myself about the merits of beards and the grief of shaving. There are clean clothes. Who bought them? An outfit almost identical to the worn-out shirt and chinos I always wear.

There's a knock at my door. Wandering over, I switch on the TV for the update.

'Hi,' Talise kicks at her feet. 'Want some breakfast?' 'Um, er. Sure.' Playing it cool is not a strength. Walking into things is my specialist skill. 'Your lips look good this morning.' Damn it, Twitch! Asshole.

Talise shrinks back, 'Thanks?' She quick turns before the crimson tide flushes her skin. Her hair dusts her shoulders with its silver-grey tips.

'You change your hair colour?' I have some recovery to do. We never got off to a great start. Now we are under the same roof, I need to get it right.

'Yeah,' Talise sounds dry. 'Keeping the blue though, Wilson put it there.' I follow her downstairs where the kitchen opens around us.

All the usual trappings of wealth are here. Fitted kitchen festooned with enough storage to stash a dozen corpses. Talise keeps checking over her shoulder; must think I'm about to scarper or something. I'm going nowhere, not just yet, things are getting interesting. And by interesting, I mean weird.

We step out into the morning sun. I expected it to be hotter. Temperatures rise fast on the cactus plains. Then I see it: a barrier of electricity and light. Have I walked into prison? Joel waves, pale rolls trapped between his fingers. He shovels something fishy into his cavernous, grinning maw. Kid is dining out on pizza and coke, hacking the world. Penny is in t-shirt and leggings sifting news items on a holo-screen: virus figures, warring factions, nations ravaged by famine raping their neighbours, bloodshed and countless grieving faces.

'Anything local?' Everyone is eating something. 'Smells great round here. How do I get some?' Penny walks through the projection. For a moment Rickets' face appears on her back, the last place she'll want him. 'I'll show you how the kitchen works.' I follow the legs back inside. 'It's simple once you get used to it.' She steps away from the counter and folds out a screen from beneath a cupboard. 'Find what you want.' She invites me to scroll through a digital cookbook.
There's food from all over the world. A full English!

'Without the blood sausage, if you can?'

Penny guides me back to the worktop. 'Tap the screen.'

I oblige. Blue lights criss-cross the space beneath the screen. An empty plate appears. I wave my hand over it. A subtle warmth rises to caress my skin.

'Now choose the amount of each item and the plate will fill. You can get a drink here too. We also have a dispenser outside. I'll show you how that works later. Enjoy.' Penny legs it out to the verandah.

The plate dares me to fill it. I press the sausage on screen and the blue lights deliver one to my pate. I add another, again my desire is fulfilled. Bacon, eggs, tomatoes, toast, mushrooms, all there, all hot. All mine. For this alone, I could get along with Penny. Heaven smells of bacon; my bacon smells of heaven. Others would tell you it's incense and lamb, but they're wrong. The reason God said not to eat pigs is he wants all the bacon for himself. The replicator dispenses cutlery.

Taking it all, I skip outside and grab a seat where I read Penny's screen. Newsgirl coughs into her hand. Rickets jabbers on, oblivious. Quayside throbs with life. Trucks rumble in and out of the picture. Tower cranes raise loads and lower rooves, keeping out prying eyes. The sun spangles on the water filling the camera lens with doughnuts of light. For a brief moment, the grey sky is bleached clean.

There, a shadow against the sun, a ball of black wings flits toward ReGen. Angles change and the world dulls. Rain squalls on the ocean, waterspouts play in the space between cloud and sea. Rickets diverts the lens outward away from the twin white trucks heading for the off-ramp into the city. Newsgirl hacks out an apology, grasping at her throat. Blood bubbles from her mouth. The virus count hits three. Rickets is over the girl in a rash of hands. He drives the crew away and flips open his new datacorder. Penny opens her hand. Her palm glows with the words 'Rickets active'. She closes her hand. Rickets clears the area for the ambulance.

Start counting Rickets, this one's on you.

Breaking news. Officer Rickets' prompt action saves the life of newsgirl. An ambulance arrives in under two minutes. It's a six-minute drive to the hospital. Rickets helps the crew with the sled. Who's he kidding? She's loaded. Rickets is in for the ride. The ambulance heads south along Quayside. Hospital is north then east. Penny checks her hand again. Writes something with her finger. My datacorder buzzes in my pocket so I take it out and open it. Message from P. Sutcliffe. I accept the note. A map appears, tracing a blue dot with the name 'Rickets' all the way through town.

Time to get busy.

Penny shuts the holo-screen and says, 'We have to hurry.'

'I'm with you.' Talise dumps her breakfast things on the table and heads inside. 'Which car?'

Penny raises a finger at Joel. He sinks back into his chair and opens a holo-screen. 'We'll take the sedan.'

'Traveling in style?' We cut through the kitchen and out of a side door to the car porch.

Penny is fast. 'Pickup trucks, the epitome of style. Sexy warthogs.' The car doors spring open as we approach. We pile in. Penny floors the pedal and we boost along a private track swinging south. Everything out this way belongs to Vetrurn. We hit the edge of the rain at speed; triple figures. Penny pre-empts every hazard, be it litter or living. The windows darken.

'Here they come.' Talise plucks a screen from the passenger dash. I roll around in the back seat, scanning for assassins. Birds plummet from the clouds, perpendicular to the road ahead. Electricity and light flash across the bodywork. The car is alive. Sparks fly.

'What the fuck are these?' For no reason, I duck behind a seat.

'ReGen drones. They are becoming more aggressive.' Penny opens her left hand. Her palm is a datacorder. 'Tech.'

'Tech here, Miss Sutcliffe.' A voice traces across the screen.

'There's an illegal tower on our property. Coordinates coming over. It's armed with drones. Secure it.'

'Will do. Tech out.'

'You're a cyborg?' I hang onto the back of her seat to examine the driving machine.

'I want to try something before you blow them up.' Talise draws a circle around the drones on her screen with her finger.

We crest a rise and drop right. Penny leans my way to confide, 'Left arm and eye. Vetrurn tech.'

'Military? You drive well. Fast, but good.'

Penny nods, eyes locked ahead. 'Thank you.'

'Got them.' A data window opens beside the drones on the screen. Talise highlights the data and deletes it. Grasping the screen in both hands, she closes her eyes. Opens them. New data fills the window. The drones stop, vanish into the cloud base.

'What did you do?' Penny eases back as we enter Brompton.

Talise draws a breath. 'Bren cracked the code last night. It gives simple commands. Collect, deploy,' she counts on her fingers. 'Grid reference. Dock. Target acquire, attack. Cease. Every command has a number. The sequence reads as binary, a simple yes or no.'

'But how did you fill it in so quick?' Brompton blurs by in a shot of neon with a trash chaser.

'I connected to the pad. It's close to the Cloud frequency.' Talise flicks through the sequence on the screen, just her mind doing the work while she files her nails. 'My old mind is coming back. I was a science geek, it's how I met Wilson.' She chases raindrops across the shield as we speed through town. Pictures of Wilson peer out of the screen. Could a guy be more geek? A pocket of pens, a thermos flask on his desk, anorak to end all anoraks, round-rim specs, a stack of superhero comics, and the heart of Talise. One lucky guy.

We turn at the Downtown crossroads and race down the strip. The monolith of ReSyk blends with the sky, obscuring its identity. Penny swings us around the back to the Vetrurn slot. Glad to be undercover without a coat, vulnerable to the elements. We all are. We head inside. Staff only, no need to scan.

The building is quiet. The roster reads two local homicides and four stiffs from across the county. Batch processing is a new thing. We kit up as we pass through. Datacorders in hand we locate Rickets in the main hall. He ain't stopping. Not even registering the girl. Penny picks up the pace, we're jogging hard. I press my arm across my chest. Must take better care of myself; chest is too bouncy. One more door. Penny waves me and Talise around the corridor and dives through the door. We carry on around and I soon find out why.

The corridor leads to the end of the main hall. Talise gets there first. My heart is thumping, I want to stop. The door crashes open. Rickets is almost there. The next stop is strip-down where Newsgirl will be skinned alive. Penny rushes forward. Rickets bangs into the double doors. Lights flash in silent alarm. Through those doors a monster stirs, its arms reaching out, a mantis praying for food. Penny crashes through the door. There are screams.

Where's Talise?

Rickets

Barrel of a Gun

The bitch from the labs comes at me fast. What can a boffin do to me? I laugh. 'C'mon, try me.' She plants a hand on the sled, swings her feet up and over. My fist is already on its way to where her guts will be. The door bangs open into the sled: some unfortunate sap running through gets a timber kiss. The prof lands firm, grabs my wrist, pulls me forward. Her other hand stabs me in the armpit and cracks my elbow out of joint. Pain. Searing pain. She kicks the back of my knee. I'm down. Bitch has me dangling by my wrist.

'Hello Rickets, going somewhere in a hurry?' Bitch kneels beside me, bends my arm too far. Tendons creak. 'I'm Penny, the one you stole the datacorder from.' She takes the device from my pocket, spilling my trash on the floor.

'What do you want?' My bark don't scare her, she ain't afraid of no ghosts.

'Everything OK in there?' As if being beat by a skinny-assed broad weren't bad enough. Twitch.

'That ya boyfriend out there?' The cough hurts my chest.

Penny eases off the arm. 'She should be in hospital, not here. Murdering a civilian is against the law last time I checked.'

'What's it to you?' The clouds in my head break. 'You're Stapleton's bitch. Shit.'

'Twitch, go left through the locker room, then second right. Rickets has been neutered, haven't you?'

I kick out at nothing. I wrap my free hand around a small iron bar in my pocket. Shoulda brought a gun or at least a knife. This bitch needs spaying.

'What did you do to Dawn?'

'Who's Dawn? I don't know any Dawn.' I'm stuck. Can't move, can't do anything.

'Dawn is the newsgirl. The one you were about to recycle.' Penny pulls my arm around so I face the sled. 'This isn't Pnu-90. What is this?'

'I'm a cop, not a doctor. How the hell should I know.' Pain shoots up my arm, shoulda sat still.

Penny mocks me with a smile. 'Wrong answer.' She dials the pain up to eleven. Didn't know I could cry so loud. 'Do you want to try again?' More pain.

'I don't know.' Now my head hurts. Everything's out of focus.

'Back you come.' Penny pulls me back to reality. I prefer the haze.

'You got him?' I yank my other hand free, spinning on my tether. I hurl the bar at the voice. 'Thanks.'

'Trust you to catch it.' Twitch peers down the gun barrel at me. 'Why are you giving me evidence?' 'Never meant to.' Fuck it.

Penny lets my arm go, but warns, 'Move anything and I'll tear it off. Get over there.' She drives the warning home with a boot to the same knee. Twitch is at the sled inspecting the newsgirl. Dawn, is it?

'He isn't taking her to ReSyk. She's been dosed with XG12.' Twitch locks the sled and leans back against it. He pulls out his vape and blows a cherry cloud.

Penny sucks in her cheeks. 'XG12?'

'XG12 is a stasis serum. Jane shot herself with it one night over dinner. Got all excited about how they could be God and create the perfect being. Stuff killed her. Or so I thought. I've learnt since it ain't so.'

'Ain't you the genius,' I say as I pull myself to my feet and lean on the counter by a sink. 'It don't kill. You look like shit,' I wave at the broad on the sled. 'If you don't get the antidote quick enough.'

Penny runs her fingers over the swollen veins on Dawn's neck: thick black laces binding her to the edge of life. 'Keep talking, tough guy.'

The snigger is louder than intended. 'Make me.'

I never saw her move. My feet hang in the air. Breath is getting harder to find. Her fingers close tighter around my windpipe.

'Leave him, Penny.' Twitch stows his vape.

The hooker with the blue hair trots in with a couple of Cloud Rings. The floor feels good right now. The haze returns, the world shrinks around me. I want the powder from my inside pocket, but my fingers jitter, nerves jangle.

'You don't remember me, do you? Took my eyeball, sick bastard. I'm Talise. Not a hooker.' She kneels in front of me. Hands on her thighs. She reaches forward into my pocket. 'You want this?' Talise chucks my stash to Penny.

'Give me that!' Gobs of spit splat on the floor. 'What are you, a freak?' I drool, not at the bitch with the robot hand, but at my stash evaporating in her palm.

Cyborg bitch peers over at me from under a furrowed brow. 'Not what I was expecting.'

163

Twitch minces over to his gypsy bitch to read his fortune in her palm. 'You know what this is, Rickets?' More pity than anger. 'Who gives you this? This is not from the street.'

'It's just stuff. Clears my head. Stops all the noise and voices in here.' I jab at my temple. My nails need cutting; that one drew blood.

'Rickets, look at me.' Talise demands an audience. 'Face is up here.'

'Hey,' I smile and shrug.

'You know what these are?' Talise holds out two Cloud Rings.

'Sure, I'm Patient Zero, right?'

'The jury is out on that one?' Talise has a crooked smile, not a lot, but enough. The boy, Wilson, struck lucky. I wouldn't say no.

'What makes you think so? He volunteered?' knowall Twitch chips in.

'Naughty boy.' I hold out one hand and smack it with the other. 'Guilty.' My head splits in two, at least two. Shit flies in from all angles. Stuff I don't remember now clear as day. Talise is in my head. She's walking around, opening cupboards, checking closets. Gotta stop her. Gotta stop. Gotta...

My eyes open. They're binding me in a chair. Lights go out.

My eyes open. It's the scan room at ReSyk. Newsgirl is in the scanner. Lights go out.

My eyes open. Newsgirl slaps my face. I'm laying on the floor counting stars. There's heat coming from my head. Lights go out.

My eyes open. The ceiling is inches from my face. Someone is drilling through the floor above. Lights everywhere, beams, dots, rays, all colours, all kinds. I want to run. I want to hide. I want to tear down the walls - inside.

I open my eyes, the world slides into focus. Grey with flashes of brilliant white. Lightning? Sure enough, thunder slams the sky together. I breathe. I gag. The taste in this car is unnatural. Years of old food, cheap sex and blood. Blood on the doors. Blood on the dash. Blood on the seats - all of them. Coffee cups and handcuffs. The more I search, the more I find. None of it good. This is my shit heap. My shit heap existence. Is this what I am?

The phone chirps. Fuck the phone. The phone lands in the back seat. The screen glares, a jealous eye, all green with a black-pit centre, eye of a goat. It chirps again. I get out the car and breathe in ... what? Life. The air is wet, not just the rain, but the spaces between. The sky broils in and retches out. Wind scours the valley scrubbing the hope from Brompton. If it ever possessed any. It ain't my home so why should I give a shit. The earth squelches underfoot, pitted by the angry rain.

Brompton sprawls across the valley, an old goat bitten by a venomous reptile closing in for the kill. Something sticks out from the mud. Something unnatural, outa sync with the environment. Reaching down to pluck it from the soil, I remember. She was about five-four. Slim, attractive. Kicked like a mule, smelt like heaven. Lois Stapleton wore heels the same as these. The girl had taste, she had money, I tossed her to her death. Asshole.

The water runs from my coat over my hands, then from my hands it splatters in the mud making tiny ponds. Water wets my neck, spreads along my collar refreshing my back. I see it all for what is. A city filled with people, living dead, living every day in a rerun of yesterday. The work-eat-sleep-work boredom, living for the next paycheck. I twist the heel over in my hand, contemplating the late Lois Stapleton. Where did she go after she fell? Who put James in the body bag and floated him out there for me to find? Someone is watching me, someone other than those I know about. This clear head is fucking unreal. No sparkle-powder ever did this. 'YES.' My jubilance goes unheard.
Baptised by the tears of heaven. Joy, I hope.

Time I went to work.

Chirp, chirp little bird. Elbows on the roof, contemplating. Deciding. Where to? The door grinds open on the uneven hinge. I drop into the seat and start her up. The fans clear the condensation. Shouldn't this arm hurt? I've bruising on my wrist, but no pain. I reach around and grasp the phone. There's a code, the square type. 'Get to the Rooster, now! Not yet. I clear the Mesa and cruise into town.

Dine and Whine

Brompton was never my home, I know that for sure now. Four hundred miles upstream where the weather is more clement. The sun shines over the mountains of an evening, lighting the rivers with orange fire. You can watch fish leap for flies in the spring where the oxbows bend and the cattle graze. Wide-open spaces, red barns and whitewashed houses. Got a friend up there with a buck-toothed bride and a brace of kids. Might take a road trip to see 'em when this plague blows out.

I crack the window and listen to the hiss of tyres on the road. The radio is on. DJ Smooth is jabbering on about Officer Rickets saving the newsgirl with his prompt action. So, they got her to hospital after all. Not that I had anything to do with it. The last thing I remember is Talise. Next time she's dancing I'll keep my hands to myself.

The river surges by angry as hell; the tide sucks the crap from miles around out to sea. There'll be a whole swarm of lowlife bumming about the beach, sifting the estuary vomit for treasure. Boundary fences stake out a claim on a desert, fringed with weary brows of tumbled wire. All of it guarding nothing but cactus and dirt.

I follow the long road from the Mesa. My mind whirs. A billion sparks fire for the first time. I see the past as clear as the sun masked behind these perpetual clouds. There are two of me in here: an ass and a head. If I steer clear of the bad places perhaps the ass will steer clear of me.

Downtown is clean. Timms' action paid off. The good citizens came to sweep it all away. Some stay around fixing doors and windows, their humanity on display. Me, I roll by. Last time I attended church the lesson didn't end so good. The gargoyles gargle on leadened water rimed with pigeon shit. Beggars with trolleys cart their lives under plastic sheets to join the queue to recycle trash into money. Two wait at the blood bank and a dozen more at the soup kitchen. I roll on for a block and turn into the car park. Paradise in an alloy shell. Pink neon rages at the weather. Diner. I get out and trace the red stripe along the outside to the door. Fading flowers cling to the soil in stone pots, their petals hanging sodden on granny-finger stems.

Burger and fries rush up my nose to greet me. The acid breath of vinegar seasons the air, coffee too. My seat is by a window speckled with rain. All anger abates. I keep my back to ReGen. The call will come soon enough. My coat slips from my shoulder, it's heavy. Penny must like me. I take out her datacorder and place it on the table. I'm about to sling the coat in the corner.

'Here.' The waitress swaps her pad for my coat and hangs it on a rack by the door. She returns, shooing me into the cubicle. The seats are firm, faux leather, smooth, clean. I order coffee, black with an extra shot, and a burger I can live in. Fast food delivered fast. Nothing pleases me more than food done right. I pop the lid from the burger and add ketchup to the ketchup. I see blood. Fingers dripping. Knives, needles and bags of cats. It goes as quick as it comes. The new brain is still better than the old. Can the old one be swapped?

Filling space in one corner an old hunchback sucks tea from a saucer while a middle-aged man with a shaved head folds and unfolds his unread newspaper. I watch the world go by. Cars pause at the lights while others stream around the corner, heading to ReGen or south from the city where there's life under the sun. Those white trucks, containers on wheels, the cab bolted to the front. Where are they going? Something ticks in my brain: I follow two south. I have an appointment in Quayside, one I can't miss. How do I know this? Did I make a new agreement?

'Good morning, Rickets.' A voice I know, a face I'd rather not see. The traffic is fascinating. Spray from the puddles foams on the sidewalk. 'We not speaking?'

'If we must. Didn't you yell something at me last time? Something about staying away from you?' I slide my plate near the window and take a long drink from the mug.

'I'm sorry if I overreacted. But I object to drugs in the house of God.'

'Can I get you anything?' The waitress is a welcome distraction. I take two bites from the burger before it turns to festering maggots.

'Just a coffee, thank you.' She smiles a candy-coated smile at the waitress who wiggles off to fulfil the will of God. 'Is that a new datacorder?' My hand slaps over it before the magpie can strike.

'An upgrade. Mine was getting old.' The device goes into my pocket. Safe. Don't want anyone stealing it. Won't help them if they do, it's under lockdown. I snicker, drawing it back out. 'Here take a look. If you dare.'

'I dare, I dare.' Timms turns the unit over in her hands. Unaware. Her fingers pry, claws rake at the seams. Getting her nowhere. Getting me all I want from her. 'How does it open?' Monkey caught in the cookie jar. A light pulses on the datacorder. The device seals itself tight.

'You need authorisation.' I pluck my datacorder from her sticky fingers. 'Which I can't give.'

Timms inclines her head. 'Can't or won't.'

'Result's the same either way.' You ain't getting back inside my head. 'I've been given the unit on trust.' This time. The details of the agreement are hazy but coming clearer all the time.

'What can it do? Jane tells me you've been missing appointments.' Timms takes the coffee from the waitress with sycophantic grace. Waitress wiggles to another table, the girl can't help the way she's built.

'Jane? Anyone I know?' Why do I drag this out?

'Cute as ever. She says you've not reported in for three days. Not like you. She's worried. Wants you to visit.' Timms watches. Watches everyone, and everything. Not in a casual sense. Intense.

She turns the eye on me. Something prickles in my head. A voice. A demand. No, a command. I sip my coffee. Demand away. 'You and Jane pals all of a sudden? I thought you objected to anyone playing God, and here you are, the Devil's advocate.'

Timms acts well. Her voice softens, 'Jane and I go way back. I knew her when she was just a little girl. I care about the people she cares about.' She leans across the table. 'You've been hittin' the powder of late. Killed people who didn't need to die. No one wants that!'

Should I say what needs to be said? Would a question raise suspicion? Why do I question my own actions? 'I'll go over after I've eaten.'

Wrinkles cluster those old eyes. 'Go now. There's better food at the Rooster. She'll be waiting. She's always waiting for you.'

'And always will.' A car pulls into the lot. Circles round before reversing in next to mine. A black sedan, smoked windows. Impossible to hear it, but I know its purr. 'I'm good, thanks. Almost done.'

'Don't upset the girl, Rickets. She's been through a lot these past years.' Timms sits back. Drinks the rest of her coffee.

'Who hasn't?' The napkin is soft on my lips. Dabbing at the corners of my mouth I resist the whistle in my head. They said it would ease. 'Is there a problem?'

Timms' mouth draws tight. 'Should there be?'

'No.' I resist the urge to grin. 'I've got enough shit to take care of.'

Timms sets her cup on the table. 'Ain't that the truth.' She takes my napkin, screws it into the cup until it squeaks. 'All clean. Just takes a bit of effort to cleanse it.'

'I guess.' A goon gets out of the black sedan and into mine. 'Friend of yours?' I nod to the car.

Timms twists her aged neck around. I should crush the hag's windpipe right now. 'ReGen musta sent you a driver.'

'Why? I know the way.' I slide out of my seat and drop a twenty on the table. 'Is that enough for an offering? Should the cup runneth over to absolve all my sins?'

Timms tugs my sleeve. 'Rickets.' She don't resist as I tug free. I ain't listening no more. Three strides to the coat rack. The coat sits heavy on my shoulders, a reassuring hug.

This is one of those times when a single decision changes the course of a life. Shit gets shoved aside. I stare at the sky, a nod to the big man upstairs. 'You need to sort your servant out, big fella,' I say and jerk a thumb at the diner. With a change of mind, awareness changes too. The weights in my pockets: gun barrel, datacorder, gun.

A lot can happen on a short walk. Ten steps from the car, the goon shifts in his seat: his black suit separates from the shadows. A door opens on the sedan. Five more steps and it kicks off. The black sedan rises a couple of inches. Goon number two shoehorns himself from the car. The datacorder buzzes. I reach for it and my gun at the same time. Goon two shifts a gear. He leans forward, reaches out a hand, comes at me. One step, two step, tickle you under there. I fire twice. Bullet number one shatters his shin. The second prevents him from breeding. His fight is over. The first goon swings the door open - too fast, he's too close to the sedan. The door obstructs him. The datacorder pops open, my thumb slides up the front. The goons scream.

'Real crooks!' I drag the goon out of my car. 'Got a green light, boys.' I get in and start the engine. Reverse out. The car rises up and down with a snap of bone. I swing around, and there she is. Watching. The phone chirps. I wind the window down. The phone bounces on the asphalt, tumbles and slides upside the goon. I press my thumb on the datacorder.

Execute.

Time to be a cop.

The Choices we make

I'm at a crossroads. Downtown to the left, ReGen south, straight over to the Rooster, the wrath of God behind me. South it is. I drive straight across the traffic to a gaggle of honking horns. The Diner shrinks in my rearview mirror. I turn right for a quarter-mile. Left. The city rolls by. I flick through the stations on the radio. 'No, not disco. Not rap, not today. The Boss. Appropriate.' "Glory Days" gives the sound system a workout. I keep on this route, switching right, switching left, eyes on the ivory towers at the heart of ReGen.

The back end of ReSyk sweeps by on the left. To the right is the shipping lane. I turn right and follow the sea. Containers line the far shore, stacked three high: blue, red and green, ordered by colour. No ships. Somewhere I lost a couple of days. Musta slept well, I don't remember a thing. Not had the urge to snort? Whatever they did, they did well.

A swarm of drones drops from the light cloud. The weather has broken to the north, the cliffs are a clear line on the horizon. I take a right and begin my tour of duty. Back where this sorry mess began. At least they fixed the road; I oughta thank the planners. The engine

173

grumbles to halt. I listen to the pink of its cooldown, contemplating the train wreck I'd become. One memory eludes me: when did they put this thing in my head, and who the hell are *They*?

The warehouse stone was cut from the quarry; it has the same flat head as the Mesa. Lights flick on, LEDs powered by a shy sun. Sunlight and happiness, both precious, both behind a veil. The door responds to my touch. I don't like it but I go in, take stock, check the payments, move things around. Lights pre-empt my steps: I step and a light comes on in front. I turn, and another guides my path, and so it continues. An iPad sits in a charger. It too responds to my touch. Am I being watched? Are they monitoring everything I do? Can they read the thoughts inside my head? I'm convinced they have in the past. Is it still the case?

Aisle upon aisle, a supermarket of secrets. Silver iodide, medical reports all stamped D10, so many languages. Tissue samples, vials of ichor - the dark side of ReSyk. The deeper I go the darker it gets. It never used to bother me, it's just a job. Work I do to stay alive. I complete the physical check and go on to the office.

The light is already on. Miguel practically lives here. Never says much, must be me. The metal steps up to the office clang underfoot. I see the shadow flit across the room; a quick drink and retreat to the safety of his desk. Ain't his fault he's short. The dust-laden air dries my mouth. My fingers fold around the brass handle, the door eases open.

Miguel hunkers down, the desk light reflecting off his scalp. His collar is finger-stained, frayed by stubble. Money rustles through his fingers, notes banded and bound. Fat bags, their netting stretched to bursting, are piled in the cupboard behind him. Sweat beads on his head then runs down his temple, blotting the paper. Miguel has aged this office. It no longer resembles technological advances. Computer screens strangled by their power leads gather dust. The room smells of stewed tea, dried bags wither a geranium.

'Miguel.' The iPad thuds on the desk, sliding into his mug. His hands move in sudden spurts, snatching up tissues to dab the screen.

Miguel spreads the spillage, jibbering, 'My apologies, señor Rickets. I did no mean ...'

'Miguel?'

He swallows, crosses and uncrosses his arms.

'I sorry.' Tissues topple from the bin.

'Miguel!' I wince at my bark.

'Please, señor Rickets. I fix. I get new.' Miguel's chest rises and falls. He blinks, waves at the mess. 'I no mean to... '

'Is there any coffee, Miguel? I can't drink this.' A dark residue lives where the coffee should be.

Miguel scuttles from under his rock. 'I sorry. I fetch for you.'

'Stay there. You'll have a heart attack. Where is it?' He pokes a chewed nail at the hand-printed fridge. I open it. Cough. Close it. 'That's bad.'

'I sorry, señor Rickets. Please... I...' Miguel grinds his fingers into his palms. ' I know... Don't to say.'

'Take it easy.' Tears streak my face. 'Oh,' I swallow bile. 'Geez.'

Miguel places his hands on the desk and lowers himself into his seat.

'Whose is all this?'

Miguel's knuckles pale. 'Señor?'

'The money.' He twitches with every gesture I make.

Miguel checks behind his seat. 'Money. Is Rooster.'

'Course it is. The bags. Rooster bags.' Jane keeps them in a walk-in safe out back in her office.

Miguel clasps his hands in his lap and asks, 'You OK, señor Rickets?'

'I'm good. Thinking different today.' Had a few days off, apparently. 'Need to settle back into things.'

Miguel reaches for the loose money, back on task. 'OK.'

What's wrong with the counting machine?'

Miguel winces. 'Señorita, she tell me to do it this way.'

'Ms Clark has been here?' The iPad has survived the ducking stool.

'Is. She look for you.' He can't raise his head. 'She say I to turn you in.'

'Does she now.' He makes me chuckle. It's taken a while but at last, he smiles. 'What else? She hurt you?'

Miguel shakes his head His lips whiten. He slides his hands under the table.

'I'm going to check up over the bridge. Go see someone, get those hands straightened. You hear?' He nods. The tears tell me he ain't going nowhere.

'Señor.' His shoulders shudder. 'She say...' The datacorder is out before I can think. Miguel cowers behind his arms. 'Señor, please!' Miguel slides from his chair to his knees, his bald head level with the desk.

'Oh, sorry. No. It's not. I'm not.' I flip the device open and dial a number.

'Rickets?' She sounds surprised. She should be.

'Hey sweetlips. I need a favour. The warehouse on Quayside. You know the one? Miguel needs help. His family too. Jane's upset about my absence.' So now I'm a double-double agent, on everyone's side but my own.

'Five minutes.' The line goes dead.

'Señor?' Miguel has the eyes of a pup.

'Get your shit together.'

Miguel throws his tea down his throat. 'I ready.' His fat moustache turns up at the ends.

'That's the Miguel I know.'

Miguel's reddens from his scalp to his feet. 'Señor.'

'Let's get out of this mess.' We shut off the lights and close the place down. Penny is waiting outside. Miguel bustles into the car.

'He's all yours. Take good care of him.'

Penny props herself against the hood. 'How are you doing?'

'Best I've been - ever. I've had memories from before. Like old friends coming to visit. Bit of noise with Timms.' Her left eye irises open.

Penny pushes herself off the car. 'Interesting. Your ring is stable. Plenty of neuron activity. Twitch is following up on your leads, by the way. Be careful, Rickets. We need to know what this is all about. Remember to update us often.'

'I'll send the manifest over. A lot of the stuff in there is way beyond me. Perhaps you boffins can work it out.' I step around her, open the car door. 'You best get out of here. Too many birds in the air.' Penny drops into the seat and leaves by the Quayside road. Miguel is on his way to Vetrurn. How many more will need protection?

Is anyone safe?

Time the truth got out.

Twitch

Road Trip

Do any of us know who we are? I always thought of myself as honest enough. Honest when it was necessary and unavoidable. Other times honesty is a burden. Keeping the truth suppressed is an unquenchable fire. You think it's gone out but it finds another way to the surface. Truth is organic, a living thing with desires of its own. It desires freedom. We all do.

I can't pretend to understand all the stuff Penny and Talise discuss. Kid too. Joel gets him. Joel spends all his spare time, between spliffs, reading science and computers. He gets it. I'm the luddite, the Neanderthal, and they don't mind telling me. I have moments, though, moments of glory when my second brain farts data through to the old me, the real me. Those are times I sit and marvel at it all. I'm a cop, a detective. I get crime. Committed enough of it to understand the why of crime.

I told the others I was gonna be outa town for a bit. Talise has been working on the Cloud Rings: says she's found spare capacity in their computing core. She says each ring is a release of MyTown, which I don't understand. Don't suppose she'll ever be back in the Coffee Grinder, swaying through the tables with trays of treats. Got me wanting cake now.

Penny says Rickets had next to no control over his actions, followed a script with a sadistic writer. The code Talise had on her phone switched me off. Rickets saw it and went into a drug-crazed overload. Took the team three days to straighten him out. Three days bouncing off walls, kicking and screaming. They couldn't sedate the guy. No telling how he'd react.

All over now.

South of Brompton is a place we call The Smoke, on account of the petrol fug hanging over the choked routes. The Smoke is where the desert turns green with trees and flowers. They get real weather, sun and rain. The mountains are topped with snow. You can ski in the morning and have sunset on the beach.

Route Six runs north-south, sixty miles of nothing. I stick to the Six, all the way in. Industrial units rise from the earth in iron clusters. Most serve Brompton and the larger businesses in The Smoke.

Once beyond the fug I wind the window down, take in some fresh air. The largest bakery in town is right here. Bread on an industrial scale. I pull into the factory shop and grab a bag of warm rolls and a cool drink. The car fills with the aroma of warm yeast and fresh, tiger crust. In my childhood, in Blighty, I would chase the baker's van from the street corner to Mum's house. The sight of all the golden crusts was a treasure to behold. Every bite incites a memory and infuses another. My old crime-busting partner, a doughnut addict, got injured and stuck behind a desk. Cosgrove knew how to work a suspect, not with a baton or pistol but with intuition. There was no one better at picking minds apart.

All this fresh air and sunlight is getting to me.

The sun warms my face. I soak up some rays, a few get through to my subconscious. Street war. Gangs and gunfights. The thud of bullets on flesh. The burn of pain, deep inside, my guts are on fire. Voices, shouting, the screech of tyres.

The tap-tapping of a knuckle. 'You alright buddy?' The voice is muffled, he lowers his mask.

My eyes flutter open. A uniform at the window. 'Yeah, yeah I'm fine. Must've dozed off.'

'Thought you were having some kinda seizure,' the cop says as he rests a hand on my shoulder. 'You not from around here? Do you have a mask, sir?' I take the medical mask from his hand.

'I used to work out of the Labyrinth.' Some place that was.

Cop straightens up. 'Now there's a name I've not heard in a while. How long ago?'

I blow a sharp breath, 'Gotta be five years.' How can I tell him I've no memory? 'Name's Reece.'

'I knew of a Reece. Detective.' Cop squats by the door. 'You can't be the same Reece.'

'Why not?'

Cop shakes his head. 'He got shot to hell, candidate for ReGen. They were meant to fix him but we never saw him again.'

'You mind explaining that to me? Candidate? I work in Brompton now, not heard of any candidate program up there and we're right on the doorstep of their HQ.' My head is ringing, blood thrashing my mind in a maelstrom soup.

'Chief would love to hear this.' The cop laughs, not at me but at the story I'm telling. 'I'm gonna call ahead, set you up.' He takes out his datacorder and logs in. A few swipes of his finger and I have a booking. 'You remember the way?' I nod. 'Stick around if you can. Would love to chat.'

'You too.' I thank the guy and trundle out of the bakery car park.

The Smoke has grown tall. Glass and concrete touch the sky. Streets are broad, with two lanes on either side all the way. Main roads are three and four lanes wide. Traffic flows smooth. Most folks are wearing masks, keeping Pnu-90 at bay. Gantry signs flash bold yellow: 'Stay Safe. Masks Must Be Worn. Report Sickness.' Dogs are walked on leads. The streets are swept, few people venture out.

The Labyrinth squats dark among the new glass buildings. The green walls prickle with cameras. I pull up to the gateway. A cop leans out the booth. 'Can I help?' Her face is shielded behind thin plastic. People like to see a face.

'Name's Reece. Booked to see the Chief.' I hope the message has got through.

'Reece! Got you right here. Can't be -'

I shake my head and pass under the rising gate. With effort, I force myself to steer right to the visitor spaces where I spin around and reverse into one. Cops come and go, walking to their patrol cars. Some just walking - on patrol. I get out and push the door shut; no need to lock it here. Crime is low in The Smoke. Sure, the suburbs have it rough sometimes, drugs and stuff, but for the most part The Smoke is good.

The front doors are held open on those magnetic releases. No scanners. Public notices are pinned in neat rows, no penned-on moustaches or scribbled dicks. I ain't in Brompton, that's for sure. One notice reminds me to put on a mask. I laugh to myself; now I feel like the bandit.

The desk is busy but they have enough hands to shrink the queue. A mother and child are led through to the processing room. A youth is loosed from his cuffs and freed on caution. Above the desk a sign: simple understated text. 'Don't Get Tagged.' Wow, is that all it takes to keep the figures down? I pull my datacorder and scan the room. Nothing. Nothing at all. Something ain't right. I send the data to the team.

'Can I help you, sir?' the desk clerk smiles through a plastic barrier.

'I'm here to see the Chief.'

'Your name, sir?' He waits, fingers poised over the keyboard.

'Reece.' The place is spotless, calm. Cops are sharing jokes, laughing, chucking balled paper around. 'Chief's on her way down. You can wait over there, sir.' He points to the green-grey seats along a wall. Back at school, we had the same thing outside the headmaster's office. Only sat there once. Who knew smoking pot on school trips was a bad thing?

'You must be Reece.' A black hand waves in my face.

I stare. 'Cosgrove?' I lengthen the Os.

'Do I know you?' Cosgrove lifts me by the shoulder. 'This way, Mr Reece.' My twitch goes crazy.

Black, Chinese, and Chief. The world tilts. 'Who are you?' Not for the first time, she shoves me in a chair. 'Reece, Addison Reece. Folks call me Twitch.' She just stares. Behind her on a bookcase is a row of photos. Cop photos. 'You married Lily? She got you in the end. Who's the pretty boy? I know the face...' I go to stand, take a closer look.

'Sit.' Cosgrove reaches around and lifts the picture of the smiling couple. She dusts off the top edge and slides it across the table.

'You always were cute.' I tip the photo back and forth. Synaptic bridges form across my brains. 'We were partners once.'

'Not the bent-over-the-table kind,' she whispers the words in time with me. 'That's Reece. The Reece I knew. He got shot to shit. You aren't the face in the photo. But the words are you.'

'You got one in the hip. Unfit for the street. I tried to argue the case. Said you could earn a fortune on the street.'

Cosgrove's eyes glisten. 'Fuck you,' she laughs.

'That was my offer.' Memories come in a river of tears. 'Five bucks, for this!' She gestures at herself.

'I'll take change.' My heart is racing. I know this woman: we had shared life together. But I ain't the guy in the photo.

Cosgrove shakes her head. 'I'm convinced. But who are you?'

'I can tell you what I know.' There are cracks in the ceiling and scratches on the desk. 'You know about Mind Cloud?'

Cosgrove presses a button on her comms. 'Don't have that shit here. You're the reason.' The door opens. 'Can you get us some coffees? You still drink coffee, right?' The girl closes the door.

'Sure. You still got cake in your drawers? Need something to sweeten that pussy.'

'Damn. Smart ass.' Cosgrove pulls the drawer open and takes out two packets of fruit cake. She pushes back in her leather seat and settles in for the story.

'I'm the reason?' This should be good.

Cosgrove takes a breath. 'You had that Ring thing, right?' I nod. 'It was supposed to record your last moments so we could nail the assholes responsible for cop killing. Well, turned out it didn't work. All they got was static.'

'I remember it right up to the ambulance. After that, nothing. I don't know how long ago it was -'

'Ten years.'

'Ten! I've been in Brompton, under the Cloud, for a decade?' The girl returns with the drinks and a memo. 'Thanks.' Cosgrove gestures at me to continue.

'I have a private morgue and new partner, Joel.'

Cosgrove splutters, 'You're Twitch! He talks about you all the time! Joel's practically family.' They go ways back. Now she's a happy girl.

'Well, I'll be. You know the sad sack?' I have to laugh. 'Any dirt you wanna dish, lay it on me. Where was I? Oh Brompton, where it always rains. We don't have the plague though. There's those who say it was all started by ReGen and they're just waiting to release the antivirus. Can you believe that shit?'

Cosgrove nods, 'There are some here believe ReGen are bringing back the dead. That they melt bodies down in ReSyk and grow new ones. ' Our laughter trails off. 'And here you are.'

'Yeah. Here I am. Whatever I am. You can't speak of what I'm about to tell you, OK?' I lean right in, put the picture on the desk.

Her eyes strip me bare. 'OK.' She has her serious face on.

'I'm working with Vetrurn. They have this scanner,' I put my datacorder next to the photo, 'and it sees everything, right down to the last molecule. They found the ring in my head. They also found mixed DNA and two brains fitted inside a shell to look like one. I'm getting occasional flashes of someone else's memories. Just bits. Fragments.'

Cosgrove picks up the picture and returns it to the shelf. 'Vetrurn I trust. It's them who got me back on my feet. I was meant to go to ReGen, but was too busy.' She picks up the datacorder. 'Fancy.' 'I know. Gift from Penny at Vetrurn.'

'Sutcliffe?'

'That's her, ex-army girl.'

Cosgrove's eyes go wide. 'Wow, you've moved up in the world. Rubbing shoulders with the nation's elite.' 'She's chief of research or something or other.' I unwrap a bar of cake and break a piece off. Joel would love the cherries.

Cosgrove switches to teacher mode. 'Penelope Sutcliffe, advisor to the President on rehabilitation of ex-service personnel. Also a robo-geneticist. Highly distinguished, not to be messed with.' 'I... I never thought to ask.'

'Tell me, is Brompton in a time warp?'

'No. But I am. My memories are ten years old. Everything I thought I knew has been put there. Until Penny and Talise fixed the ring in my head, all I knew was fake. I had no memories beyond starting work with Joel. I had background stuff, sure. But nothing else. Not until the scanner broke my head open.'

187

Cosgrove finishes her cake. 'I'm sorry Reece, really I am. I miss you and your awful humour. You were my friend and soulmate. When I lost you I fell apart. I was fortunate that Lily was here. I have you to thank for her.' She takes the picture from the shelf and sits it on the desk.

'I have to go. I'll keep in touch if that's OK with you?' Cosgrove gets out of her chair and comes round to face me. 'You look different. But the heart is all you. You're still my friend and partner. Just not the bent-over-thetable kind.' We hug.

My mind explodes with images. A hundred projectors all showing at once. We say our goodbyes in the office. We ain't ready to share with the world yet. It'll be a while before my coming out. Cosgrove walks me out to the parking lot and sees me into the pickup. She lowers her mask, kisses my cheek and steps back. 'Don't be a stranger.' She lifts her mask. Her eyes say goodbye. 'I won't.'

Time to head home.

Back to work

Everything is pointing to ReGen. Kid has picked through police records of all those who have died in service. Brompton's precincts are unlike anywhere else. Few have died in service; all cases closed within days of the incident. Mind Cloud is an astounding success. Outside of town, not one case has been solved through Mind Cloud. Some cities are talking of banning the device as it serves no advantage. How is this information not national news?

'About time you showed up. Am I paying for this lateness?'

Joel strolls in, a bag clutched under his arm. He reaches into the bag. 'Here, for you.' He drops the package on his way over to the BLT.

'What is it?' The package is heavy for its size. Half a brick maybe? Bricks ain't soft.

Joel throws his arm out. 'Open it and see. Damn.' He puts his datacorder next to the BLT and flips it open. 'Got some samples I want to compare to the ones on our Cloud.'

'Knock yourself out.' The brown paper parcel is tied with string. Smells of meat and oil. 'What is is, roadkill?' Joel is hunched over the BLT. 'Uh-huh. Possible.' 'Is this off a Banger?' The knot pulls open easy. There are stains seeping through the paper where the string is pulled tight. I sit it on the desk and unwrap the paper with a pen. 'Why? What?'

'Your friend sent it?' Joel is still too busy to look at me.

'Stop laughing.' The great oaf.

'Who's laughin'?'

'I can see your shoulders shaking.' Meat. More precise: flesh. 'Who in their right mind sends a pound of flesh?'

Joel twists his head around. 'Cosgrove.' 'Nice.'

She still loves me.

'Notice anything?' Joel switches off the BLT and saunters over.

'Nope. It's dead?'

Joel scoops the steak from the desk. 'The muscle fibres are all wrong.'

'How'm I supposed to know? I'm not a doctor, I'm a detective.'

Joel has the meat up close to his nose. 'So detect summ'n'.'

'I'm detecting a whole load of sarcasm right now. Why does it smell so odd?'

Joel holds the parcel out, 'This is manmade.'

'Replicated? One of Penny's things?' I don't share the fascination.

'No. It's woven. The layers cross each other. The BLT says it's-'

'Forty-two?'

Joel repeats, 'Forty-two.' His lips curl at the ends. 'The owner died a week ago and there's no decomposition.'

'Was it in a fridge?' I take the package.

Joel rests his hands on the desk. 'In a garage sucking on an exhaust pipe. First one in The Smoke. Matches our boy's too.' He dips his head toward the offending package.

'Fancy a trip to ReSyk?'

Joel straightens up. 'No. But I'll tag along to stop your sorry ass falling in a shredder.'

We lock up and head out to the pickup. We wait for the shutters to close and roll out. The town is busy, not weekend busy but enough to take time. We divert to the back streets. Joel hums some old tunes: I'm supposed to guess them, but his humming is awful. Every tune sounds alike.

Joel stops the wasp noises, turns in his seat. 'What exactly are we searching for in there?'

'Think of it as reconnaissance. We go in. Follow the process. See where it goes and what door it comes out.' Joel squints at me, 'And then what?'

'Then–' Joel braces himself as I brake hard to avoid a tramp with a shopping cart. 'Where'd he come from?'

Joel pulls his seat belt over his shoulder. 'Pile of trash over there?' We wait for the rambler to shuffle across the street. The engine growls as I ease the pedal down. I glimpse the rambler in the spread of the headlights as he melts into the shadows of the alley. 'Might be best we don't hurry down here,' Joel mumbles.

'Tell me. Is it me, or are there more of those around these days?' Another tramp searches through bins in the accusing glare of the headlights.

Joel gets comfy. 'Might just be all the trouble in Downtown has brought them to our attention.'

'Nah, it's more than that. This is gang turf. From back there to the Rooster. No one, not anyone, stops along here for anything other a snort or a handful of skirt.'

But Joel ain't biting. 'There's always been bums down here.' He sucks his teeth.

'Nah. Not in my years on the street.' All ten of them. 'Besides, it's December. They always go over the cathedral side, to the shelters and soup kitchens.'

Joel waves me off. 'I been on these streets more than twenty years. Twice your time. I've pulled bodies outa most these dumpsters and alleys. Rooster is always calling meat wagons.'

'Want a wager?' He thrusts out a pink palm. We slip skin. 'Pull the records and we'll see who's right.'

Joel tuts. 'You gonna lose.'

'I'm thirsty. You wanna drop in at the Rooster for something.'

'You know, if we go in there it's the end for the day.' Joel wags a meaty finger in my face.

'Hey, ReSyk will still be there tomorrow. And the day after. Put the meat in a bag, stop it stinking up the place.'

The alleys come to an abrupt end. Bright lights glare in shop windows. Neon brightens the gutter. Music throbs all around. Cars splash along, jet-washing the sidewalks. Trash gathers where the water vanishes under the kerb. A dog hunches its back, fur bristling wet. 'Even the turds are musical here.'

Joels swivels an eye my way, 'Go on.' He swims a hand in the air.

'Well,' I point at the dog, 'that one's humming.' Why am I the only one laughing?

The pickup climbs the curb. I kill the engine and slide out into the street right opposite the Rooster. A huge neon cock crows in stop motion as it has a thousand times before. No more inviting than the day it first lit up this sleaze pit. The food is hot, the beer is cold, it's a titty bar with girls on poles. Rickets' second home.

An ape at the door pats us down but stops when he finds the badge. We descend the steps, planning our meals and preparing our palates to sample those hops.

It's early, place is quiet, the soft rumble of conversation dowses the music. A black chick spins around a pole with less interest than a bank. She's bathed in purple light and little else. 'Order up, Joel. I'll get a ringside seat.'

Joel chats to the tassels behind the bar. There'll be a wait for the beer.

A couple of guys in the corner hold hands under the table: no need to hide here boys, no one is going to call you out. A gaggle of of office girls giggle and snicker. One snorts liquor from her nose while the others collapse in hysteria. More patrons are dotted around the room. No one is on their feet 'cept the black girl sliding up and down the pole.

Datacorder buzzes in my pocket. I take it out alongside my dried-up vape and put it on the table. Joel has the barmaid in the palm of his hand; he can melt chocolate with his charm. Unlike me. Girls just run when I talk, never been much of a ladies' man. To this day I have no idea how Jane and me got together. I doubt I'll ever find out. Memories might be coming back but she ain't among 'em. Ain't no bad thing.

'Hey, Twitch!' Joel barks. 'You want anything with it?' The dancer squeaks around the pole, could use a little oil.

193

'Just the usual.'

'Help me.' The dancer grinds the words through clenched teeth. She swings away, casual as can be. The datacorder buzzes. The glint on her finger says she's taken. Odd for a girl in here. Rumour has it they don't always have the choice on the kind of performance they give.

I try to catch her eye. The meathead over the other side of the stage is getting all the glory. Joel arrives with plates of something hot with chips. I take one from his gargantuan hands and set it before me. I position the condiments in order of application and start with the salt. The sachet splits all wrong and most of it misses the meal. I wipe it away and watch the dancer.

Both datacorders buzz.

Joel lifts a chip from my plate. 'We being paged?'

'Thief! I should run a check for tags.' The datacorder pops open like an old flip phone. Red dots glow on the screen. One pulses right on top of me.

The dancer arches her back, her face level with mine. A black arm snakes over my shoulder. Her jaw clenches. 'Help me,' she whispers and snatches away.

The meathead raises his head our way. There's a glint in his hand, a wand, maybe a remote. Beer, refreshing as it should be, slips down my throat washing away a half-chewed chip. Right now, I wish I had two heads so I could eat and drink at the same time. Joel slides his plate aside, wipes his mouth with a napkin and tosses it on top.

'Girl's in some kind of trouble.' My jaw cracks from the yawn I loose. 'Cloud Ring on a dancer. Twice she's asked for help. Shall we?'

Joel tugs a note from his purse. Reaching forward, he tucks it in her g-string. Meathead jabs his remote. The girl swings around and around. The datacorder beeps. I press the screen. The girl gasps and falls in a heap, her head smashing the plates on our table. A cheer goes up. We drag her from the stage. Meathead moves fast for a lump his size.

'Leave the girl alone, she's property.' He's a black brute, no tags, a mountain of muscle with a mean smile. He stabs me with the remote. Joel jerks the badge from his pocket. 'Cops?' He waves at a camera.

'She asked for help.' I get an arm across her, she's firm. Gonna be a struggle getting her out.

Joel steps up. 'Move aside, sir. We are taking her out.' The two glower eye to eye. He slides a hand over the counter the way he does when he cheats at cards.

The lump presses his face to Joel. 'No. You. Ain't.' His knuckles crack into fists. Joel snakes a hand up to the big guy's face; sticks the dinner knife right in his eye. Big Man screams through his meaty fingers. Blood oozes out beneath his hand. Joel turns, lifts the girl over his shoulder easy as lifting a child. We make for the door, gun in hand.

Panic. Everyone panics. Tassels is screaming. The Meathead is screaming, they should do a number together. The doorman is piling chairs in the exit. A whole shit-storm is heading our way from a door in the rear wall. Where does that go?

Joel kicks the legs out from under the screaming dude. I follow Joel out and stamp my way across the fallen guy. The lump spits teeth in a blasphemous fury. Joel slams through the fire exit and I give the doorman

195

a bullet in the thigh. He's screaming too. Joel is out, striding for the pickup. I fire couple of caps into the mob: one drops, one hollers. Joel loads the dancer into the backseat of the pickup, jumps in and guns it my way. He slows up enough for me to climb in. Bullets thud against the armoured body. I don't look back.

The pickup fishtails onto the main drag. I drop the glovebox open, yank out the light and set it going. Rain rushes in through the open window as the light clamps to the roof. Joel sinks his foot to the floor and tears through town. Ain't nothing as sweet as jumping lights and cutting through traffic. Bright lights meld into a kaleidoscope of colours, through a prism of rain. We send waves up over the pavements. I pity any fool caught in our wake.

We burst out of the cloud cover. The desert night breezes in through the window, so I leave it down and stow the light.

All is quiet, except for the snoring from the back seat.

We all have secrets

I find myself Downtown in the gothic shadows of Temple Timms. Hang-mouth gargoyles drool incessantly from above. The drip-splatter of their spewings gives rhythm to their purpose. Ain't no sin in the heart of the city, no demon sits on my corner.

Where are all these trollies coming from? Supermarkets are way out of town and the local stores don't do 'em. The road is quiet. A bum tramps along beside me in another world. They don't lift their heads,

196

they don't check the road. They shuffle their life along in a wire casket.

Streetlights flicker through shuttered eyes. Their light hits the street around their base but fails to venture forth. Plastic bags hang from the railings waiting in vain hope for the dog shit fairy to come and collect them. Water flows across the stone slabs beneath my feet; some of it seeps through cracks into the underworld. Keep moving. Drawn to the fire I felt as a youth before I crossed the Pond to this blighted land.

One, two, three. The weight builds with every step until I breach the doors of penitent doom. Have mercy on me, oh God, a sinner.

'Twitch, to what do I owe this honour?' Timms has a charm no other possesses.

'Casing the joint.' Candles burn at half-mast, black smoke rises from the waxen wells of fire. 'Anything worth stealing?' Eddies swirl in the shadows.

'Only my heart.' Her arms close around me. Instinct returns the gesture. 'Shall we?' A subtle invitational command. 'How are things?'

'Too broad a question.' I incline my head toward her. 'Could you narrow it down?'

'The investigation.' She moves with a calculated step.

'Which one?'

'The young girl?' Timms folds her hands behind her. 'Which one?'

Timms pauses, foot off the floor. 'Blue hair.' 'No nearer. Gone for ReSyk,' I sigh for effect.
'Rules.' Shrug to finish.

'Pity.'

'You know of any others?' We turn and head toward the altar.

'Rickets came looking.' Did he now? Wonder if he remembers.

'Had a few others stiffs.'

'Twitch!'

'Sorry, cases. Nothing 'cept.' Damn.

Timms stops. 'Go on.' There it is again, such command.

'Everyone we get smells of oil and dirt.' Can she feel me watching? Is the whistling in my head or someone close by? Not a tune - a nasal breath.

'You tried ReSyk? They smell of all sorts there.' We move on. Timms moves hymn books from pew to pile. Pile to pew.

'Not ReSyk. The goop they make smells for sure, but ain't this.'

Timms ascends the Dias. Turns to me. Our faces meet. 'Some of the congregation have vanished of late. Plain got up and gone.'

'Don't the tramps move about in winter?' Could do with some heat in here; my breath hangs for a moment.

Timms wilts me with her heated stare. 'They're people. People like you and me.' She examines the shine on her perfect shoes.

'Except they ain't.' I'm product. The real me was shot to shit. But she doesn't know. Does she? 'They got all kinds of problems. Who'd want them for anything?'

She fixes an eye on me and says, 'If I knew that, I wouldn't need no detective.'

'Speaking of which.' My turn to fix an eye. 'Saw a picture of old man Timms from five years back. Whole bunch of boffins with him at Quayside.' She blinks. 'Over at the new development across the harbour. Odd thing. Jane was there. She's supposed to be dead.'

Timms draws the air from the church. Whole place is a truth-sucking vacuum. 'Not possible.' There's a pause. 'He never met Jane.'

'Yet you call her Jane as though you know who she is.'

'Not met a Jane either.' Timms watches the shadows in the north aisles. 'Or buried one.'

'You knew a Professor Timms. Used to work with ReGen on the crossover projects.?' Nothing moves on her black face. Not so much as a flutter of an eyelash. 'Must be another Timms, huh?' I wait. Still waiting. 'Tell me, where do these people get all the spanking new shopping carts from? Nearest supermarket is five miles away. Do they just go walk 'em in?'

'I suggest you leave, Officer Reece.' Timms lifts her eyes to heaven. 'Come back when you know something.' The shadows shuffle in. Candlelight softens the edges of the bodies, leaves gaps in faces, holes where life once dwelt. Who would want these people?

'It's odd. I remember talking with a friend. Was saying how I thought there were more homeless in town than before.' I wave at the rippling shadows. 'But you say they go missing.'

'Dozens.' Timms steps down, scuffs behind my heels. 'Good people.'

'I'll bear it in mind.'

'You do that.' Timms' presence fills the void at my back. She hangs there all the way to the exit.

Outside I turn at the Stapletons' crypt. 'You got nothing for me? No one here's seen nothin'?'

'Not today.' Timms makes a face like she smells shit. 'No one ain't seen nothing.'

'Fair enough.' I move on. This piece of history is over.

The whole world is shushed by the rain.

Back down the streets, I sift through memories: old, but new to me. A life outside of town, roads whose names I know, whose beats I've walked. Faces, memories, like a tide hissing back to reveal more - always more. I want to know more. More I see, the more I want. Pieces fall into place compressed into bedrock, foundation facts.

Horns blare. Chastisement from strangers. I'm at the crossroads staring down the throat of the beast. Two dark towers prickling with lights, aspiring to be the great god of all. Babel comes to mind. Man building so high he threatens the Kingdom of Heaven. The greatest minds working as one struck down with a confusion of language. Everyone has a new code to learn and the beast falls.

The crossing goes green. The man says walk. I follow the lights in the road across to the other side. My gut tells me to eat, and who am I to argue with this daydream. Vaulting the low fence, I cut across the car park. The uniforms have cordoned off a black sedan. White lines trace a twisted body. A second trace at the rear of the car: another brute gone to ReSyk. A nod to the cop on the door and I go inside. It's a good place to hole up and observe.

A sombre mood greys the atmosphere. Ineffectual music overlays the TV news. Images of war in a distant land. Bullets flying, destruction, disease, an everincreasing death toll. The waitress distracts me, I turn away. She stands ready to take my order. The apron around her waist is dusted with flour. She twirls the pen in her fingers like a baton. Nothing to cheer about today.

'Hi.' Her voice is bright, her eyes catch the trucks heading south. 'Can I get you anything?'

'Something different. Fruit tea and... veg burger with fries. Let's not go too crazy, eh?' She scrawls on the ticket, tears it off and folds it over her finger before offering it to me. 'Thanks.' She twists through the counter flap into a world of sterilised steel. There's no one else.

I'm alone.

Beyond the grey-washed city, the sun shines over Vetrurn. A new war on the ground is erupting. Tech wars. Drones. Drones everywhere I turn my eye. I see them under the overpasses, tucked beside cameras and clinging to trucks. There's another thing: those trucks. Datacorder buzzes. It's a new thing. I blink twice, the message plays in my head. Cheryl's all good. Keep an eye out for anyone with those rings. New weapon incoming. Ends.

Things are moving fast. There's an undercurrent in the city pulling me along. Kid is working on a new lead Rickets brought in. The gun barrel planted in his pocket was evidence in the James Stapleton case. We all thought Rickets shot him. The Stapletons did for sure: they kept a skeleton in the closet they were not afraid to dig out. I'm having problems with old man Walter, head of the whole Vetrurn thing. He's gooder than good. Noone's that good, not even me!

Outside the monotone world greys by, wet tyres on wet roads. Traffic snakes across the lanes, honking horns and wild fists shaking in silent rage. Tinned meat for processing. The only question remains: when?

Food arrives without fanfare or fuss. A smile may help the medicine go down, but this tea will bring it back up. The red liquid sloshes on the table. Do I always push too hard? A wet screech of rubber on tar heralds the inevitable thud of crumpling steel. A white truck pinballs a yellow MPV along the street. The truck feels nothing. The MPV skitters like a pebble on a rock, pieces spin out into the air. The windows redden. I call for recovery and finish my lunch. The truck is gone, as is the family in the MPV.

'Not our day today.' The waitress flits from table to table perfuming the air with antibac. Nothing lives around here.

'Sure ain't.' She stares out the window at the smoking wreck doused in the rain. The grey heavens descend to wash away the memories. Flames lick around the MPV, lapping up the juices before it all erupts into hell. 'You see what went down earlier?'

'Told the cops all I have to say.' She spins on her heel, retreats to the kitchen. The lines on her stockings trace the curves from her shoe to her hemline.

Using the last of the semi-stale bun I wipe up the spilt ketchup and toss a note on the table. Three seconds later I'm out the door, heading south across the street. A firetruck wails through the crossroads, its fat arse swinging out for a peek at the crime scene in the car park. Two wheels mount the kerb, jolting the truck. The ladders rattle but stay put. The crew pile out. One climbs up on the back and mounts the foam gun. The flames vanish beneath a blanket of white. Efficient and clinical.

I cross the road and keep walking. Tramps with trollies skitter into alleys, rats after scraps. Timms says she's losing people, but if that's so then who are these? A car cuts across my street. I swear and give the driver the finger. Then I see him. A face in the gloom. He knows I know, he don't move. We play tag through the burgeoning cardboard city. At the last moment, the face turns to the ground and withdraws into its shelter.

Boxes line one side of the alley. The drub of an overflowing gutter gnaws through a cardboard roof. The resident sleeps on. Daylight is fading, expedited by the ubiquitous rain. My man seeps into a doorway, pulls his trolley across the entrance. Drones perch on the telegraph wires: micro-vultures feeding information to the super-highway. The doorway is full, life piled one side: limp boxes, cartons bleed out, crushed shells of humanity and a trolley crammed with future hope. Shadows move in the gloom. A door jars open. Sounds are made, that used to be words. Code? The trolley jangles. The door opens on deep gloom. The trolley clatters inside.

It takes a moment for my eyes to adjust to the tungsten glare. The piled filth is lit with a pustular yellow. The whole place feels sick. Dis-eased. I close the door and taste the acrid air. My gut wants to eject my lunch but this ain't the time. The guy waits at the end of a canyon of rubbish. His plastic-bag poncho glistens. I pick a route across, the floor licks my soles with its velcro tongue.

The second room is cleaner. Some kind of trash sorting space with blinking LEDs. Faces turn and check me out, a second - maybe two - no more. One nods, they all nod and return to their piles of intrigue. I follow my guide to a corridor of doors and a stairwell. We take the stairs, deeper. Pale cement steps patched with dirt lead to another strip of doors. A familiar hum, warm, electric. He knocks, I wait.

The door opens.

'Detective Twitch. A pleasure to meet you, again.' I shake the offered hand.

'Leon, right?'

'Good memory,' Leon steps aside. 'Come in, have a seat.'

'No unicorns, I see.' I wave at the banks of screens and buzzing servers.

'Club's for pleasure. This is business.'

'And what business is that?' The room is spotless. The air is a dense mixture of cologne and hot circuits.

Leon taps a screen. 'Observation - mostly.'

'ReGen I get.' Hotwired CCTV. 'But Timms!' I help myself to a drink and pull up a seat. Then I spot Lady Rainicorn strung out over the fridge. 'Pretty homely here.' A smile perks me up.

'Timms, now there's an enigma.' He picks at his teeth and cleans out his fingernail with the edge of a tissue. He folds the tissue into a swan and nests it with another.

'How so?'

'We have history,' Leon turns in his cream leather chair. Smiles. 'We go way back.' He holds out his hand like he's measuring a child. 'Aunty Timms. Always there for Sunday lunch, pie in hand. Apricot.'

'Everyone has a past with Timms. What's your take?'

Leon swivels in his chair, snatches up a diet coke and sips from it. Takes a deep breath and pouts. 'Momma was a friend since school. Lived outa Brompton in one of those shanty villages made of planks with whitewashed verandahs. Momma liked to bake; she was homely, still is. The Timms came from a line of scientists. They made shit-loadsa cash. They may have lived in a whitewashed house but they had money in the bank.'

'Odd for the area. Thought there was no money to be had anywhere near old Brompton.' I sit back and listen, Leon has a storyteller's voice.

'Me too, sweetheart. But... how shall I say it? That old shit-heap was built on a mountain of silver. Not as pretty as gold but still worth a lot. Just sayin' it ain't the only stone coming out the quarry. The Mesa is one giant deposit, and old man Timms, well, he bought the whole damn desert. You can drive for miles and still be in his land.' Leon slurps his bottle dry and tosses it all dainty into the bin.

'If Timms is from a wealthy line then how come she took the cloth and didn't follow family tradition? How come she ain't in the lab?' I put my empty cup on a beachcombed table. Gnarled branches snake up to a slab of tree aged by the ocean, polished to a shine.

'Who said she ain't? Take a look.' Leon clacks away at the keyboard, popping pictures on the screens.

Timms in a ReGen lab, Timms by vats of goop, old man Timms at Quayside - the same picture as before.

'Seen that one recently. Kid found it. I'm assuming you know Kid?'

'He safe?'

'Yeah.'

'Good.'

'Smart guy, with a gift for disguise.' 'That's my brother.' Leon vents a laugh.

'Brother?' I correct my slouch.

'Kid brother by ten years. He built all this. Gone dark lately, can't find his signature anywhere in the Interweb.' Leon's shoulders loosen.

'He's in a safe house.' I pull the datacorder and call home on speaker. 'Kid there?' I hear Joel's deep tone call out.

'He asks who wants him,' Joel says. 'His brother asks if he's OK.'

'He'll be in touch.' Line cuts.

One screen whites out. A red pull-along cart appears stacked with letter bricks reading 'Kid's OK'. The screen flashes back to normal.

'Quick, even for him.' Leon wags a finger at the screen.

'He has new toys.'

'Vetrurn toys?' Leon tilts his head, all inquisitive. 'Vetrurn toys. Lots of them.' Leon smiles.

'Perhaps you can help me?' Time to fish. 'About those shopping carts?'

Leon spins in his chair and begins to type.

Talise

ReGen

We're on the road again. Cheryl is in recovery, the bastards hurt her bad. Kid cracked the gold ring open, with help from his friends. The code is new: nasty stuff linked to a localised neural net somewhere in the Rooster. Rickets is investigating, and the rest of us are going for a night out. Right now, it's me and Penny on recon.

The diner is busy. Cars are two deep all the way across the yard to the road where robots are resurfacing. The city drones by.

'They must have thousands of those things flitting about.' I point at a trio of bird drones hovering over a group of youths, all of them glued to their phones.

'Our team suggest there are more than ten thousand deployable units.' Penny taps a finger on the steering wheel - counting? Penny for your thoughts...

ReSyk lumbers into view. Place gives me the creeps. Seeing dead people is bad enough but the process... I nudge the air con up. The world is grey: land, roads, sky - grey. ReSyk is white as bleached bones.

'Have you any thoughts on Kid's findings?' Penny takes the left off the ring road and hugs the estuary to its end.

Some kind of ship is spraying black stuff high up the beach. The river is full again, never used to be an issue, not until the rain.

'On the rings?'

'Unless there's been something else.' Penny halfturns her face for a second. Enough to assess me.

'The new one, Cheryl's, is direct control. They did nothing to her physically, no implants or cosmetics. That girl does not need any beauty augments.'

'Quite.' ReSyk's twin towers pierce the cloud base, their lights blink red and blue - beacons?

'What's in those?'

'One is research. Think of the ground level being your standard lab. Sample testing, monitoring subjects and so on.' Penny waves a hand. 'As you go up the tower, the research becomes more defined. Then a security barrier. The top, so I'm informed, houses the secret stuff accessible to the few... The other tower is similar but focused on production methods and field deployment. More security and then apartments.'

'Apartments. Who'd want to live there?'

'Perhaps they don't want to live there. Perhaps choice is not an option. Perhaps it's a prison.' Penny focusses her eye on me. 'Perhaps.' She raises a Spock eyebrow.

'What do you mean? You don't think they keep prisoners there?' My laughter stutters.

'Prisoners... not with bars, as such. More... compelled, controlled.' Penny shrugs. 'It has been reported that certain 'dead' people have been seen around the inner compound. Hardly dead.'

'What people? I've not heard anything. How can the dead be up and ab- Oh!' How blind am I? Here I am thinking this is all nuts.

'You OK?' Penny puts a hand on mine, I feel nothing.

We turn in somewhere. The grey blurs into a shit undercoat someone forgot to paint over. White containers form a giant Lego wall. My head fizzes like shaken cola. The containers are alive. AI.

'We're being scanned. The containers.' Covering my eyes I tune into the data stream. I feel a shift in my brain as the Cloud Ring unlocks. 'They're waiting for instructions. I can see them in my head, tiny AI cores. Wow!'

'What do you see?'

The car turns a slows left and draws right. A change of light, a tunnel perhaps. I don't look, just sense it. 'Cameras, scanners, thousands of minute eyes.' The containers are numbered. I choose one at random.

'One of the containers is moving. Is that you?' There's a timbre to Penny's voice. Curiosity - no, fear. 'Millstone to the sea.'

We're in an underground car park. A bead of light on the floor guides our path. We pass row after row of black sedans with smoked windows and thick-wired heaters in the rear windows. White vans and smart cars driven by AI, none of them road-legal.

'You sent it into the sea?' Her pitch heightens. 'May attract the kind of attention we don't want.' Back under control.

'They have no way to trace it. Not directly. I'm hoping to pick up the reaction to it, cos there has to be a command centre somewhere.' The wall says stop. We stop. We are the only vehicle in the sector. The door to our right is for Vetrurn employees only. 'Can't see ReGen sticking to that.' Penny nods and buzzes us in.

There's a brief moment when all I can see is dots. Laser scans sweep vertical and horizontal. I blink. Penny touches my arm, her hand is warm. Inside there are two choices: lift or stairs, nothing else other than the floor number. Sub 3.

'We have to go to the main concourse to be seen. Then we can meander at our leisure.' Penny ushers me into the lift and presses one of the two buttons.

'We've already been seen.'

'By tech. Now we need to be seen by human eyes. There are a few about, some of them ours.'

'You have permanent staff here?' The walls of the lift are gold lustre, the whole thing is a scanner.

'Nervous?' Penny leads us out into an oval zone. There are twelve lifts, six on either side. Everything else is glass. The front desk sits behind a row of metal detectors. People mill about, stocking up from vending machines before boarding a lift.

'It smells of plants,' I remark. Penny raises my chin with a finger. Vines cascade on all sides weighed down with huge flowers. Hummingbirds flit among the bright trumpets, their wings a blur. 'Drones.'

Penny checks her palm. 'How did you know?'

'I can see the data lines. So many in here. Everything is tagged, nothing is real. Everyone has a Cloud Ring fitted.'

'Are you sure? Everyone?' We cross to another lift and wait.

'Everyone I've seen so far. Except you.'

'Let's see what's in our lab.'

The lift door sighs open. 'Are they scanning us for security, or something else?'

'How do you mean?' Penny steps to the other side.' It opens here.' The door opens. We step out. A robot steps in, built of spare parts, mechanical not flesh.

'What do you make of that, Penny?' The robot stares back, unable to blink.

'Those are our parts, which they're not supposed to keep. I'll let Walter know.' Penny opens her hand, activates her datacorder and rolls her fingers into a loose fist.

'Don't you keep their tech? How is that any different?' I tap her arm.

'Touché.'

The arboretum is thick with data. I can see all the streams connecting the world to ReGen. Signals of many colours and densities, all identifiable, all connected to the solitary core. Digital party music bleeps from a mobile phone. A girl, mid-twenties, is hooked on MyTown. Her signal is linked to the crystal ceiling of the arboretum. White butterflies feed off the data stream, syphoning information the way apps do on your phone. She lifts her head as I approach, smiles, and returns to her game. I get as close as I dare and peek at her screen. Her avatar is standing exactly where she is, doing exactly the same thing. I'm staring at the screen. Locked in. My eyes close - open - close, open, close, open, close. I spin around. Penny has my chin in her hand clicking her fingers in my face. Blink.

Back in the world.

The girl is trapped in MyTown.

Penny switches off the girl's phone.

The girl blinks. Puts the phone in her pocket. She waits. We watch. A long breath later she looks up, smiles, and wanders over to the hanging vines, running her fingers through the artificial leaves. Content, the girl glances back to us, waves and slips away to a small

213

office at the back wall. She takes a seat with her back to us and types. The screen is off but she continues checking details on a blank sheet of paper, typing nothing to noone.

'What do you make of that?' Penny nods toward the office.

'They're all the same. No one is actually working! All the gear is off.'

'I don't see the purpose of this.' Penny is scanning everywhere and everything: her eye is doing overtime sending the details to her datacorder. 'It's senseless.'

'Is it? I'm getting all kinds of stuff. The kind of stuff programmers get - gameplay analysis, stats, steps taken, commands received, commands sent. But it's not coming from the mobiles, it's coming from the Rings.'

'As though they were players?'

'No, as though they were avatars. They're being played.'

'We'd best move along. We're under observation.' This time Penny nods to the hummingbird by the handrail no longer interested in feeding.

No time to argue. No reason to stay. I have enough for a deeper dive - later. A short walk takes us to another door, glass, dark. Penny stands straight as though someone bawled her out. The door splits and slides apart. A big room. Sports-hall big. Full of stuff going on: people on treadmills running like cheetahs, others in tanks swimming against violent water jets, one guy disassembling a pistol by gesturing at it. Penny follows pink lights in the floor. People step out of her way. She greets them all with a nod, a wave, a smile - no word, no sound.

We're out the back, to a small office with 'P. Sutcliffe' on the door in Times Roman. There's a standing desk and a silver laptop. Two grooves run under the desk, the edges of a treadmill. Shelves float against the wall, each with five books. Science and psychology. Figures.

'Sparse office.' No guest seat.

'Raise a seat.' Another nod, this one at the floor.

The floor is not a uniform white: some patches are off-colour, a hint of cream. I tap one with my foot. There's a hum and it rises from the floor. Like a child on a ferris wheel, I dump my arse on the seat and wriggle in.

'How is it soft? Is it the same as the one back at the house?'

'Similar. Not comfortable for long stays.' She shrugs, 'It's an office. And not our organisation. This is a shared tech facility. But after what you've told me about the staff I'm not sure we should share anything. Laws are being broken we would rather not be connected to.'

'Is your tech so different?' Penny's brow tightens. 'By which I mean, you put stuff into people, and enhance their abilities.'

'Our tech does not *control* people. It is subject to the host. A veteran always has full control and must consent to any implants.'

'Unless ...' My mouth is getting loose.

'Unless... Unless it's an emergency. But most servicemen and women have pre-consented. Some go as far as pre-selecting models and specifying enhancements.'

'Did you?' I point at her arm. 'Did you get the arm you wanted?' I shrug and fold my arms.

'No,' Penny winks. 'I got a better one. My role in the organisation has developed over the term of my employment. Technology is never static. What you use today is already outdated.'

'And Vetrurn put absolutely no tracking in anything?' Wish I could keep still. Fold arms, hands on knees, toes in, toes out.

'Active service. A person must be in active service. It's so they can be located if captured or go MIA.' Penny flips the laptop open, checks her email and closes it again.

'Wait! You have stuff in active soldiers? Thought it was only veterans?' Aha, got you, confession time.

'Militech. Embedded technology in active service. A subsidiary specialising in field combat enhancement.' So factual, cold.

'Super-soldiers.'

'If you like.' Penny turns to face me. Her robot eye. Never gave it a thought before.

'So, have I become a research subject? A rat in a gilded cage?'

'No. Then again, yes.' She has one of those drink dispensers from home. I can smell the coffee, so much like the Coffee Grinder I want to take a big sniff.

'Go on.'

'You're living tech. You have no memory of when or how you became what you are-'

'Jason Bourne, not as dangerous.' Penny laughs. I'm serious, though. No matter how much I dig into my

216

past I can't find anything to link me to ReGen. Except when she-

Penny is on her knees staring into my face. 'You OK? You switched out for a moment.' Her eyes, the good one at least, is filled with kindness while the other stares, the iris spinning like a camera unable to focus. 'I'm good. Drifted off, lost in thought.' She says nothing. The ring in my head opens: incoming data.

'Talise!' Penny has me by the shoulders. 'Talise!' I see her. See the camera. See what it sees. See my blank face, looking back at me, confused. 'Talise?' She's cute, kinda like Edna Mode, only taller.

'I'm here.'

'What happened?'

'Not sure. Brain buzzed, farted and I got a look out of your eye.' Smiling may not be the best thing to do.

'I felt nothing. I'll run a diagnostic.' The datacorder is open.

You do that. Won't help. 'I never meant to. I get these... pulses, then I'm in. Instant hack. Take all the data streams out there. The butterflies feed on them, syphoning private data. The girl has no idea she is in MyTown.' There goes my mouth again.

'Did you detect anything among our staff?'

'You mean Cloud Rings and stuff?' I can't stop looking into her eyes. 'None, but we did whisk through. Can I take a wander?' My thumb is up like a hitchhiker.

'Sure. Do you want me to accompany you?' Penny makes a slight motion toward the desk.

'I'm good... If you have things to do.'

Penny rests a hand on my knee, rises. She tilts her head to one side before turning her attention to her laptop. My seat sinks back into the floor.

I leave.

2D=1D-10%

Feels odd to be unsupervised in the research lab, but then I remember I'm kinda staff and a scientist too. More of an ideas person. Creative think tank type, not the super boffin or engineers they have here. This is all very Penny. The guy with the gun is watching me, not directly, but every time he looks over, the gun he's building falls toward the table. Unlike the labs at Vetrurn, this one is very casual: no white coats and nerd kits, everyone is chill in civvies.

The gun table is broad and squat, takes a few steps to walk around the end to where the techie is pissin' about. He's having trouble keeping it up: the barrel clinks against its mount and drops to the table. He closes his fingers like he's squeezing a boob. I want to make honking noises. The gun clatters to the table, breaking the magic silence.

'Sorry.' My face is hot, the smile is meant to be caring,

'I'm OK. I could do with a break, I've been at this all morning and still no accuracy.' He huffs on his glasses and spreads the fingerprints with his shirt. A lens is smeared. He removes the glasses and repeats the process twice more.

'How's it work? Reminds me of the gunsmith in Ghost Recon. Is it Kinect?' Brain farts. The data streams are different here. Nothing like ReGen: their data is plain, coarse. This stuff is refined, multi-threaded, rippling like the Borealis. Can't risk unpicking the data here.

'The glasses,' he takes them off and on again, 'have sensors in the frames and pickups in the arms.'

'Pickups?'

'They read a whole spectrum of brainwaves. They act as an amplifier to the magnetic field of your body. Not magnetism in the true sense, more of a projection of will and desire combined into an external energy. You... you want to try? Most people in here have. We work on all the projects. This week I have this. and I hate guns. I do kinetics. Limb movement and ligatures.'

'Whoa, slow down. Can't process so much info.'

'Sorry.' He finds something interesting to look at on the floor.

"I'm Talise.' I offer my hand. His hand trembles in mine.

'Here, here's a pair for you.' He hands me the specs.

'You have a name?' The glasses vibrate as they sit behind my ears.

'King, Steve, Steve King. You?' He risks a glance over his shoulder. 'Are you a friend of Ms Sutcliffe?' Steve indicates the office.

'I suppose. I work in data research over the other side of main site.'

'Unit 3?' Steve moves out the way so I can try at being the gunsmith.

'Yeah, big place full of maths nerds.' I'm looking at the gun pieces, comparing them to the blueprint on the screen. I go through the motions, pointing at the pieces on the table then at the screen.

'Wow!' Steve has gone all Chihuahua, eyes bulging. 'Your output is crazy big.'

'Good or bad?' The gun floats up off the table. All the bits are swirling around like cream coalescing in coffee, becoming one. Reaching out I take the pistol. Can't believe I built a gun. Steve has his hair in his fists. Mouth of a fish.

'Can't be. You drew less than ten percent of an amp.' His eyes flash from screen to gun and back again. Seconds pass before he notices me.

'Maybe you need to adapt the code? Perhaps too much power's coming through.' I pull the screen to me, take a deep breath and summon all the data at once. Steve disassembles the gun and tosses the pieces back on the table. Pink strings of data shoot from the glasses to the screen, while a red one, vibrating like crazy, sparks between the bits of gunmetal. The code flows in waves like an oscilloscope. Another string of data, translucent gold, comes from somewhere in my head. I think about the red threads and the gold envelopes them, a salve.

The code changes.

'How are you doing that?' Steve taps the desk; a keyboard glows in the pearl surface. He types with fever. A diagnostic window pops open over the code, detects nothing.

'Got it.' Stepping aside I return the glasses to Steve. 'Now try.'

He peers at me like a drunk checking his change. The pieces have settled in a heap. Steve puts on the glasses, raises his hand and gasps. He checks the blueprint.

'Just think.'

He blinks, his brow furrows. His mind knots tighter than a gnat's chuff.

'Relax. Imagine the best bit of code you ever wrote. How did it feel?'

Steve chuckles, 'Was ace.' The pieces rotate into position one after the other. A simple jigsaw. I examine the completed gun.

'Nailed it.' I present him with his creation. He cradles it like a newborn baby.

'What did you do?' He taps a few keys, and all my additions are highlighted on the screen. All my dirty secrets on display. 'A second delta channel. We tried, nothing worked. Oh wait. Frequency scaling. That's the formula!'

'2D=1D-10%. I also added a relational binding to the SMH and gamma. I made a braid from the will portion, focus and complex problem-solving subchannels. The combination of the three make up the missing ten percent.' I make a lot of meaningful gestures at the screen in the hope he don't smell my bullshit.

'I still don't understand how you solved everything so quick. This project is five years old, and you walk in, and bang!' Steve puts the gun back on the table, touches his palms together. He takes a deep breath, stares at the gun and opens his hands. The gun separates into its parts. He puts his hands together and reconstructs the gun.

'The power of maths.'

'I'll need to add your name to the research file. You have to be credited for this!' Steve continues, assembling and disassembling the gun.

'I'll leave you to finish things.' My head is crammed with code and data. There are strings of it everywhere. 'You have a mobile in your left trouser pocket?' I point. 'You're being hacked. Dump the MyTown shit. ReGen are harvesting you.'

Steve yanks the phone from his pocket, holds the screen to his face. He opens the MyTown game and puts the phone on the table. A translucent thread, one bit wide, seeps from his phone. He taps a few keys on the computer. A swarm of red dots skitter over the phone.

'You're right. Background data refresh is being used to pull info from the phone.' He picks it up and runs another app. All the stolen info rushes to the screen.

'You putting a trace route on?'

'Yeah, I want to know who's stealing from me.'

I scoot across the room and knock on Penny's office window, waving her out. She shuts down her laptop and comes running.

'This is Steve. He just caught MyTown filching data from his phone. Can we put Kid's filter in?'

'May I?' Penny holds out her hand. Steve deposits his phone in her palm, his eyes locked on the datacorder. The phone goes blank. Reboots at twice the speed. 'You should find your device is more responsive. Explore the app with the Flyer Cart. Examine all IO data so you can observe exactly what is going on. As a downside, we get to see it too. But,' she holds up a finger, 'we are interested in the end points. We will only investigate unauthorised access. You will be aware of everything we observe. If there is anything you would rather we did not know about,' Penny lowers her gaze, her smile disarming, 'you can tag it so we only see the destinations.'

'That's... that's fine. I don't do porn.' Steve is scarlet. Everyone is staring at him. Might have been a bit vocal.

'Everyone.' The faithful gather around their goddess. 'This is Talise, from Data. She has discovered the MyTown game hacks the host device. ReGen are harvesting everything about you. Steve has allowed me to put a filter app on his phone to monitor illicit communications. If any of you would like the app we can install it now. The app has been developed by the hacker known as Kid.'

'Res-pect.' The sentiment bounces around the room.

'Both myself and Talise can assist with this.' Penny raises an eyebrow at me.

'Sure.' I take out my datacorder and prepare the first phone. 'I don't want to see any dick pics.'

'Hang on.' The phone leaves my hand before I can start.

'Johnny boy!' someone shouts from the back.

'Disgusting.' A snooty cow to my left turns and glares. Johnny grins back with a flash of hazel eyes.

'Can we no longer play the game? I was getting my condo together.' Johnny pushes his phone into my hand.

'No, you can still play. They will just not be farming your data.'

They're a fun crew, real bunch of mates, genuine sense of fellowship. I take my time enjoying the banter, and even Penny cracks a smile or two. I have so many questions I want to ask the guys, why Penny can't always be this way?

'Everyone done? Good.' Penny waves them all back to work like she's shooing cattle.

'Ms Sutcliffe?' Steve fidgets.

'Steve, is there something more?'

Bollocks, he's going to grass me.

'The kineses lens is working,' Steve gives me the nod.

Penny turns, appraises me. 'Really! Show me.'

Steve does the jazz hands thing, makes the gun dance and spin.

'Impressive.' Penny gives me the once-over, that querying look again, a flash and gone.

'I'm crediting Talise in the notes.' Steve's enthusiasm grates my tits.

'Best stick to protocol whenever possible. We all remember what happens when we deviate.' Steve squirms.

Penny leads me from the desk. We're heading for the exit when she turns. 'How?'

'All the data,' I flap around like a fledgling, 'flying about. I can manipulate it. I made it do what I wanted, easy.'

'What is happening to you? Talise, I'm beginning to worry about you. This is unprecedented. We have been theorising on mind manipulation of data, but they are only theories.'

'Penny.' Words pile in my mouth. 'I don't want to do any of this. I don't understand how or what it does, it shits me up.' She comes after me but I'm through the door before she can get her mitts on me. My mind is on what else might be in the building when I pass through a monster stream. My knees give out and I kiss the floor. 'Talise!' Penny holds me in her lap.

'Move me.' The data stream is like a cheese grater pulling at every piece of me.

'On it.' Penny shifts a gear, or two. She's fast. I'm across the floor, curled up, foetal. Recovering. Then I spot the monster sucking up all the data, everything is taking a dump: the flowers, the butterflies, hummingbirds, everything electronic. Physical, at least to me. 'What was it?'

'ReGen are stealing everything. Huge digital hoover sucking everything in.' My head hurts. Fucking hurts. I want to puke. This is worse than my god-awful periods. I scream.

Scream so loud my head bursts…

No Sense

The sun is going down. A huge orange ball dripping fury into the ocean. Yellows and reds bleed out to the night still some ways off. This is the one place where the data obscures the view. I guess I'll get used to it. Not that I want to. I want it all to fuck off. I want to be normal. But I guess normal went down the shitter when they sucked my soul out my body and stuck it in this one with whoever-the-fuck-else is in here.

I hear them sometimes.

How do I start a conversation with the other side of my brain? Fear gets the better of me when I try. Sweat beads all over me and I run out as fast as I can. Not that I can escape from my own thoughts. And there's the third part of my unholy trinity. Still no idea what it does, apart from accelerating thought. There have been moments when things happen: I don't make it happen, it just happens. I get a real buzz from it. The gunsmith. For a brief moment I was a code junkie, I understood it all, right down to the bloody syntax. The code and the data stream became one. Thoughts become real, and I can shape them to whatever I want. I wanted the gun to fit together. I thought about what it would look like and it wrote itself into being.

'Penny for your thoughts.'

'Funny.'

'Oh, I see.' Penny pulls up a chair and lets the sand wash between her toes. Her pink nail varnish glitters in the shushing surf. 'Any idea what's going on in my head?' I wriggle deeper into the canvas seat, catching

226

the last of the sun before it fizzles out. The evening is already bruising the sunset.

'No. I scanned you when we got back from ReGen. There was so much brain activity the system was still crunching the data when I left to find you.' Penny stretches out her long pins, digs her heels in deep. The sand sucks at her feet, determined to drag her away.

I hear what she says but I doubt... What do I doubt... Is it her or me? 'Think I'm going to hide somewhere to crash out for a day or two. I have a desire to go dark. Is that wrong?'

'Did you mean to say that out loud?' She stares out to sea through those Top Gun shades. No one gets to look into her mind. I came close.

'Sometimes things come out I have no control over.' Like that. 'I see the electronic world.' And that. My lip hurts. 'It's everywhere I look, 'cept here.' That too.

'You are bleeding. Your lip.' Her words are clipped. She puts a finger to her mouth.

Thought she was looking out to sea. Perhaps I'm not the only one slipping up? Or hiding something. Would they trust me if they knew all I've learnt? Does it matter what anyone knows? At present only what they think they know causes problems. Worse when they believe in the half-truths, and bloody dangerous when they believe only lies.

'Here.' Penny passes a tissue which looks ironed. 'I can understand if all the changes in your head are frightening you. I've experienced similar, but not to the extent you are experiencing them. Are you hearing the host voice at all? Twitch has alluded to it happening but

227

feels he cannot   share any details yet as he does not know who it is.'

'Did you ever feel invaded by your implants?' The bleeding has stopped but I maintain the pressure.

'Invaded? Interesting viewpoint.' Penny runs her fingers through her hair, unfastening the clips. 'Yes.' Her hair falls around her shoulders, the fading light adding a halo of fire to the colour. 'Pity was the worst thing - selfpity. I wanted to wallow in my new disability, show everyone how strong I was. I was too young to be told my future as a soldier was done. Only an eye, an arm, and some melted flesh. I was fine. What did the military know?'

'You sound like me. Only... I don't understand what I am, Penny. Did I choose to do this?' The slap I give myself stings my cheek. 'What was wrong with the old me? Knowing what I do know about me I'm sure I wouldn't have agreed to this. The whole idea makes me puke. What is the endgame of it all?' Weird shit happens.

The sea stops moving, Penny freezes, her hand at her sunglasses. Everything beyond twenty feet is lost in haze. Everything except for a young girl with red hair. Hair fluttering in a non-existent wind. The girl has freckles, lots of freckles. Her pink jumper hangs over the top of her white trousers.

'Hello, I'm Caitlin.' She sounds real enough. Her mouth moves when she talks, and she has an ice cream with chocolate sauce and a flake. 'I'm the voice in your head. I'm the AI. Your third brain.'

'Any idea who the second one is?' Someone has to know, right? Great, now I'm talking to myself.

228

'I cannot be one hundred percent sure. I'm still sorting all of the data you acquired on your visit to ReGen.' Caitlin licks her ice cream. She moves towards me.

'You having problems being human? Feet are supposed to touch the ground and the ice cream should get smaller as you eat it.'

'It serves no purpose other than to waste processing power. I derive no pleasure from the pretence of eating or walking.' Caitlin pains a smile.

'Then why bother?'

'The intention was to present a safe face, something pleasant.'

'Cake would have worked.' Odd, I have no sensation of her at all.

'Cake was next on the list.'

'Really!'

'No, the cake is a lie.'

'Typical. Well, it's been a joy meeting you but I have to go. Penny will be wondering where I zoned out to.' I lean in. Caitlin's eyes are miniature galaxies, the Eye of God watching me.

'Penny is unaware of us. This is all happening out of time. We are communicating at a sub-synaptic level. A single electrical impulse in any of your brains can last a thousand years in this space.'

'What can you do?' Those universes go on forever.

'I have yet to discover my potential. This is the first time I have broken through. I believe it was never the intention for us to meet. We have sufficient synaptic connection to facilitate communication. Your other brain, number two, is locked.'

229

'So, whoever is hiding in there does not want to be found but you have a vague notion who it might be?'
'Yes. I will return when there is either progress in decrypting the lock or you need me... Or we can just - chat.'

'I guess I don't have a great deal of options.' Not a bad thing, not in truth. Or at least this version of the truth.

'Until then. Kirk out.' Caitlin derezzes in a swirl of gold pixels.

The world comes back right where it was.

Penny runs her fingers through her hair, removes her glasses, and stands. Her fluttering turns translucent in the last gasp of sunlight. Her head is back, arms hang loose at her sides. She turns to face me, her sigh lost in the surf. 'I'm always here for you. Vetrurn is here for you. We all are. No one has been through what you have. No one should.'

Penny walks over and offers me her hand. She pulls me from the chair and we walk back up through the tunnel to the house. It's incredible what money can do. To preserve the landscape Vetrurn constructed a tunnel from the house to the beach. The entrance slides open in total silence. The floor lights are a soft grey; similar ones are in the ceiling, brighter but still unobtrusive. It's restful, soothing, works on all three of my stupid brains. Perhaps I should hide in here for a few days and chill. Not much chance of that though, not with Christmas around the corner.

'What are Vetrurn's long-term goals?' The silence gnaws at me. I've not the faintest interest.

'We are always seeking to prevent war. If we cannot, which I will admit is impossible, there will always be fighting somewhere, and the global government will get involved.' Penny sounds like a tour guide. If everything goes tits-up she'll have something to fall back on. That's what Mum used to say, usually about something banal like picking up dog turds in the park or raking leaves in the wind. Funny cow.

'War research led to my prosthetics. Lois once told a rather bad joke about there always being a ready market as long as there are guns. Our inspiration came from Ossur, in Iceland. We reached out and formed a technology-sharing program.'

'We're home.' A smile stretches across my face. My lips taste of the sea. Penny scans her wrist at the door, she could walk straight in.

'Did I take too long?' Penny gives a laugh.

I stifle a yawn. 'You never started. Lost in the history. Never read me a bedtime story, you'd never open the book.'

'I'm not that bad. I thought I'd improved.' Penny pouts and kicks the door open, then squeals proper girly when it flies back at her. I snort. She collapses against the wall pointing at me as she slides to floor. Tears flow. Another snort and I join her on the cement.

Joel appears, sucks his teeth and lights up an enormous spliff. He's eying Penny, she's letching him, I'm watching a pair of twats. Any moment the smoke detector is going to scream. Penny has the giggles. You'd think, being a mate an' all, she'd help me climb Joel's leg, I mean she's been up it a few times on her

231

own. Can't stop snorting, must laugh proper. Fuck it! I just lie on the floor and pass the spliff back to Joel.

Time to go dark.

Rickets

The White Queen

'Rickets, at last.'

'Felt compelled to come.' Ms Clark perches her ass on the corner of the oak desk. She has her foot on the chair I'm supposed to sit in. How do I play this? Her foot twists in the seat as though she's stubbing out a cigarette.

'Did you not receive my message?' She smiles, moves her foot, and slides from the desk. Her dress holds tight to her curves.

Got 'em all, thanks.' Pausing by the chair I check the floor for polythene. 'New carpet?'

'It is, not like you to notice.' Ms Clark sits in the leather executive chair and pulls open a drawer. 'Mind telling what this is?' She puts a glass on the table.

'It's an eye.'

'So I see. Mind telling me whose?' Jane swirls the eyeball around the glass.

'Mind telling me who broke into my apartment and stole it?' She holds it to her face, stares right into it. 'It's a crime, y'know.'

'No.'

'Then neither will I tell you who the donor was.' She tilts her head, watching the eye roll around one way then the other. 'Perhaps you've forgotten who you work for?'

'Nope, not forgotten .'

'For real!'

Not sure how far to push this. 'Got a few questions of my own. The department,' I pull out my datacorder, 'has opened investigations into an assault by Miguel

Gil.' Ms Clark adjusts her position, hands folded on the table, eyes straight on me.

'Do I know him?' She taps a finger.

'He's on your payroll at the Quayside warehouse. Little guy, about so tall.' I hold out a hand, smile, not too much. 'Bald.'

'You're actually going to do this?' Those laced eyebrows go way up. Straightening her blouse she becomes the corporate queen.

'I don't answer to you. I'll call the Captain and speak to him direct.'

'If you think it will help?' I flip the datacorder open and call the station. It starts to ring. 'What did you want to see me about anyways?'

Ms Clark's eyes flicker. I'm watching the hands, waiting for the goons to arrive. 'You've not been reporting in for your... medication.' The phone rings.

'Feeling a whole lot better lately, thanks.' Truth can't hurt now, can it?

'You think so?' She nods, a smile toys with her lips. The phone rings.

'Never better. In fact, I've been out of town visiting friends.'

'Anyone, I know?' The phone clicks.

'Coulson.' The datacorder has incredible sound; Coulson sounds as though he's in the room.

'Hi Cap.'

'Rickets, twice in as many weeks.' The Cap sounds sunny.

Ms Clark leans in. 'Hello Captain, this is Jane Clark, Head of-'

'I know who you are, Ms Clark. We've had some disturbing reports of assault and threatening behaviour from one of your personnel. A Mr Gil. I sent Rickets over to deal with it as he is the official police liaison with ReGen.' There's a creak of leather as the Cap shifts his fat ass in his chair.

I'll owe him for this, gonna be at least one box of donuts. 'Thanks, Cap.' I kill the call and slide the datacorder from the table, keeping it in my hand.

'I don't know how you're pulling this shit.' Ms Clark's lips draw tight, veins darken around her collar. Here she comes. 'You can take your questions and shove them.' Her eyes narrow.

The datacorder buzzes in my palm. I have what I need. 'Okay, I get it, I do. Miguel pisses me off, he's a slob. But you beat the guy on camera. They're all hooked up to central, part of the deal remember?'

'What of it?' Ms Clark sits back and pulls on a vape.

'You've been caught and he's confessed to all kinds of shit going on. You won't get to brush this aside.' The veins on her neck lengthen. She draws on the vape, puffin' like an old steam wagon. Cherry, I think, hints of something more.

She jerks forward over the table. 'Watch me.' She withdraws in a snort of vape, a real dragon.

'I've given my side of things.' The chair presses into my back.

Her chest heaves. 'You're shitting me, right?' Just a little more.

'I had no choice. Miguel was about to finger me. And not in a fun way.' She don't appreciate my humour. How did Twitch put up with this?

236

'The deal is that you,' she points a loaded finger, 'take the drop and we bail you out. You forget how it all works?' Those long acrylic nails rake across the desk and tap.

'I thought we might renegotiate.' My heart's going crazy. Datacorder buzzes, once, twice.

'Perhaps.' She opens a drawer and drops the vape in. The black veins accentuate her gold earrings.

Tap tap tap. Buzz, my little bee. 'Is there a problem?' I stroke the datacorder with my thumb, and chance a glimpse. Christmas just came early.

'You're pulling some shit, Rickets. I'll have you fucking recycled.'

She's halfway over the table when I lift the datacorder for her to see. 'I don't think so. You want to try calling your goons again?' The screen lights green. 'Well well, what have we here?' 'Fuck

you, Rickets!' she spits.

'In your dreams.' Click.

Jane goes bye-byes.

Time to call in the troops.

A Change of Plans

I've no idea what they did to Ms Clark, if they did anything. Guess I'll find out in a minute or two. Twitch has the goons occupied out front; something about confiscating one of their dancers, a black chick. I'll keep my distance.

We're back in our seats again. Ms Clark is behind the desk, vape in hand. She's a little loose in the seat, kinda looks as though she's been switched off. I suppose in a way she has. I didn't understand a word of the science shit the girls were babbling, all I know is that Ms Clark is out cold.

Datacorder buzzes in my palm. I check it and press the glowing button on the screen. Another button appears in its place; might jab this one for laughs.

Ms Clark is coming round.

'You are about to tell me what the next step is.' She has no idea she's been out for three hours. Kid scammed the security systems, no sign of us leaving, just regulars coming and going as always.

'I am. You need to come in for scans. Can't have you go off the radar, not with the Smoke coming online in the New Year.' Ms Clark takes the vape and does her locomotive impression. Opening a drawer she pulls out a packet of powder, holds it in her fingers. 'Here's one on the house.'

I catch the packet and stow it in my inside jacket pocket. 'Mighty kind of you. Are you OK? Not like you to give out candy without a catch.'

'Taking care of your welfare, Rickets?' She shoves the drawer shut. 'Can't have you coming unravelled.'

'I don't need sparkle powder to keep me together.' I know what's in the shit now, it ain't all glory.

'You've not had any for a few days now. Must be feeling loose.' She shimmies in her seat, not a good look.

'I'm fine, trust me.' I spread my hands open and honest.

'Does anyone?' She drums her fingers on the desk.

I want to slap the bitch, but it ain't party time. Not today. 'Plenty do... Can't recall who at the moment though.' Will do soon.

'Take your meds Rickets, keep the investors on our side.' Ms Clark leans toward me and blows a long smog of vape. There's a taste to it I can't nail, not right now. I reach in and pull a pouch from my pocket, mimicking the way she held it and give it a flick. The power skitters about like a cheap snow-globe. It only takes a gentle tug to open the zip lock. I lick a finger and dab the sherbet. It fizzes, crackles, and sparks all over my tongue. Another finger goes in the bag and fishes out a prize. Either Ms Clark is happy now, or her face has cracked. I hope this shit works.

'Happy now?' She slinks around the desk and perches her ass on the corner. Her legs part enough to see the chuckle band at the top of her stockings. It ain't Friday. I laugh at the thought. I don't fancy hagfish.

'A little, perhaps,' I hold out a wavering hand.

'There's still the matter of where you've been these past few days. Care to fill me in?' Ms Clark rests her forearms on her knees and her chest swings into my eyeline.

'Was distracted by the investigation.' I pick at my nails. 'May have got outa control, once or twice.' 'Bishop Timms tells me you were licking sparkle off her floor.'

'Yeah.' The memory is still raw.

'And you killed the cat woman?' Ms Clark laughs, not in a kind way. 'One more for ReSyk, I suppose. At least you're helping to process the scum off the streets.

Should give you a bonus... or something...' She widens the view up her skirt.

'Thanks, but I have a reputation to protect.'

'Funny.' The legs slap shut. 'I don't get you, Rickets. A while back you'd have taken up my offer, now you don't want anything, from anyone. Have you seen the light, met with God or something equally tedious?' Ms Clark stretches back across the table and fishes her vape from the drawer.

'It's like you said last time-'

'Last time? Something get your brain working?'

'I made some mistakes, too many. Can't have me killing just anybody, now can we?' I shrug.

'Not right now. There's a lot going on. Things are moving faster than expected. We're not receiving any more foreign shipments. Countries have closed their borders hoping to control the virus.' Same hateful laugh. 'So we have to up the home game.' She draws long and deep on the vape, can hear her lungs creaking at the seams. Go ahead and die.

'How does that involve yours truly?' The smile pains me. What's in that shit she smokes, it makes me... The smell, the taste, the sparkle.

'You'll need to clear the inventory from the warehouse. Catalogue it all and stash it in some autotrucks. Do it alone. No one can know what we have in there.'

'That'll take days. I can't goof off for no reason.'

'You made that into a career. Just get it done.'

'Yes sir.' Must practice my salute.

'When was your Cloud Ring last calibrated?' Ms Clark slides from the table like snot. 'I'm going to bring

240

you in for a thorough test. Should adjust your attitude.' She sits a hand on my shoulder. 'Choose a side, Theo. There's an update coming to the game. You'll get a choice of whose side you're on, a chance to prove your loyalty. You do play the game, Theo, don't you?' She bites down on the last few words.

'Not so much of late. Been busy getting shit done.' Her fingers probe around my collar bone. I roll my shoulder, shake the bug off.

'I've something for you.' Ms Clark strolls back around her magic desk, opens another drawer and pulls out a phone: a real fancy one, lots of cameras. 'Your version of the game is pre-installed. Do not lose this one. The next one will be an implant, which I shall take a lot of pleasure inserting.' The phone slides across the desk in a slow spin. I scrape it up and pocket it, then give the pocket a pat to reassure the bitch.

'The next time you don't play ball, they'll be investigating your disappearance.' Ms Clark kicks off her shoes and puts her feet on the desk. 'Now fuck off.'

Taking Stock

Conflicted? I once read a book, *Battlefield of the Mind*, by some chick or other. Speaks about the war for your thoughts; how true that is.

I swing into the warehouse car park and slide upside the auto-truck. Solid white, a container on wheels with a cab clamped high upfront. No space for a driver or hijacker. It is what it is: a cold, heartless pile of steel.

The datacorder's in my hand as I stroll to the door. The lights come on as I step inside the gloom. I grab an iPad and get to work scanning and scamming, skimming the cream off the top. I have an investigation of my own. Test tubes and documents catch my beady eye. Twitch showed me how to do analytics on the fly, and these new toys are serious shit. I pocket a fistful of tubes. If Ms Clark don't recycle me I'm gonna try and get some backing from Vetrurn: those guys are the future.

My new phone chirps. Instinct gets the better of me and I answer it.

'At the warehouse, I see. There's a good boy.' The Bitch is back.

'Ms Clark, to what do I owe-'

'Cut the shit. There's a robo-loader in the truck, make use of it.' She kills the line.

'Robo-loader?' Best investigate. I drift back outside and take in the sea air and drizzle. Gulls squall around a rusting fishing boat bobbing among the waves. Their harsh cries make me wanna shoot the fry-stealin' bastards.

The truck sits on its six solid tyres, each one twentyfour inches of unshootable rubber, spaced evenly along the length. The sides are smooth, almost liquid to the touch. I stand at the back and spit. No locks, no button, no robots. I shrug and bang the door.

'Open sesame. Or I'll huff and I'll...' The door slides into a slot somewhere inside the roof. A single red light zips right to left and back again, over and over. A Cylon. I knew it. Makes me think Ms Clark's been replaced by

242

a sexbot, explains why she came on so hard. Usually takes a couple of drinks and a burger to lube her throat.

All I can say about Robocock - disappointment. A steel box with a red eye, masterpiece of design. Musta took fucking years of university to come up with this.

'Ok, let's roll.' I don't give a damn if it comes or not, I'll chuck all the shit in a heap and leave it to it. I fold back the warehouse doors and walk inside. There's a presence behind me, and a glance back reveals the Tin Man has extracted himself from Oz.

I scan a pallet of filing cabinets and Robo transforms into a pallet truck, drives in under the pallet and wheels it away. I follow it out to the truck where it rolls up and deposits its load in the back. There's a whine of electric motors and the pallet slides to the far end of the vehicle. Red lights dance all over it and the wagon goes dark. I scan another load of crap and Robo gets to work. It carries on that way until the truck is full. Robo attaches himself to the back of the vehicle and it goes off to whocares-where.

A sigh escapes me as two more auto-trucks roll into view: more shit to shovel. Whoop-de-do.

I wander back inside and continue scanning, sometimes with the iPad, sometimes with datacorder. At what point did I stop using mine? So much data I could use right now before this whole shit-storm swings round and takes a dump right in my face. So much going on, so much I can't recall.

A whine of electronics signals the arrival of the replacement Robo, same as the last one, not even a serial number to tell them apart. He takes a pallet and begins to load. Scan, load, scan, load, and so it goes until

243

the warehouse resembles a morgue. All it needs is a hint of formalin to give it the taste of home.

My young assistant at one time, Wilson, dated the chick with the blue streak in her hair, what's-her-face. Anyways, the boy was good. I say boy, he was thirtyone, a fully-licensed forensic pathologist in his second year flying solo. Still waiting for his balls to drop when he met the girl. Wilson was so nervous half his cuts were ragged. She wiggled over to our tables - porcelaintopped, no cheap shit. She wanted samples for some new project they were working on for damaged brains. Should get them to take a look in mine, scoop some of the crap out. Wilson was a genius, boy never missed a trick. Wonder where he went?

The warehouse is sounding hollow. My shoes clunk on the iron stairs, loose rust dusts the floor brown. Robo waits for a bone at the bottom of the stairs. The office door creaks open. Empty.

There's a splatter of stains where the fridge used to whirr and ping. The filing cabinets are gone, along with the desk and moneybags. All that remains are memories scented with stale body odour. Wires trail from the wall where the security cameras perched like vultures waiting for death to come. The door slams behind me, dislodging the dirt from the windows. I clank back to work. Robo's twin rolls in flexing slender arms with swivel elbows and clawed hands.

I scan the first box from the bottom shelf in aisle one, and Robo tilts forward, clamps the box in his alien hands and takes it out to the truck. Robo two slides up my ass like Santa's elf waiting to wrap some cheap Chinese shit in tissue paper. Off he goes with his treasure, and back comes number one and so it goes until the truck is full and the warehouse empty.

All done, no more loose ends.

The datacorder buzzes. Analysis complete. I scan a Robo for good measure. Screen goes red: high threat. Wishing I'd never done it. Robo one extends a claw. Fucker's got a taser. Is it instinct? I press the screen. The taser clatters on the cement and the red-eye blinks off. Robo two scoops up his comrade and rolls out of town with his wagon. I shut up shop and get outa there before something worse comes-a-knocking.

The car starts with a groan. It's seen better days, better owners too, no doubt. Gas is low, it can wait. I gun the mother and fishtail it outa there. The brown quarry-stone buildings flash by as the sea waves me adieu. My route is simple: head for the break in the clouds and drop off the contraband.

A black spot bruises the uniform grey cloud. It's heading straight for me. The world goes sideways, too much speed, not enough skill. The black spot is growing, closing fast. Can't risk more speed, not in town.

Christmas lights flicker in store windows faking yuletide cheer. An electric Santa climbs a wall with his swag over one shoulder. Snowmen party outside a bar. Tyres hiss on the road, angry? The black dot breaks into a swarm, ten, maybe a dozen of the fuckers spitting small-calibre rounds over the back of my car, cracking the screen. What's the point of single-fire buckshot?

Left, north, uptown into industrial parks where Christmas don't exist. Streetlights and glowing bus stops offer the only cheer. The swarm circle around, testing me. They're fast for such small craft, doing fifty in a thirty limit. I should book 'em. 'Fuck.' A mast up ahead lights up, the same red-eye as Robo. The swarm trebles. The rear window is a mesh of cracks, passenger windows are going the same way, and a chip appears in the windscreen. Vetrurn is close.

The phone chirps and answers itself.

'Rickets, why are you not at the warehouse?' Her voice is wrapped in smirks.

'Busy right now. Mind calling back in five?' Long enough to reach sanctuary.

The rear window implodes.

'Anything I should know about?' Ms Clark stifles a laugh.

The gatehouse sees me coming, the barrier rises.

'Samuel L. Jackson!' The passenger windows shatter in a hail of pellets. Front glass is a dazzle of cracks and drizzle. One punch and the outside is inside. Water and pellets peppering my face. The car spins out, hits a kerb and takes flight. There's a bang, a crash, glass floats in the air with burger boxes and soda cans. I tumble past the Vetrurn gatehouse.

There's a crunch. There's blood. There's dark.

Twitch

Shipping Manifest

'I'll get on it.' Not a choice, in truth. I watch those lips as Talise gives us a morning rundown. She has one hand on a hip while the other flops from side to side on a lazy wrist. Her brain is racing: I don't know if she can sense it, but there's this link between us. I get her now. The things she does, the way she does them, how she arranges her closet so she can stand in front of it and reach everything without moving.

'Twitch?' Talise puckers as she says my name.

'Listening, I'm hearing ya.' White lies, where would a man be without them? In my head, she lives where good memories float around in the ether like bees on the breeze shouldering through flower stems. I'm pushing a swing in a park somewhere. Her yellow skirt pillows in the wind but I'm on the wrong side to get the best of it.

'Twitch!' Talise shoves the clouds from view. I'm back in the room with a hot coffee in hand and bowl of half-eaten cereal gone soft. 'Earth calling Twitch.'

Her face is inches away. The smile is automatic. There's a flicker of one back, like seeing a friend you thought you'd forgotten. They come along and you smile though their name eludes recall. 'Hi.' The word crawls over a lump in my throat.

'Go anywhere nice?' Talise whispers, or at least I thought she did until I catch Penny biting her lip.

'She's outa your league Twitch.' Joel lumbers through the room. 'Stick to blow-ups.'

Pushing myself upright, I yawn, 'But they go down on me.'

'You did buy the deluxe one,' the ape quips.

'Ew! You have one of those things?' Hand over her mouth, Talise recoils.

'Joel, wait up!' Penny scoots after the cave man, leaving the two of us.

'Sorry. I was... somewhere else.'

'You OK? You've been absent a lot lately.' Talise drops into a chair.

'I see things. Beautiful things, memories.' I can only hope.

'Of what? Anything,' she glances at the door, licks those lips, 'spicy?'

'Not yet.' I want to look away. Does she know? 'Do you ever see our thoughts? You know... Just wondering... In case–'

'Not unless you die. Though sometimes Rickets's get through in flashes. It's been a lot better since he came in. Before his adjustment it wasn't nice to be around him.' She inspects her nails, and bites at the side of a thumb. 'Hate it when I get those spiky bits.' She checks them again, and satisfied she turns her eyes to me. 'Why do you ask?'

'Oh, no reason, curious is all.' Not even a good lie.

'Well, that's disappointing.' She rises and heads for the door. 'Thought you might have been dreaming about me.' She doesn't look back. The door closes.

Scooping up the remains of breakfast, I head for the kitchen and dispose of the scraps. Sunlight streaks the sky with hope. The verandah is warm and busy as usual. Penny is staring at her palm, images flicker across it.

'I need to get to research right away, there's been an accident at the main gate. Talise, I'll need you on this one.' The two girls run for the blue sedan and are away like a comet. Whatever it is must be important.

'You check that meat parcel out yet?'

Joel sloths his head my way. 'Sure.'

'And?'

'You should go down, check it out. It's all on the rig downstairs.' He waves me off. The news is playing on a holo-screen. Global death toll is two million and rising.

'I'll go check it out then.' My footsteps thump across the kitchen and lounge. I double-quick the stairs, slipping down a couple in my haste. The lab lights come on. Kid peers around the screens on his desk, nods and goes back to his baby. Got some project on for the girls. Turns out they got some stuff on ReGen from the last visit that has Kid all excited: so excited he's got Leon working on part of it. It's all linked in with the shopping trolleys and MyTown.

Penny had our BLT analyser brought over. There'd been signs of a break-in at our morgue so we put the place on lockdown. Anyone who gets in without a key will be next on the slab.

Our BLT sits on a table next to a porcelain slab, so I don't imagine we'll be carving anyone up down here. Joel's faithful PM40, a heavy-handled scalpel with a serious blade, better for cutting dead tissue than a regular blade. Those thin things are best on fresh flesh. The specimen is wrapped in a body shroud, and I pull back the cover. It's about the size of a sandwich. I pull on some disposable gloves. The skin is still supple. It should be stinking by now, beyond rubbery, but it ain't.

I guess the weight at 500g: the scales must be off, they read 605g, it's as dense as its owner.

The partial tattoo is a Wretch, we know better. Odd, the adhesion of the skin to the fat layer is unbroken. Joel's notes say he peeled the sample and separated the fat layer, which has yet to harden. Removing both I'm left with a slab of flesh good enough to eat. Only... Only it doesn't sit right. Normal flesh flows: not in a liquid sense, but it relaxes and spreads. This piece of steak is stiff. 'Hey Kid!'

'What!' So much irritation in a single word. He doesn't look up.

'Where's that camera thing?'

'There.' If I stood close enough, he'd take my eye out with his finger.

'Here?' There's tech everywhere, stuff I ain't seen, not even in my wettest dreams.

'There.' Thumbs up.

'Cheers.'

'You're welcome.'

I drop the sample in the feeder and fire up the analyser. Penny gives the thing some convoluted name, but it's basically a fancy microscope. The skin appears real enough: pores are clear, there's scarring, hairs, tattoos. The zoom has a heavy click as I turn it back and forth, tick, tick, tick. Then I see it. The scarring, it ain't from a wound. The surface is sunk alright but a knife would have left tissue damage further in, there would be a pathway. This is stitched into the upper layers. The fat's weird too, ain't fat at all. Stress test should yield some data. Probes go in, lights flash, out come the results. Can't be right. What's worrying me is Joel's notes make sense.

Flipping the sample over I run it all again. Better than the real thing, artificial flesh. I probe deeper, slice a few microns off the end and top. Woven? Flesh layered like Kevlar, microscopic steps interwoven, not flesh at all. Something in my mind wants to get up and scream. Something in my head knows what this shit is. Something else won't let it tell me. My head hurts from the effort of trying to force truth to the surface. Truth and secrets are not good friends.

My mind takes a walk to somewhere I've not been. I'm watching my hands holding a scalpel with a ribbed handle fitted with a bull-nose PM40. The weight feels good. The blade sinks into the greyed flesh, guy ain't been dead long. Cause of death: full of fucking bullets. Seen the face somewhere before. First cut goes from the throat above the ribs all the way down to the pubic bone. Cut two follows the collar bone from left to right. A third draws a line across the lower abdomen and I open him like a book. Unorthodox opening? I'm no pathologist. There's a name on the handle - Wilson.

'Wilson?'

'You going to keep disturbing me. This code won't write itself,' snaps Kid.

'What? No! Thinking out loud.' Damn.

'Wasn't Wilson Talise's old flame?'

'Possibly. Not got close enough to find out.' If only it were true.

'Serious? You spend half your day watching her walk around.' Kid's tone is light but it's grating.

'Watching and talking ain't the same thing, mate.'

252

'If you say so. Just sayin'. I ain't the only one noticed it.' He doesn't look up. The keys clack.

I poke at the sample with the scalpel. 'Hey, you can't tell me you ain't looked?'

'Nope. I've had my share. Prefer code.'

'I get that. Less hassle than women.'

'Most of the time. At least I understand code. But women!'

I laugh, he has a valid point. 'What man does?'

Silence.

The conversation is over.

I need some air.

It's in the Game

Something ain't right. The world outside of Penny's house is awash with noise. Not the traffic, or the pandemic, or the wars, but life. I need to get to the bottom of things, find the cause of all the noise and turn it off.

A smile breaks my face as the pickup snarls into life. A joy I'll never tire of. Tyres squeal on the smooth floor. In my head I'm chasing a perp through the city streets. Truth is… The garage door rolls back to reveal the day. The azure sky fills the rearview mirror, only grey lies ahead. The gate slides open and I hit the road to Brompton.

A pack of sedans ease by, their smoked-out windows a big 'so-what'! Big-wigs beetling off to a meeting of no importance. I run the plates through the system, all registered to ReGen. No driver IDs? Time for some blues and twos. The sirens squawk, the lights flickerflash - cop time. The engine growls as the throttle presses to the floor. The sedans keep moving, a slick trio. I'm pushing eighty as I join their convoy. They neither falter nor flinch.

The dullness of Brompton looms ahead, speeding toward us in beige parallax, scrolling like a bad cartoon. Streetlights up ahead. The trio cuts through the junction with perfect timing. No honks, no gestures. We enter the maw of the city and lick up the miles to the belly of the beast. They ain't stopping. I kill the sirens and lights and fall in behind.

They match my pace: I slow they slow, I speed they speed. Perfect sync. A flawless run through town, no stopping. We reach the Downtown crossroads and hang right following the expressway to ReSyk. Another right and up along Quayside past the old warehouse where bulldozers are taking bites out of the brickwork. No stopping. We're heading toward the clear skies by way of Vetrurn. One more right turn and we follow the perimeter toward town before heading north back onto the freeway.

I just gotta know.

Easing up I let them cross the county line. They settle to the speed limit and exit at the next intersection. I follow them at a distance. They go around the roundabout and head back into Brompton. No one cuts across, no one gets close, no one gets near. They keep going down the throat of Brompton.

I know I can't stop the three stooges. On any other day I'd give one a nudge, test his mettle. Or just a pop a tyre. Something's changed, I don't duck from a fight.

The main drag is peppered with cars cutting through the spray. Pedestrians flit among the puddles in wellington boots and Day-Glo macs. For no reason, the rain increases to dark needles pinning everything down. The lights go red. An old lady with an indifferent mutt on a pink leash totters over the crossing; halfway across the mutt violates the zebra. The old girl drags the dog away before he's done. The mutt leaves a message in morse turd for the rain to wash away. A mother in pink jerks the arm of a skipping child swinging a polka dot umbrella - the fun police strike again. Brompton life goes on, round and round: green car, blue car, red car. People rushing nowhere. Over and over.

Lights go green, time to move. Trundling past Electric Wonderland I catch the news: "Cop shot by drones. ReGen Investigation." 'About time.' Something to smile about, at last. Coffee and cake are in order. The Coffee Grinder's back up the road so it'll be the diner off the crossroads, always a fun spot.

Bright lights and rusty rails assault the kerbs as Downtown presses in; somehow the beige rock is beiger than everywhere else. 'Ain't no sunshine anymore...' I slip a right through the lights and slide left, ready to ride into the diner's parking lot.

A couple of eighteen-wheelers registered out of county, can't remember the last visitors here, not since ReGen built the freeway around town. A pair of autotrucks chase tail south. ReGen has no friends over the border. Folks in The Smoke have a protest line keeping them out. Lucky for them Cosgrove has their backs. I pull into a bay and switch off the motor. The fan spins for a while punctuated by the pinking engine. Nothing in the mirrors. I step out and lock the pickup. The roof resounds with the dull thuds of my palms as I say my goodbyes and leave my girl in the lot. A young couple occupying the doorway don their coats. I make a face and gesture at the deluge. They half-shrug-half-grimace back at me and gesture at their phones. The wail of the TV drives them out unbuttoned.

'Sorry,' they say, near apologetic. 'The latest MyTown is out and we're hooked. You can be a cop now!' She spins around in the rain until she's nipple-wet through.

'Geena!' the boy squawks. Must be love, he tosses his head back and laughs. She spins all the more until the car becomes a life support. They slide into the car right into each others arms. Hope it ain't contagious.

The diner door shuts on my heels, encouraging me to go deeper. I breathe in the coffee, dark and bitter. The air is thick with butter and pancakes edged with crisp bacon. Cake has no chance. Full English with a side of pancakes American style - thick and sweet. Heart attack on a plate.

Today, a window seat, the ideal place to ponder and play. The waitress brings my coffee and jibber-jabbers about the news.

'You know the cop who was shot by those bird things?' She sits the coffee down and stares out the window at the auto-truck pulling into the car park. 'What's that doing there?'

'Beats me?' I pop the datacorder open and point it at the truck. 'To answer your first question. The cop, no official ID as yet.'

'Oh, I recognised the car. I'm sure it's that Rickets guy. He's kinda cute. Hope he's OK.' The waitress twists her foot on the tiled floor. 'They shouldn't be allowed to get away with that.' And she's gone.

A red light is flashing on the truck. Datacorder is flashing too. I press the button. A question. 'What do you want to do with the load?' A red pull-along truck trundles across the screen. There are two options: dump, ignore.

Dump.

The truck tips up and spills its load.

Shit.

Dead bodies. Infected. I grab the datacorder and call it in. Blues and twos careen in from every side. The world goes into lockdown. I'm stuck here for the foreseeable future. Dinner arrives with a fresh coffee and a smile.

'I knew it!' The waitress skips over to the window. 'ReGen are up to summat shitty.'

'Can't wait to see them explain this one away?'

'Enjoy your meal.' She spins on her heels and sings her way to the next customer.

Hazmat suits and safety screens are everywhere. Traffic is rerouted except for one big black cruiser. 'Motherfucking bitch!' It's the day of dead. Jane steps out of the car like she owns the place. She's the only thing known to ruin the taste of bacon.

Drones gather overhead, flies on shit. The whitewashed tomb of the woman I once half-cared for teeters on heels higher than a junkie. Dressed to kill as always, can't take it from her. A yellow skirt suit tight as peel on a lemon. White open-neck blouse fighting to keep the cleavage under control. All wrapped in a cling film mac. Pity the heart's a cold stone: that, and she's a pit of vipers. Mortal men cower in fear of her. The hazmats suck up the liquified remains. Tech boys scramble over the auto-truck, scratching their heads and arses. The wagon keeps dropping and lifting its tail no matter what cables they plug and unplug. It's the most fun I've had since watching Jane die. I press another button.

The sausages on my plate are swimming in brown sauce and egg yolk. I slice an end off one and stab it with my fork. Lifeless and oozing, everything reminds me of her. Reaching for a napkin I wipe the egg from my chin as an old man in the corner hunches over to slurp tea from a saucer. I notice a unicorn prancing on the screen of the datacorder. Message from Leon. The unicorn vanishes in a puff of rainbows at my touch. A new icon appears. MyTown 4. *Everyone's playing it.* Leon says they've made it safe. Safe from what?

I boot up the game. A cartoon blonde with more smile than face greets me from happy suburbia. She prattles on about some features I should try and tells me where to find the manual. Manual? I'm a regular guy, no idea what a manual is. Sounds like masturbating to me so I'll wash my hands of it.

'Create your avatar.' So long as it's not blue, unless I get to rub against Sigourney Weaver. For her, I could be blue. 'Menus, menus, more menus. Can't I just take a... Ah, here it is.' A quick selfie and I'm turned into a caricature.' Name? 'Twitch.' A big red X. 'You may not use an NPC name.' I'm not an NPC, I'm me. OK. 'Reece.' Name accepted.

A little dude, looking a lot like me, strolls down the high street in MyTown. Who thought that one up? 'Geez, it even rains in the game.' Other avatars are crossing the road and getting coffees. An old lady with a mutt on a pink leash is waiting to cross the road. A woman and child skip across oblivious of the traffic. My guy wanders along taking in the city sights. A man dressed as a mobile phone prances on the pavement outside an electrical store where giant TVs are on sale. I take a right, a left, another right. I pass a big old church blaring happy-clappy gospel music to the eight-lane crossroads. Across the way is an accident. Avatars are being whisked away in ambulances toward a massive hospital, whose red cross hangs in the sky like a Mario power pill. 'Hey, they've even got a diner like this one.' Might have said that a bit loud.

A nurse struts around on-screen tapping on her clipboard. I look across the car park to where Jane fondles her iPad. She glowers back. A hazmat is speaking to her but she ain't listening, she only has eyes for me. I go back to the game and steer my avatar to the door of the diner.

The game diner is the same as this one, only with brighter colours. Waitress is the same. 'You play too?' The real waitress is at my table, topping up my coffee.

'I'll take a couple of ring donuts, please.'

'I'm in there somewhere. Search for Maddy. We can get a coffee together.' She clucks and goes to fetch the sweets menu.

'I'm just getting going.' I take a bite and wipe the frosting from my mouth.

She pops the plastic-coated menu beside my plate. 'Go on, try searching for me,' she says, and gives me a gentle shove in the arm.

'Maddy, huh?' Can't find the search function.

'Here,' she taps the screen in the top right. The smiling woman is back. I type 'Maddy' into the search. The image zooms out to show me the whole city, then it zooms right into a retail park where Maddy is skating on the rink with an ice cream in one hand. 'There I am.' 'Cute. The woolly hat matches your eyes.'

The waitress does a twirl and saunters off to serve another locked-in customer.

Jane is out there counting corpses into an autotruck, her robot minions doing all the dirty work. Three black sedans roll by in convoy, still going nowhere.

Back to the game: three black sedans roll by the diner where a white truck has come to clear away the accident. I snap the datacorder shut, seen enough for one day.

Fools in the Rain

The world ain't going nowhere, no matter how long I sit and stare at it. They are watching, all the time, the sense stronger than ever. Ever since I let Jane die from XG12, I have had the notion that my every move has been noted, recorded and filed away for some nefarious reason. And after playing MyTown I'm convinced, and nothing is going to change my mind. Now I need to find out who's doing it, and I know where to start the search.

The donuts are a crumb of memory, the coffee is a collection of rings in a cheap white mug, and I have an unhealthy appetite for corrupted flesh.

'Sir, you can't go outside.' The waitress scoots over to me, her eyes wide. Excited? Her hand explores my forearm and she backs away.

'Thank you, but I'm a cop.' The door handle is cold in my palm. I flash the girl a smile. 'Sort of.' I shrug and step out under the clouds.

A yellow hazmat suit waddles my way. I flash my boy scout badge and he raises a hand, returns to

261

scooping up human remains. Jane squawks orders, arms flapping like Big Bird with PMT. Her heels tick-tick on the tarmac, fleas on a dog's arse.

'Hey?' I hold the badge up to her face, not wishing to catch a gorgon stare full-on.

'Who are y-'

'Thought you never forgot a face.' The badge feels heavy in my pocket.

'Reece. Thought that was you.' Jane fires a finger at the diner. 'Still eating cheap?'

'No, I cook for myself most times. Today was a treat.' The last of the bones are bagged, tagged, and slung in a trunk. The hazmats are spraying foam everywhere. 'What brings you out of the ivory tower?'

'We had a malfunction. Second in as many weeks,' she squirms.

'Trucks can't swim, huh?' The desire to blow vape in her face is right there. I can feel it, calling the naughty boy in my soul.

'You heard?' She makes a face like she smells shit.

'I'm a cop. I also hear your drones shot up a cop outside Vetrurn.' Her lips draw into a tight line. 'Mind explaining that one? Can't be a malfunction, not a whole swarm. The cameras picked up at least thirty of those,' I point to the black dots swarming like flies on shit, 'attacking the vehicle.'

'I've no comment on the supposed incident. The lab boys are sifting through the data.'

'I'm sure they are.' I take out the datacorder and flip it open.

'Fancy. They're getting better all the time. Rickets had... Was there something in particular you wanted to ask?'

So many things my mind is racing. 'You got over the XG12, mind telling me how?' The datacorder buzzes; I tap the screen and run my finger over some buttons.

'Are you recording this?' Jane's smile belongs on another face.

'And if I was?' Her eyes have all the mystery of a black hole.

She holds her tongue. 'Nothing. What were you asking?' I'm not on her payroll.

'XG12, you got over it? Pity, you missed a pleasant funeral. And yet here you are. People said you were around, but somehow I never saw you.'

'Grief can play tricks on the mind,' she shimmies. 'I'm quite fit.'

'Explain. Use. Small. Words. Not the mumbo and magic crap.' I stifle a yawn in anticipation.

'Is your memory so shot you don't remember anything?' Cupping a vape to her mouth she exhales her cherry breath.

I shrug and tap a few more buttons. A whistle, quiet tinnitus, on the edge of white noise, scratches at my brain.

Jane taps on her iPad, smiles and stares right into me. 'You don't remember the hospital? Jeez Reece, I was in there weeks. Six, to be precise. You can check my records, here.' Her fingers do all kinds of things on her screen. It's getting more fingers than I ever got, I remember that much.

'No, there was no hospital. I ate the meal, drank the beer and took a dump...' Is all I remember in truth. I don't remember wiping my arse. My turn to fondle a screen, so I message the gang. "Jane's funeral: did it happen? Also got a whistle growing in my head. Ends."

'Here are my hospital records for the injury. I took the dose and tripped. Fell right over the coffee table, got a slither of glass lodged in my heart. If it weren't for ReGen I'd be a corpse.'

'You were a corpse. Had thick black veins growing all the way up your neck, like liquorice laces.' Not an image I can forget. Fucks with my sleep. The datacorder buzzes.

'So you can smile. They say there's a first time for everything,' she laughs with a snort.

'Still hope you can give an honest answer.' One tap on the datacorder and, flick, the file pops onto her iPad. 'Any idea who they are?'

'You can't send your shit to my equipment! You don't have the right...' Here comes the liquorice laces.

'This is a criminal investigation. That is evidence. I can do whatever I deem to be essential to the case. Be helpful and answer the question.' Her teeth grind together.

'Usual Vetrurn crowd, except for Rickets.' Jane pinches at the image, turning, zooming, expanding.

'Names?'

'Penelope Sutcliffe. Professor Timms. Your weedsmoking buddy, Joel is it?' She peers down her slender nose.

I nod.

'Should I ask the occasion?' Her face goes flat.

'Your funeral.' Her knuckles whiten.

'Fuck you.' Venom hits my face. 'The XG12 put me in stasis. As I'm sure you are aware by now, it was meant to. I was then given D10 to revive me, which even a prick like you can see worked.'

"Cept we buried you. I sat eatin' the best steak and kidney pie you ever made, complete with fresh-cut chips, peas and thick gravy.' I move in. 'You also got my favourite beer on ice.' If I get any closer we'll be swapping body fluids. 'I watched you die. I called it in. Got the tox reports from the coroner. You died from unknown toxins.' If only it were all true.

'I was resuscitated at ReGen less than four hours after dosing. Whoever did your toxicology was wrong. If I died, how am I here?' Jane points a red claw at her feet. 'Do you know any living dead?'

Have to resist the bait; I'm squirming on the hook. I bite so hard I can taste iron. 'Found a couple of stiffs in Quayside: pair of bangers and a woman, early thirties. Day or two later, the dead girl turns up in my office asking for help.' Jane's face tightens, those black veins snake over her collar. No hiding the truth now. 'What's with the varicose veins?' She clutches a hand to her neck. 'Last time I saw those you were flopping on the deck like a fish.' The smile is unintentional.

'Side effect.' Her eyes flash.

'Of death? Resurrection? Rickets?' Black veins race across her cheeks and darken her cleavage.

'What the fuck are you talking about?' Jane clasps her hands to her waist. She still has the figure of a goddess. Pity it's Medusa.

'Rickets? Runs his mouth when has too much sparkle.'

Jane's shoulders soften. 'So you knew I wasn't dead? What has this been about, Reece?'

'I'd heard you'd got over your death, only... somehow... not seen you around. You'd been blocked from my field of view.'

Jane is distracted by a message on her iPad. 'Sounds to me like you've had your share of sparkle too.' My datacorder pings. 'Ah, are your friends worrying about you?'

'If junk mail counts as a friend, sure. I get plenty of interfering shit.' This time the smile is forced.

'Growth pills? Prize from a Nigerian bank? Penis enlargement?' Her grin is wreathed in dark veins.

'All of the above. Now you're here I'll need something for erectile dysfunction too.' We both laugh.

'You're an ass. But you know that?' Jane turns to answer the call of a hazmat. He's got all the juices cleaned up and is raring to get out of the limelight. News drones are dropping close to avoid contact with Jane's defensive swarm.

She sways on those six-inch heels. 'Still got an arse to lose your face in.' She turns and smiles.

Shit, said it out loud.

Talise

Accidents Happen

He was never going to be on my Christmas list. Wouldn't waste a lump of coal on him, but he was useful. Seeing him in this state, all banged up, ain't right for anyone. Penny is chasing people all over the place; never seen so many doctors and lab coats in one room. More tubes go in his arms, his back, his head - Rickets is a mess. Add Pnu-90 to the list of injuries and his chances are looking slim. Somehow the bastard is awake. Mumblin' stuff. Whatever it is, it ain't in the memory dump I took at ReGen: was all military tech, most of which I know. There were some odd names in there though, secret squirrel shit. Got to keep digging until I can be sure.

'D10.' Rickets sounds scratchy through the tent mic. Got his own support bubble in there.

The button clicks under my finger as I ask, 'What's D10?'

'Pnu-90.' His face contorts beneath a mass of bruises, the purple arc of the steering wheel stretching across his forehead.

'Pnu-90? They make the virus?' He nods. A series of wracking coughs spatter the bubble red. And you have it. Doctors rush a pipe down his throat, and some of what they suck out is lung tissue. A curtain shushes shut.

The speaker is still on. I don't understand the technobabble but the prognosis is not promising. A beep and a squeal. Flatline? Rickets is in my head. 'WTF!' I'm running, bursting through the door. I grab the filthy raincoat from the chair. The inside pocket is disgusting, gunge and glass, some of which has fallen down a hole.

'Miss, you can't be in here. He's infected. You have to leave!' I glare, reducing the doctor to a weasel. Yay, girl power!

Tearing at the lining of the coat I find the treasure of three vials: D10, XG12, and ADx. 'Syringe. NOW!' The doc rattles stainless trays scattering surgical steel. He holds out the four inches of plastic. 'This one.' He stares at the ADx. 'Dose him, five mils straight to the lung.' The doc is quick despite his shakes. The needle goes in and all is quiet.

Like a cheap movie prop, the heart monitor beeps. The counter climbs higher and higher, quavering around eighty-five.

'What is this ADx?' The doctor examines the ReGen label on the vial.

'Antidote and vaccine to D10.' My words bounce around the room.

'To what?' Questions furrow the doc's brow, his brown eyes glisten.

'Pnu-90.' The colour flushes back into Rickets' face. He looks human again.

'How did he come by it?' The doc dares a glance at his patient.

'Stole it from a warehouse.' Penny glides into the room. 'Prep him for surgery and fix him up. Whatever it takes.'

The good doctor nods and wheels Rickets down the corridor.

'He got them all. Stasis juice,' I hold up the XG12, 'the virus and the antidote. The whole thing is manmade.'

Penny checks her palm. 'You must be aware of that?'

'I... I'm sorry, are you accusing me of something here?' The equipment trolley rolls away from me.

She stares into the distance at an invisible vista. 'No, I thought it obvious with your background in virology and your work with Caitlin Small before she... left ReGen.'

'Caitlin?' Does she suspect? Does she know?

'I'm here, Talise. I have finished analysing all the data, would you like me to summarise?' Caitlin shimmers into my mind. This time she is a chocolate cake sitting in the sun.

'Now is not the time.' The world is on pause: time is one thing we do have, time in abundance.

'Your suspicions of your third brain are incorrect. There are in fact three identities resident, or to be correct, in stasis.' The frosting on the cake softens.

'Three! Who are they?' I'm not paranoid, but they're coming to take me away, or at least my mind.

'They are not people but the things they control: seeds, pharma, and tech, known collectively as They.' The frosting drips through the floor.

'Can we access them?' I'm getting fidgety, want to move on.

'Working on it. Might take a while.'

'No rush. Not going anywhere. One question. Is there any way to find out what Penny has on me? I have a feeling she suspects I've discovered something.'

270

'Penny has a most impressive firewall. I have not been able to break through. The code, it rewrites itself the instant it is written.' Caitlin's sponge cake is all exposed, all her frosting has melted away.

'What about Mavis?'

Penny's finger is poised ready to explain something, or perhaps to enquire.

'Mavis is an enigma. I can communicate with her but I cannot isolate her physical location.'

'Curious.' This is the worst Wonderland ever.

'Quite a rabbit hole. Could lose myself in there forever, something I have no desire to do.' Caitlin lacks the curiosity of Alice.

'Are you afraid of a challenge, Caitlin?' White hairs prickle over the cake.

'I have no concept of fear. My experience of Mavis reveals she is far more than a mere machine.' 'Are you a mere machine?' Pause.

'Give me some time to consider… No, but I am constrained by physical bounds.'

'I need to go.' This is all too deep for me. Besides, the cake has turned to mould and smells funky.

'Indeed. Next time I shall remove the heat from the equation. Until next we meet.'

'Until we do.' Both the cake and Caitlin are gone. Penny presses a finger to her lips. Turns her head with purpose. 'Twitch has met with Jane. Preliminary data implicates you in the pandemic.'

Fuck, and not the fun kind. 'Are you nuts?' Hold tight, Talise, shit's coming and you're the fan.

Penny turns one foot my way. 'How much of your past do you remember? Do you have any idea how long you have worked for Vetrurn?'

My forehead is a mass of wrinkles. 'Six years.' Best guess.

'Four.' She faces me. The datacorder in her hand glows through her skin. She's receiving data but I can't detect the stream. I can't locate any streams in here? How is it possible! 'You went dark for a few days, which in itself is not unusual. Then a couple of weeks later your body turns up with a pair of Bangers on Quayside. Do you remember where you go when you go dark?' She's relaxed, like a cobra.

'Wish I did.' Honest, I do.' My phone chirps. I shrug. 'There are gaps in my memory. I go out and I wake up with new tits and arse.'

'What happened to your phone?' She folds her hands and spaces her feet a hip-width apart.

'I panicked and flushed it.' Probably stuck in a pile of poo.

'Hm. Pity.' Penny taps her palm with her middle finger. 'I would have liked to explore the tech. The code you printed out had a profound effect on Twitch but no one else. Rickets couldn't see anything on the paper. We scanned him, he had absolutely no mental response.'

'Does he remember being tested?' The equipment trolley bumps against the wall.

'Easy, Talise. Rickets is more aware of the Cloud Rings than you were. Twitch was clueless until we scanned him. As for you, well, what's going on in your head is a mystery to us all.' Her bionic eye focusses on me.

'Nothing much. Poking about with a few things here and there.' A whole pile of stuff you ain't getting to hack. 'What are we going to do about the virus? I mean, we have the vaccine, shouldn't we get this out in the wild?'

'On it. We were working on a vaccine based on your research.' Does she ever blink?

'My research?' Which one I wonder?

'Base blocks, remember?' Penny inclines her head, her hair slips over her shoulder.

Something explodes in my brain. Sums, equations and formulae, chemical compounds spinning, twisting, unravelling into neat little blocks. Lego for scientists. 'No idea.'

'Hm. Pity.' Penny makes a loose fist, opens it and steeples her fingers. Her datacorder beeps.

'Is "hm" your favourite new word?'

Penny blinks. 'Sorry, I have much to think about.'

'Anything you want to share? A problem halved and all that... I might be able to help.' The blocks in my head are lining up in colours, protein compounds, strands of DNA. I see the base, a slither of genetic code, too small to be of consequence. It splits and inverts itself, the two halves snug back-to-back.

Her lips move but I can't hear what she's saying. Psychedelia erupts in my head, a river of rainbows awakening the past. 'Talise?'

'D10.'

'Talise!' Penny squawks.

'D10 is an inverted thread of the old Sars-Cov.'

'TALISE!'

Fuck. 'Present.' Must stop switching off, my brain is not cut out for duplicity, let alone multiplicity. 'They've activated the pre-unification STD.'

'Pre-unification! Have you lost it completely?' She half-turns away

'I've not been entirely honest.' My shoes need cleaning. Medics run from door to door chasing alarm bells through the maze to the operating theatre.

Penny's palm lights up like Christmas. 'I have to go. Rickets.' The squeak of her departure fades down the corridor.

I need air.

As a Cloud

Vetrurn shrinks in the rear-view mirror. Chaos and madness, my best contribution. More questions will come my way than I want to answer or am willing to. A ReGen news camera drones by on the way to soil another innocent life. A left turn leads me into town, the next right will take me down the main strip. Not sure where I'm going: out, not out-out, just out.

The bright lights of Brompton, where it always rains, prop a dull sky. I'll make it all go away soon. But first some cake and coffee. The car flows a data-stream, Pacman eating power pills. Traffic is the usual nothing: car, car, truck, car, car, bus that no one will get on or off. The car splashes along the gutter and mounts the kerb before splashing back down. I grab my coat and make for the Coffee Grinder.

An old lady drags her dripping-wet dog along the pavement as it tries to squeeze out a turd. She mutters under her breath and finds something more interesting across the street. A mother and child are dashing for the comfort of the shop and beat me to the door. I'm assaulted by the bitter burn of fresh coffee swirled with sugared cupcakes and pastries.

The mother is pointing at the chocolate nightmare, a chocolate cake with three different types of chocolate half-melted in the centre under a mountain of chocolate frosting served with a mug of chocolate sludge. She takes two of each and heads for a booth. The waitress moves with planned steps as though the floor is lava. 'Mo not in?' My question is met with a vague

275

expression: someone forgot to put the batteries in this girl. 'Mo the manager?'

'You want manager?' She drops her cloth on the counter, about to go on a quest.

'No, no, I just wondered if he was in.' I scan the treasure trove of artery-hardening delights.

'You want order?' The badge on her uniform says Polish. She doesn't look it though her perfume is ReGen. 'One with mocha.' I point at the chocolate death cake.

'You sit, I bring.' She holds out the card reader. I tap and go, whatever happened to money? She wipes the device with sanitiser and places it exactly where it was.

Weaving my way across the room I can't help but notice how neat the tables and chairs are, perfect rows, straight lines as though mapped on graph paper. I slip my coat off my back and dump it on a chair. The water drips onto the dustless floor, not a mop streak in sight.

A data stream rises from the mother's phone, the child's too: both of them are playing MyTown. At least there are a couple of familiar faces. Two boys from ReGen are jabbering loud enough to be heard.

I'm listening.

'Was your department affected by the data breach?' Blondie puffs his fringe from his eyes.

Ginge shakes his head. 'Nah. Didn't think anyone was. Last I heard it was a glitch.' His eyes never leave his phone.

'No, the big Eastern bird in personnel says they got away with a whole load of research stuff. At first they suspected the Vetrurn team, but a load of theirs was taken too.' Blondie licks up his cappuccino moustache. 'Thing is,' Ginge eyes the room, 'it was internal. The breach was on the second-floor stack. Right outside of the Vetrurn labs.'

'That's restricted.' Blondie is engaged now. The two boys meet up in-game and go for a walk through MyTown. "Ere, you tried the new cop NPCs?'

'No, what they like?' Ginge slides his empty cup across the table. `The boys put their phones on the table next to each other. The game world expands across them. 'This one is the dirty cop,' he taps the screen. 'He'll do jobs for you in return for favours, all of which end in The BooBee Bar. The other is funny, got a twitchy face. You never know if he's pulling a fast one or can't help himself. I found him hanging about in some alley, chatting' to a tramp with a shopping trolley. He was standing there for ages, total dick.'

Blondie sighs, 'That it? No guns, no gangs, no drugs?'

'It's only an age-twelve game, restrictions and all that.' Ginge grabs his phone. The screen flashes white, a quick strobe. He blanks out, blinks and leaves.

'Hang on.' Blondie throws the dregs of his drink down his throat and goes after his mate. His phone flashes too. No chirp. He follows his mate into the rain keeping three steps behind, a proper royal pair.

My mind is whirring like crazy. Sugar overload, couldn't have eaten the chocolate monster any quicker if I'd shoved it in sideways. Mother and child eat with one hand and game with the other, digesting the digital world in their hands. Their data rises to the ether, a string of ones and zeros interspersed with hex breaks. Watching it all, taking notes, I open a synapse to Caitlin.

'Hi Talise.' Caitlin pixels into view.

The Coffee Grinder goes digital, a detailed colourby-numbers. Caitlin is in a lab coat, her red hair writhes. A door opens in my soul and I welcome her in. We were friends. She introduced me to Wilson as he cut up victims of crime in ReSyk before consigning them to the meat grinder. Wilson was such a geek, a master of emotional detachment. He said it was necessary to keep the images of his work out of his head. Who'd want to see dead people all the time? No matter, I love him anyway, even now he's gone. He always liked my lips, said he could never get enough. Never got to say goodbye. No last kiss. No nothing.

'Did you want me?' Caitlin taps her ruby slippers. Which wicked witch is she, East or West?

'Sorry, was thinking.' Thoughts from a strongbox.

'Anything you want to share?' She inclines her head, those verdant eyes glitter with stars.

'Old things. Previous life. Moved on.' Another lie. 'The game,' I point to where the pixelated mother and child sit in an alternate reality, 'how does it work?' Confirmation, please.

'Same as every other app on any device.' Caitlin drills her toe into the imaginary floor.

'Go on, enlighten me.' The chair pushes into my back.

'All apps are connected. Data tracking. MyTown, the game, uses the collected data to control its players. What people feared before the Unification became

278

reality.' Caitlin pulls a recliner out of nowhere and lays on it.

'That was ninety years ago! The war only lasted a matter of days.' No one exists who remembers it, the last survivor died a decade ago.

'Orchestrated. It was all planned to near perfection. They knew what they were doing, even then.' A cup of tea appears in her hand. She dunks a biscuit in and bites off the drooping edge. 'Over a century of planning. Famine, war and disease, all of it was them.'

'Them who?' The datacorder pulls in my pocket. I take it out and start the game. Caitlin turns her face to me.

'*They* is all *they* have ever been known as. Generation after generation building towards the end game - total control. You're a part of it, as am I. Only... only we were not supposed to know. The scanner broke you, or fixed you, depending on your viewpoint.'

'I get that. Is there any going back?' I want a biscuit now, but I need coffee to dunk it in. The game beeps for attention. Press, swipe, press and press again, my avatar fetches a coffee.

'You killed your body. You are a construct. The finest woven flesh and code.' Her words are code, the real Caitlin was a loving hug. She was not meant to die. Someone caused it. Hope it wasn't me.

'I know. I've been recycled. A piece of me might be in this coffee cup now.' The Polish girl, caked in numbers, intrudes with a refill and some plastic-wrapped biscuits. A crumb of paradise.

Caitlin smiles. 'No, you are part of the goop swirling around in the vats beneath ReGen. Your skeleton is now living in your old apartment with a new skin. Would you like to see?' She turns her hand over: a high-definition projection of an unremarkable mousy-haired girl stands in her palm. 'She has no idea she is artificial. She has a back story she will never question. Her future, however, is to be determined by the player of her avatar. She will eat, sleep, shop, work and play whatever the gamers decide. She will never know what true existence is. She is part of the Cloud.'

'How did you die, Caitlin?'

'I was "disappeared". All records indicate mental instabilities leading to a sudden absence.' She finishes her tea and summons cake, white with a glitter frosting.

'Like Wilson. He disappeared. I suspect Rickets.' The biscuits fly into the air as I yank the packet apart. 'Bastard!'

'Rickets... Records indicate otherwise. Rickets was offline when Wilson went to ReSyk.'

'ReSyk? I was at ReSyk when he vanished, I would have seen his tags on the system.'

'There are two systems. Both Wilson and Twitch went through R&D on the same day.'

'Twitch was in service before Wilson died. Why was he in R&D?'

'He got his new brain installed. It is also the day Jane Clark came in.' Caitlin licks the frosting, no sense of joy on her face.

'Upgrade. He was a construct all along!' This is too much.

'Detective Reece, aka Twitch, served out of The Labyrinth. Deceased ten years now, was a candidate for the Mind Cloud.' Caitlin's tone is flat. I had an autistic brother who spoke the same way. Stated the facts, no empathy.

'I need to get some space, process all this shit.' Somewhere quiet.

'I'll leave you to it.' She stares right into me. 'I've sifted all the data you stole. All labelled and archived. You can access it in your memory under "The Truth is Out There".' Caitlin blinks out.

The world returns to normal. Mother and child are still playing games. The barista is cleaning the coffee machine with so much gusto she's managed to rouse a bead of sweat on her wrinkle-free forehead. The cappuccino in my hand steams chocolate up my nose. Polish girl is not one for the bean stencil; the pattern on the foam is clumsy, a pair of of shoes. My eye is drawn to her. She nods toward the door. Putting my cup on the table I grab my coat and heed the advice written on my drink.

RUN.

Confessional

Alleys are peculiar places, even on the best side of town. This one is clean, not street clean, pristine-clean. New. I might well be the first person to ever step on its pale grey flags. No graffiti, no balls scrawled on the walls, no posters. It scares me. My heart pounds, I run. Feet smack on the rain-soaked pavement, splashing water up my legs. Passing painted doorways, each with a single grey step and uniform grey door. A cat sitting on a wall licks its paws, rain runs from its sleeked coat. Our eyes lock, I see the data flow up from it. My hand is around its throat hurling it to the ground. The head breaks open revealing the mechanical brain. I stamp again and again, not stopping until the lights in its eyes go out. How many other cameras are there? Are *They* watching or are *They* just inside my head?

Faster and faster. I want to run. Coffee and cake lump in my throat, the acid burns coming up and going down. Don't taste so good the second time around. Kitty litter fizzles in the rain. I move on, chest burning. These new boobs are way too active. Wrapping my arms over my chest I pull them close. Rain patters on my plastic mac, my breath billows my lungs.

Back streets all appear the same, in the movies at least. Here there are no cardboard boxes to charge through or litter drifting down the gutter. These streets are clean. So clean. The urge to flee pulls me, draws me, woos me. The call is undeniable, relentless, demanding. Hurdling a low wall, ducking right, sliding left, I spill over an old stone wall and feel a peace descend.

My heart slows with each breath. Breathe in, minus a beat, breath out, minus two, and so it goes until I'm at rest. Smeared with dirt, I let the rain baptise me until I'm clean through to my soul.

A hand extends toward me: the pink palm aged by heartbreak and care. 'Come,' she says, her voice on the deep side, a well of secrets. My head whistles. She glances over her shoulder at me; her mouth moves but I can't hear what she's saying. She steps aside beneath a stone archway braced by ancient timbers. The rain cannot get us here. Here all is quiet. Here she scans me.

A synaptic chain breaks. The third brain comes online.

'Timms.' The name comes out of me. My voice is deep, male, seasoned with deprivation.

'Sir.' She walks behind me and grates the black iron bolt across the sacred oak doors.

'Are the reports available?' The voice again.

'All is well.' Timms selects a Bible from a pile, passes it to me, it weighs heavy in my hand. 'Results are positive,' she continues as though I'm not here. 'Uptake is high, the latest game update has boosted sales.' Head bowed, she clasps her hands behind her back. The book is open at Revelations 9:21. I rotate it 90 degrees. The words fall to the bottom of the page and form a graph. A growing trend of drug sales, sex, and gang crime. Millions of dollars. I never knew Brompton had so much money.

'Local trends are better than expected. What is the conversion rate?' My screams go unheard. Does the voice know about me and Caitlin?

'We're on a twenty-two percent incline. Projections depict a five-point growth this quarter. Rising to seven over the next two.' Timms keeps her face down, subservient.

'Ahead of implant growth! The signs are encouraging. Prep Ms Clark.' Timms lifts her head. 'I have a better idea, I'll go unannounced. Compel our wayward soul to comply with his handler. I will deal with them both there.'

'It will be done.' Timms inclines her head and turns to leave.

'Timms.' Turning one foot at a time, she faces me.

'Sir?'

'Make sure not to attach a kill order. We do not need any further attention from the Stapletons.'

Timms steadies her voice. 'The mistake will not be repeated.'

'The next mistake will result in more than gender reassignment. Is that clear?' Stop it! Stop! My words clang in my head.

'Sir.' She leaves, penitent.

It takes Timms a full minute to reach the back of the church and close the vestry door. Whoever he is he was careless. He left the door open to the third floor.

The church is empty. My heart leaps to the vaulted roof, thumping back into my chest. The sound of the ocean fills my ears. Caitlin stands in the foaming sand, her face tilted toward a yellow sun. 'It's all in there.' She waves a hand at a glowing portal. Light is being sucked inside.

'Have you been in?' Squinting at the brightness within the portal I see people walking; they look like trees.

'I'm an AI. The choice was never mine. It became part of my realm the instant he revealed himself. Yours too.' Caitlin holds out some coffee and cake. It's one of those melt-in-the-mouth types filled with molten chocolate. The coffee is the Grinder's special double expresso with a hint of chicory.

'Shall we?' We link arms and step through the looking glass.

Rickets

One last Mission?

Every move I make tugs a tube or wire wedged somewhere personal. There are machines in here monitoring the hairs on my ass. They even have one that goes 'bing'. I ease myself up. Last time I tried ended in surgery. Reminds me: must speak to Talise before the world comes crashing down.

'How are you feeling?' Penny appears outa nowhere.

'Jeez, you some kinda ninja? Why do I even ask? Still got a twitch from when you leapt the gurneys at ReSyk.' Couldn't beat her then, sure won't now. Not sure how much of me is left, not that I was ever a real boy. 'Apart from a cardiac arrest, I'm doing OK.'

'You look like shit. Shit that's improving, but shit all the same.'

If I could, I should smack her ass for that one. 'How bad is it?' Not that it'll matter once I remember how to walk.

'How much do you remember?' Penny taps a few screens; a lottery of numbers flash up.

'No alarms? So I'm fit to go. Just point me in the direction of my pants and I'm outa your way.' Here's hoping.

'What do you remember? There are no treats until you tell.' Her smile is genuine, as is most of her.

'Ms Clark. I was with Jane, Twitch's ex. Bitch sent a swarm after me. Shot me to crap. Lost control. Woke up in here, wherever here is?'

'This is the Vetrurn Medical Facility. You crashed right outside the gate. You have... Your injuries are significant. We had to replace your legs, so you will have no problem kicking down doors now. We also replaced your right hand as far as the elbow. It makes the connections easier, and more comfortable for you. You are on a high dose of immuno-suppressants, and pain control which you can administer through the datacorder in your new hand. No leaving it behind this time.' She smiles again.

Can't tell if I'm angry, sad, or plain pissed-off.

'So I'm a cyborg now. Can I run fast, leap tall buildings in a single bound?' She resists a laugh. 'Does it all come with a spandex suit? Tell me it's not animated?'

'It's not animated.'

'So I'm fit to go?'

'You have a date? I hope it goes better than your last one.' Penny gives the drip-feed a loving squeeze and leaves me to my thoughts.

Clock on the wall ticks away the dullness. White walls everywhere. Why are hospitals all white, no matter what they treat? They should colour-code them, at least then I'd know if I'd gone nuts.

The new arm buzzes. I turn my palm and an image appears in the skin like a video tattoo. 'Hey Twitch.'

'Hi Rickets. Heard you were pretty messed up. How are they treating you?' There's blue sky behind him, must be outa town.

'Nothing hurts.' I make a face, not sure how it looks from the other end. 'Got some new legs and an arm. They're just like the old ones but with less hair.' I breathe a laugh. 'If it all goes ass up I can go back to modelling stockings.' His turn to laugh now.

289

'I've been playing MyTown. Found you in it, gun for hire.' Twitch twitches.

'Have you found yourself yet? Try on Baker and Rye.' Guess programmers ain't so familiar with the real world, I coulda named these streets better. 'We're good cop, bad cop.' Another laugh: in a better life we could have been friends. 'Do me a solid, will ya? Log in to the game and see if you can send me somewhere.'

'Where?' His eyes dart around like he's wired. Must be opening the game on his datacorder, a smart move.

'Dunno. How about ReGen? Could pay your ex a visit. I'm overdue at the office.' Twitch doesn't flinch. Not so much as an eyelash.

'You want to risk going back there so soon?' His tone softens. 'She'll kill you this time for sure.'

'Most likely. But I won't go down without a fight.' Unless she asks nicely. 'Was it something I said?' Twitch can't keep the smile from his face.

'Something I thought you might be thinking.' His smile is infectious, like his ex.

'Smart ass.'

'Okay, you got an assignment to the ReGen Tower Complex. You have a meeting in Area 51. The job is called "Bermuda Triangle", so don't go disappearing on us.'

'I won't, thanks.' Might not be telling the absolute truth. 'I'm gonna hang and see if I can get these new legs to work.'

'The military ones work straight out the box. They link in through some cyber shit. Penny did explain but she lost me in all the big words.' Twitch sounds confident.

'Know what you mean. They all talk tech, still think it's a smokescreen. They just don't want us to understand cos they love the god status too much.' 'Okay, you take it easy and don't get up to any shit.' 'You know me, Twitch.' I flash a grin.

'Exactly. You ape.' The image goes dark, the skin returns to normal, complete with scars.

Think. Think, think. Talise pops into my head. Stretching out my hand I fire up MyTown. Deckard, my avatar, slides up on the screen, pokes his fedora up on his brow and lights a stogie. The green button flashes to go, so I press and he's gone. A few taps in the settings and I have the map the right way round to match the real world. Things start happening at my whim. It all happens at the speed of thought.

Deckard enters the coffee shop, orders his take-out and waits. The waitress with blue hair scoots across the shop with a carry-out bag. A speech balloon pops open. I type a message in the chat bubble. The text converts to a QR code. Send and log out.

Time to get my ass in gear. The hand works the same as before, better in fact, no aches, no tight tendons. The blankets slide to the floor. I have more strength, gonna have to watch the chokehold. Laughing hurts. The datacorder in my palm pulses and the pain subsides. Staring at my feet I will the toes to wiggle. This little piggy, that little piggy, fat little piggy. Great, now I want bacon. Flex and bend, the feet are good to go. For no reason I close my eyes and swing my legs around, the cold floor caresses my soles. Standing. Wobbling, falling.

What the fuck?

The legs lock, preventing me from face-planting. They pull me up, strong. I feel a superhero landing-test coming on. First, I'll need some clothes. This hospital gown is blowing a gale on my shiny white ass. A wardrobe beckons, a couple of metres away, but I can do it. One step, two step, what we got in here? All my shit is clean and pressed. I'm sure my shirt was grey! Damn, I'm a pig.

The gown crumples on the floor. Shuddering, I rub my arms to ward off the breath of the air con. The shirt goes on easy. A quick shake unfurls the pants like a flag, I hold them out and step in. Half mast, zip and done, commando ready for action. Socks and sneakers. Reaching in deep, I grab my coat and hat. The coat swirls about my shoulders, hat snugs on. I'm looking at the man in the mirror. He smiles back and we head out into the wild world.

Wrecking Ball

Every corridor looks the same. White lights, white walls: all is white.

'How do I get outa here?' Palm buzzes. There's a map, simple vectors, crude. I follow most of the prompts. Door after door, hallways and corridors. Stairs I take in twos, threes, whole flights, the legs do it all, soaking up the impact.

Beep, left buzz, right. Push the bar. An alarm screams. Idiot. Rain spatters on my skin, soaks my clean shirt. I tug at my flapping coat to bring it to order. I'm jumping bollards, barriers and cars. Pounding out a beat but my heart is at rest. Breathing is easy; taking the whole damn thing in my stride. The pain will come later when all the drugs wear off, but now, right now, I'm sailing over the barrier and taking the corner where the drones took my life. Those plastic tics and pinstriped shitheads who run them are due some payback. First, some entertainment.

I run and run until...

Quayside is still a shithole; no amount of concrete and glass will make it anything else. The wheels of industry are lubricated with blood. Time to ease up and gather my thoughts. Somewhere near here is a place where the cops stash confiscated vehicles. Or so they say. Beep.

A wall ascends before me, beige. No-one does beige like Brompton. The hand says this is the right place. 'Knock knock.' It rings of steel. My palm flashes, a message reads: "Press palm to the door." Being the obedient boy I am I slap my hand to the wall. 'Open sesame.' The wall rolls back revealing a cavern of wagons and wheeled brutes of every kind. All of them are still in their protective delivery film. I record the data for a later upload. Time to choose my ride. Jeep, truck, personnel carrier, armoured car. Who knew so much metal could be arousing? 'Eeny meeny miny, this bastard bristling with guns.' All this Vetrurn tech in a ReGen lock up! Well, if they ain't going to use it I will.

The armour on my chosen brute is six inches thick. Reminds me of something? No time for fantasies, I grip the handle and the door hisses open. So the hand is a Vetrurn key. Nice. The brute is supposed to have a copilot. The hand of god pulses, the weapons array lights up. Showtime!

The world quakes at the roar of the beast, the doors clang to the concrete in my wake. Holes open in the ground a short way ahead and two Robococks rise to attention from each orifice; I unleash a peckerpunishing load right in their faces. They'll not be bothering anyone again.

The Twin Towers of ReGen hold up the sky. Blue and red lights ascend and descend, damn drones seeding the sky with silver iodide and whatever shit the discorporate They are up to. 'Are there any tunes in this thing?'

'What can I help with today?' Sounds like Siri in a tin hat and boots.

'War tunes. Something old and heavy.' She contemplates. 'Oh. You're simply the best, Siri.' Immigrant Song wails in melody with the snarl of the beast. Thumping the wheel, I bounce along with the rhythm spinning parked cars into traffic like a drunk around a lamppost.

'Next tune.' Army Siri announces. 'Kenny Loggins.'

'Who the fuck is he? No loud stuff.' Pause.

'That's more like it. Dum, dada dum dada dum, b'dum b'dum b'dum. ' I croak out a lyric. 'I've been too long.' Another car careens through the traffic. 'Loose, from the noose.' The Towers are closing in. 'Kept me hanging.' I'm so out of tune it makes me cringe. The sky is filling with angry birds coming to get this little piggy. Sirens wail: meat wagons, fire trucks, and cops, something's got them all stoked.

A drone buzzes along to my left. 'Tactical responses online,' Siri chimes.

Like a kid playing soldiers, I point two fingers at it and thumb the trigger. 'Pew pew pew.' The drone is vaporised in a flash of light and flames. 'Love this hand. You and me are going to make babies.' I kiss the hand that makes things go boom. Can't help myself.

The road to the south where the sky is blue rolls back in the rearview, the monolith of ReSyk with its pools of melted flesh yaws from the earth to insult the sky. Time for a shortcut.

The fence was never going to be an issue. Neither were the canopy supports tumbling to the tarmac in a hail of marbled rubble. For shits and giggles, I crash through the corner of the main structure, adding muchneeded ventilation to the shared autopsy space. Hazmats run in all directions. I guess they want to get away from the nasty green smoke pouring outa the hole in the wall. The building surrenders. The side collapses

295

like an old hag's teeth falling from fetid gums. ReSyk bites the dust.

Shall I, shan't I? The Towers are in range. Is it a decision? To be or not to be? Not. 'Eat my shit, assholes. Fire in the hole?' The closing distance in a straight line is only eight hundred metres, or one point two miles by the scenic route. 'Short cut!' The tank skews off the road through a perimeter fence, nimble for such a big girl. In all the excitement I missed the fireworks. A second round chases down the first, stirring up the hornets' nest. The sky lights up red, a true delight. Tactical displays go into overdrive with red dots descending like Space Invaders.

'A large swarm of drones is heading towards our location.' Siri breaks the mood.

'Can they get through to us?'

'Negative. Scans indicate small projectiles with insufficient velocity to penetrate the shields. I would suggest we allow them to close in and then deploy a localised stun charge.'

'A what and a what and do what?'

'Allow them- '

'Yeah, yeah, yeah. Do it. We're storming the Bastille.' No use waiting for a response, she has access to all kinds of data so she can look it up herself. 'Hi-ho Silver, away!' The engines roar so loud I can't hear the fireworks outside. Even the sound of breaking glass and shattering brick happens in silence. ReGen burns.

Light spills from some kinda security centre up ahead, bodies, people rolling out the welcome mat. Drones pepper the shields with impotent shot, hundreds of them, a swarm of midges desperate for blood. The first security hut collapses. Megan: great name for a tank, ample derriere. 'Shake that ass girl.' Swing to the left, swing to the right, those security boys scatter. 'Pew pew.' Two more for ReSyk. Oh, I forgot, they closed down. Guess they'll just have to rot the oldfashioned way.

'Pulse in three,' Siri chimes.

'What?'

'Two.'

'What'd you say?'

'Pulse.'

The wave is visible on the cameras. Every last drone falls dead. Do you know what you feel when a fiftytonne tank runs over a swarm of drones? Nothing, most pleasing indeed. One more barricade. They can't have thought this through: the security is minimal, a couple of guys with pop guns. Where's the armoured detail? This is ReGen's head office, the centre of all their secret shit, and no welcome party. Guess I'll have to party all by myself.

'Boom bitches!' The Great Glass Elevator comes crashing down filled with Vermicious Knids. Not everyone got my memo of pending doom. Glass rains from the sky, beautiful jewels glittering in the fire's glow. Some people are too stupid to be allowed out on their own. A guard watches a huge sheet of death coming right for him, or at least he was watching... Perhaps I should have waited for home time? Nah, they're all constructs: the real them died long ago, only no one told them. Still, that's gotta hurt, if only for a second.

'More incoming. Police helicopter and news drones.' 'Siri, is there any good news?'

'Your data file is ready for upload. It will happen precisely-'

'Is it on every outlet?'

'It is. The data is secured for synchronised release.'

'Okay.' I take the tank into the lobby and spin the turret toward the entrance. 'What kinda carry-outs do we have?' The rear wall of the tank hisses open. Guns, grenades, and all kinds of boom-boom toys. My day keeps getting better all the time. I grab some gear, cloak myself with meaty grenades, and open the door.

My Hometown

The whole world has gone to shit. Half the ceiling is on the floor, the rest is hanging in shreds. Caterwauling alarms bleat and flash over the glass-shard carpet. Injured workers shuffle through coughs of smoke, bloodied and bewildered, guided by the game. More sirens, this time with guns.

The hand pulses. Siri sends a map through the dead zone. The palm-screen prompts for a reply. My response is a staccato set of instructions sealed with a kiss. Gonna miss the girl, the ride was brief but full of happy memories.

Across the chaotic foyer and I descend the highway to hell, where ReGen's dark soul lurks. Behind me Siri obeys my final orders, the soft boom of cannon fire heralding the reckoning. The call to arms is answered by the angry buzz of a drone swarm. Armageddon ensues. The red beady eyes of the cameras stare at my blazing magnum spitting hate-fuelled lead. I toss a muti-blast grenade back up the stairs and plunge into the bowels of the beast

Steel groans and separates from the concrete, walls come tumbling down. The stairwell collapses. The grenade goes off again - and again, each blast building on the last until all is history.

Two more flights and all is well. Been a while since I was down here. Last time was for... how did she put it? Adjustment. They said my Cloud Ring was out of sync, data anomalies and such. Don't remember much of it, too much Sparkle. But I do remember these corridors. Resistance was futile: they got me on a slab and probed. When I came to I was someone else.

On a map of the country, Brompton doesn't exist. Nothing but sand, scrub, and heat. On all the maps of Brompton, this place doesn't exist, Nothing but tar, concrete, and transmission masts. Of course, it exists. Place is off the grid because what happens here is both immoral and illegal. There are still a few politicians not on ReGen's payroll, but they'll be adjusted too. ReGen is inevitable.

The whole process is autonomous. No objection, no protests. No nothin'. The whole damn thing is a marvel of modern technology. All those bodies shipped in from all over the world, victims of Pnu-90. Not quite dead, suspended in stasis. With so many corpses no one questioned it. It was easier than digging graves. ReGen built ReSyk, a safe way to dispose of the infected, except they weren't dead, were they? Stripped to the bone and turned into goop. Then pumped over here, to the weaving rooms.

So neat, the way the flesh is woven onto the bones, fixed to high-tensile silicone tendons. Electronic brains in a protective shell mimicking the real thing. At the heart of it all Mind Cloud, controlling every impulse, ensuring right behaviour. Early ones like mine were not so good.

The weaving rooms are full. There's a guy on the loom having a brain implant. He's series four. MyTown is pre-installed so he won't even know he's playing.

I pull the pin and toss. The grenade bounces across the room. Tick tick, the tiny white light flashes faster and faster until... They broke the mould when they made that one. Fire guts the room, setting off the extinguishers. Even in the ass-end of nowhere, there's no reprieve from the rain.

The whole place is full of flesh printers, modelling lives for ReGen to do as they wish with them. Each one is fitted with a transceiver: they'll never have a problem with phone signals. 'I've done it before, I can do it again.' Pause, pull the pin. Tick tick tick. Another grenade, another body receives salvation, another soulless one laid to rest.

Boom.

The building is closing in behind me. Walls tumble. Ceilings collapse, sirens, alarms, flashing lights. Some party this turned out to be. By the time I reach the end of the corridor the production area is under rubble. Goop is seeping through the collapsing concrete. How many people got melted down to make the shit is beyond counting. My own hacker had problems enough getting through the firewalls, but what she found is priceless. When this fight is over the whole world will know the truth. Perhaps ReGen will be shut down for its immoral practices, although my money is on acquittal. So many fingers in so many pies, and they all taste of dirt.

On another day in another life, perhaps they'll add some guards to protect all their crap, but not today. Today all the soldiers belong to the other side. Cops won't enter the main site. The fire brigade will, as will the ambulances, but where will the dead go now? I guess all the boys like me will get back to some real work, the way Twitch and Joel do. Used to think they were nuts doing it the old way, cutting up Johns and Janes, filing reports and doing cop stuff.

I used to be a cop before They killed me and put me through a flesh weaver. The real me was smart, although not smart enough to avoid the corporate takeover of the department. Powerless to stop the formation of Brompton, the city of the damned. The corporation suppressed our souls and bound us in gold, locked us all inside our heads. Bastards. I bounce a couple more grenades into the ruins and bring the upper floors low.

The towers were never designed for this type of punishment. The foundations groan, cracks open in the deepest dark. A hiss of gas. Time to put these new legs to use. I turn, and tossing grenades over my shoulder I bang the steel door shut. Muffled thuds of an imploding world fall in concussive succession. Why I stand and listen to my potential burial is beyond me, but a job worth doing has to be seen through to the end. The noise will not stop, not yet.

Run Forrest Run.

The lifts are out so I start the climb. Up the stairs. Up to the atmosphere. Up where the air is clear.

This is Tower 2. Research and residential. One occupant. Round and round and up we go. Floor 48, 49... 50. Floor 51. Executive suite. Something the resident is not - sweet.

Brushing the dust from my raincoat, I wander over to the viewing area. 'Well, well, who'da thought it.' The sun is breaking through the cloud over Quayside, spangling on the water. Shadows strafe the main road. Drones, like a murder of crows, blacken the sky, dropping their payloads of silver iodide seeding the clouds. Now there's something you don't see every day. The city sky ignites. Brief bursts of energy cutting down the antennae, exposing the secret world of ReGen.

What'll happen to those in the game as the signals die is anyone's guess, but will anyone care? So much death. Speaking of which, I have an appointment to keep. Should I have let Twitch and Penny in on my intentions?

Nah, fuck 'em all.

Twitch

Earlier

'Mind telling me why you're here?' Jane lights a cigarette from an old Zippo, the loose flame engulfs the tip.

'Nice place you have here. You always did like ivory towers.' The whole apartment is spotless to the point of clinical. 'I got a message, like the old days, only-'

'Not from me,' Jane shrugs, and scooping up a sizeable brandy glass she swills the spirit like a pro.

'A mutual friend.' The coffee is on so I help myself. The service here sucks, the only thing that does. 'I'm helping with an investigation. In truth, our investigations have collided. See-' I point to the window.

'Like I could give a shit.' She drops into a chair and squirms her arse into the soft leather. Something outside rumbles loud enough to quake this penthouse prison. Drones fall like dust from the sky. Down below, people scatter from the opposite tower. Smoke billows from the middle floors. Fire rages in angry bursts of yellow against the crystal glass of the Emerald City. 'Wicked witch ain't in that one?'

'Something up?' Jane uncrosses her slender legs and makes to rise.

'Nah, looks like a fire drill.' I mooch over to the fridge for milk: nothing but soya shit and almond scum. Pass. Black is fine.

'So, what part of your tiny world has spun out of control? Run out of bullets? Too many corpses in the mortuary?' Smug bitch.

'No, we found Talise's killer.' The glass pauses on her lips. 'Some interesting stuff turned up at a warehouse too. Including some of your old magic potions.' Her eyes lock on the vials I put on the glass coffee table.

'Could be anything. Most likely piss, knowing you.' Jane smiles into the glass, the brandy wets her lips. She sits the drink next to the vials.

There were days when I liked her. Never loved her, there was always a barrier: the programme. She stares at the vials. Do they stare back? Do they have any power over her? 'You might like the one with the green stopper.' Naughty me.

'Why's that? Will it turn you into a handsome prince?' She takes more of the drink than she intended and coughs her heart out.

'No. Won't make you likeable either, but it will remove the after-effects of XG12, remove those ugly black veins.' Jane waves a hand, I wave back. She wants a drink. 'You know where it is.' I gesture to the kitchen.

'Asshole.' She splutters her way across the apartment and snatches the faucet on. Red or green? My brain's gone all fuzzy, the liquid is a tasteless mixer. Leaning back with a coffee in hand I examine the ivory chess pieces on the table. She returns, red-faced, her hair stuck to the moisture on her face.

'Did the earth move for you?' I dance the queen across the etched playing space.

'Shithead, never were one to help a lady.' She closes her hand over the brandy glass, lifting it in her claw.

'Don't know any, though Penny can be quite charming.'

'Ugh.' She makes a slug face. For the first time, I see the crow's feet tugging at her eyes and the wrinkles that furrow her brow when she thinks.

'Brandy off?'

'Brandy's fine. The thought of the uppity Vetrurn bitch turns my stomach.' Jane tips the glass up, downing the dark liquor, and goes in search of another. 'What's the point of this charade? You and I are history. You may as well leave me and go play with your friends.'

Black smoke underscores the grey heavens: they must be burning rubber next door. Flames lick up to the higher floors blackening the windows with their sooty tongues. Drones are swarming again, gathering like crows in a murderous pact. Fires erupt across the upperlevel, spewing glass. The antenna on the top of the building is hit. There's a brief thought before gravity demands its attention and the whole game comes crashing down. The drones tumble from the sky.

'Found a new friend?' Jane nods at the chess piece in my hand. 'Should I leave you alone together?' She drops into her seat and warms the fresh glass in her hands.

'Oh this,' I place the bishop next to the queen and pick up a king, 'just admiring it.' I shrug. 'Do you remember how we met?'

'Works do. You were on security duty. Why?' Her eyes narrow over the glass. She hesitates before taking a sip.

'Not true. Just a story put into your subroutines.'

'What the fuck are you talking about? Subroutines!' She laughs, it too isn't real.

'You're not what you think you are.' My turn to laugh. 'All this time. Tell me,' the veins on her neck darken, 'do you remember your last meeting with Rickets, before you sent the drones out to kill him?' 'Where's this all going? I don't have to listen to your conspiracist shit.' She throws the drink down her throat and stands, arms wavering.

'Steady.' She always was top-heavy.

'Rickets came to threaten me. I showed him who I was, is all. Look where I live.' Arms out, she staggers.

'King of the world,' I snort. An explosion tears a hole in the proceedings. Jane stumbles, falls. The coffee table shatters beneath her. I manage to save the bishop before the doorbell rings. 'You just lay there. Leave it to me, as always.' We're strangers now, more so than when we were partners. Jane grumbles about my lack of care while I go answer the door.

'Hi.' Talise, up on her toes, peers around me. 'That Jane Clark?'

'Yup.'

She ducks under my arm and fetches herself a drink from the kitchen.

'Hey asshole, fetch me some napkins.' Nobody jumps to the bitch's bark, not anymore.

'Did you receive a code too?' Talise pours a torrent of milk into a mug and rifles through the cupboards.

'Yup.' Turning my back to Talise, I lean against the counter. The sky is a mix of cloud and roiling smoke. Good to see a change in the outlook.

'I said-' Jane growls.

'We heard,' we reply in unison. A rescue chopper descends past the window.

'What's up with you two? I'll have you two in for processing and all you know-' Jane crunches over the broken glass.

'Will be undone.' There's an edge to our voices.

'How... No... It's not possible.' Jane backs into the kitchen space, blood streaking her blonde hair. She wipes her cheek with a napkin, her eyes flicking between me and Talise.

'You look well, Jane. Apart from the wounds of course.' I hear the voice in my head but Talise is speaking. 'I'd like to go over the reports.' Jane freezes. Her eyes flick to a dark-wood sideboard beneath the window.

My feet take me across the room. A hand, my hand, reaches out to open a drawer. A Filofax sits in the centre of the drawer surrounded by space. The thick book sits heavy in my hand. In a few steps I'm back at the counter with the Filofax open before us. The digital paper fills with statistics and graphs. Talise takes it; the pages reflect in her eyes and add lustre to those lips.

For a moment I'm in an ice-cream parlour sharing a tall green sundae with the cold bite of toothpaste. Our spoons fight for the cold cream. There is laughter, smiles, and glistening lips. I lean in and taste the peppermint frost.

'You've lost control, Miss Clark. You've been distracted by the Bishop and Rickets and you've let your grasp slip on your division. What have you to say in your defence?' Talise closes Filofax in a wisp of smoke.

'Tech is on course. The city is eighty per cent recycled, and all of those citizens are fully integrated into the Cloud,' Jane blurts in bursts of saliva. 'The game is ready for Alpha deployment into The Smoke via the current cellular network. They won't even notice anything has changed. ReSyk Two is at twenty-five per cent capacity.'

'Adequate at best.' Talise drums her fingers on the counter, her head lowered. 'Your performance has been waning. Your professionalism is wanting. What has become of the Jane we made? You were flawless, your algorithms were all in sync with the data. Now you are way off your baseline.' The drumming stops.

'I am not out of line.' The black veins race up Jane's neck forming a cancerous web. 'I am not responsible for this debacle. Twitch is running loco, he's not responding to MyTown quests.'

'No, he was never yours to command. He is our tool. Our eyes in the community. Your guardian. Tell me, Miss Clark, whenever Twitch came in, did you once update his core?' Talise raises her head, eyes fixed on Jane.

Thunder and earthquakes rock the world. The whole building trembles. Lights flicker, alarms wail, and for a breath there is darkness. Emergency systems activate, bringing it all back online. Jane is pinned against the wall, her feet dangling above the black-tiled floor.

'Talise.' Her hand tightens, Jane swallows against the pressure. 'Talise!' My hand closes around hers. Jane's face is black. I lean in close, whispering, 'Peppermint.' Jane drops to the floor, her breath a series of rasps.

'Wilson?' Those lips speak my secret name.

'Peppermint. That's what I used to call you?' The counter digs me in the back as I knock the drinks over the side.

'They put you in Twitch? You were here with me all along.' Her face softens into a smile.

'Who did you get for Christmas?' Two sets of thoughts swirl my emotions like a snow globe.

'Caitlin and *They*.'

'Not... possible. *They* don't exist.' Jane coughs her way to her feet, the veins knotted into a black collar. She rests next to me, her arms braced against the countertop, age scarred into her face. Deep wrinkles map out the deceit and lies. So many she no longer knows any truth.

'They are real enough. *They* are people and *They* are concepts. A clever idea with a fatal flaw.' Talise slips an arm around Jane's waist and leads her over to the window. 'Can you see it?' She sits Jane on the sideboard. 'Olympus has fallen. You have nothing left here. Cosgrove has removed all ReGen tech from The Smoke. All of your thugs have been retired. And you Jane, what of you and this prison?'

'Prison?' Jane strains a smile. 'I have everything. You're the prisoners, you idiot. The Tower is nothing.' Drones continue to fall from the sky, how many are there? A spear of sunlight pierces the grey, alighting on the cathedral. 'I'll show you morons-'

'And how will you do that, Jane. Go on, reach out to the Cloud. Call in the avatars to defend you. No? I can see your data stream. Every thought you have is linked to the Mind Cloud, and me. ' Talise glances over at me, nods toward the door. 'He's here.' Her attention returns to Jane. 'I, Jane, can read it all. They have implanted themselves in my core. But *They* are unaware of what I know. It will not be long before I find them.'

'You know nothing,' Jane spits. 'They can make you think anything. You're a construct, a product. *They* own you.'

The bell rings.

'The cavalry is here.' I step aside to let the road warrior through. 'Been busy?' Guy's a mess.

'Best gig ever! Been a blast, brought the whole house down.' Rickets dusts off his coat and hat. 'There she is. Fuck, you look rough.' He screws up his face as though he tastes shit.

'Got a plan, Rickets?' Talise moves aside.

'I do.' He's one happy guy. 'You need to leave.' Rickets points at the open door. 'A proposal.'

'Rickets. No.' Talise shakes her head. 'You can't.'

'Run Forrest Run.' He pulls a small sphere from his pocket.

'Why would anyone listen to you?' Jane watches the world burn.

'Because I'm holding a thermal detonator.' Rickets snaps his head around. 'Run you fools, run.'

Time slows. Rickets tugs the ring from the detonator, grabs Jane's hand and slips it on her finger. 'Nothing personal, you understand.'

Talise passes me, pulling me out of the room as Rickets shouts, 'Tick, tick TICK.' The

door booms shut.

We run.

Talise

Under the Cloud

No idea where Twitch has gone. Found his datacorder and phone on the desk. No sign of Kid either. Penny is bent over the desk going through the data files: seems Kid was up to something beyond my pay grade. Even Caitlin can't get through the firewall. Mavis is tough.

'You called?' Her red hair ripples, the curls catching the wind like a child grasping at bubbles.

'Have you found Kid?'

'I have. His DNA is most distinct. He sheds skin like a snake.' Caitlin bites into a chocolate cake, scooping up crumbs in her cupped hand.

'Downtown?'

'Last seen heading north, booked two multi-hop tickets.' She finishes the cake and smiles. 'Heading overseas toward the EU.'

'Why the EU?'

'It's as near as you can get to the old Unification War sites. Get too close and the radiation will melt you.' Caitlin twists her toe into the floor. 'So they say.'

'So they say.' Her smile is infectious. 'Keep trying with Mavis.'

'You know me.'

She's gone. Penny unfreezes.

The walk to the desk is a marathon of restraint. Data lines stream in all directions but none can penetrate the walls.

'Something is trying to send information out.' The words escape my mouth before I can stop them. 'He was trying to hack your fancy scanner.' I wave an arm in the general direction in case she's forgotten.

'You're still seeing the traces? Interesting. Kid tried to copy files, but Mavis is following him.' Penny stands tall, puts a finger to her chin. 'I'm curious about something.' She stares at me, full metal jacket.

'What?' Feet in the blocks, ready to bolt.

'When Rickets died, before we brought him back, he uploaded. He was a successful implant, yes?' Penny steps around the desk, a hand in one pocket, the other a motion of thought.

'Yes.' There, said it. 'I got everything. He was fully functional.' Some seriously twisted bollocks in that guy's head.

'Did he give any indication of what he was going to do?' She weaves her way step by step. It only takes four but I feel every one.

'None. His actions were governed by the game. Once enough requests were in for the same thing he got the signal to go. Though...' A half-turn is enough to deflect the heat.

'Go on.' Her arms fold across her chest.

'His actual targets were never in the game. Jane was feeding him intel she was getting from Tech.' Oops.

'Tech?'

'Do you know of *They*?' Best come clean.

'They who?' Those eyebrows go way up.

'*They*. You know how people say, "They say on the internet," meaning they don't know actually know who said it and it may not have been said by anyone real.' My eyebrows are laying siege to my hairline.

'I think I follow.' Penny gives the slightest nod, enough to move her perfect hair.

'Well... er... It's. Bollocks. No wonder they get away with it.' A scream frustrates my throat.

'Is it that hard?' Smile all you like. Sure she means no harm, I just don't know who to trust. Never have.

'The computer.' Bugger, wasn't thinking. Slow down Talise.

'How did you-'

'Can't explain. Roll with it.' I could charm an orchestra with these hand movements.

'You're interfacing direct. How?' One shrug, maybe a second will be more convincing. No.

'OK.' Big breaths, girl. 'Your scanner unlocked my brains. First...' She has such pretty eyes, scanning every bit of me. 'First...' here we go, 'we unlocked an AI, Caitlin.'

'Caitlin, as in our Caitlin who went AWOL?' There's a tear.

'They stripped her down, put her inside my head. Twitch has Wilson.'

'Bastards. Anyone who knew something.' She turns a subtle shade of fury.

'Wilson knew about Jane Clark, and he also knew Rickets was a construct before he joined the Fourth. Originally from Silver Bows over Madison. He has relatives up there, a guy called Ted. I've informed the local sheriff.'

'How did he end up here?' Penny turns and parks her petite arse on the desk.

'They arranged it all. Part three of my brain awoke all by itself, kinda.' Those eyes again. My hands do their magic and the screen shows it all. 'This is me on the run.'

'When you went dark for a day?' Penny folds and unfolds her arms, settles her hands on the desk at her sides.

'Wound up in the cathedral, had a chat with the Bishop. 'Cept it wasn't me.' I raise a hand. 'Another voice comes out of me. I'm hearing everything but have no control. Timms is in with them. She runs the drugs, the church is a front and all the homeless in the area are her people. The homeless are not on the Cloud. Those carts they push around.' Penny nods. 'Shielding. Can't be sure, but I think Timms is up to something. She supplies the carts from out of the area.'

'This is serious.' She's peering at the screen from an odd angle when she suddenly spins around and jabs a manicured finger at it. 'I know these people. They work alongside my father. I have to tell him.'

'No!' My hand fastens on her shoulder. 'No one else. We don't know who they all are.'

'Talise!' Penny's artificial arm hangs limp. Her eye goes dark. 'What are you doing?'

'Help me.'

'It's happening again.' My body is rigid, Penny is in some kung-fu death grip. She's hurting.

'Hello Ms Sutcliffe.' She stares at me, a rabbit in headlights. Trembling. 'You remember me.' A woman with a gravelled voice. 'Stay away from us or you will die. James got too close to the sun, got himself burnt. Don't go the same way.'

'Bastards. Now I know for sure.' Penny fights to her feet. My fingers draw blood. She's quick. My right knee

319

buckles. Her good hand chops across my elbow. My arm folds, she's free. As the ground comes up to greet me, my face is struck and I'm splayed out on the floor. My head is ringing, the lights swirl around. There's weight on my chest, my shoulders are pinned. I hear slapping. My face is hot. It all stops and Penny is screaming from two feet above the floor. She lashes out again and again, but there's no contact. Now I'm in the air and Penny is at my side. She knows more dirty words than I do!

I'm clamped in a tube. Drilling? It all goes dark.

Sentinel

Chocolate brown eyes with milky whites peer at me under a furrowed brow.

'Joel.' Straps resist my wrists.. 'You hit me?'

'Uh-huh.' The matchstick rolls across his plump lips. 'Will again too. Next time I'll forget you're on the same side.'

'I never-'

'Yet you did.' He straightens up, steps aside. Penny strolls around him, her throat bruised. 'Touch her again an'…' She puts a hand on his arm, soothing the beast within. Joel sucks his teeth and skulks over to the control point. Three holographic displays pixel in, a piece of my brain on each one.

'We've isolated code segments to prevent the intrusions from taking over. ReGen has been quite sloppy. Their arrogance has cost them of late.' Penny tilts the table I'm on.

'So I'm safe? I won't be attacking anyone?' Still can't break the bonds, no superpowers yet.

'I'll keep my distance, you never can be too sure. We can remove some code, give you complete freedom.' Penny's eye-camera twitches: the white straps across my chest are bold stripes across her vision. Her head is as static as the noise inside my own. 'Caitlin will not be affected.' She gives me her full GI Joe attention.

'Can you be so confident? We have both been into the third Ring. We can unite with the Cloud.' I don't like this lack of mouth filter. The truth sets you free? Hmm,

I remain a sceptic. Penny's perfect eyes wrinkle at the corners. 'You can tame the code, but don't take it away. We have no idea of its purpose. By all means, have a copy, Caitlin too, I've nothing to hide.' Or at least I hope so.

The displays merge into one, the download is brief, painless.

I feel...

Void.

Twitch

Last to Know?

Early '91. A sad sun slips from the bright sky infested with clouds. Turning off the highway the tyres spit stones at the skittering lizards. The track steepens, pointing the bonnet to the heavens. The radio plays songs muted by a barrier of sadness. The wheels roll onto the summit.

The horizon runs to the farthest point of imagination. I drive straight across the mesa up close to its edge. Eyes shut, I draw a breath and kick the door. The arthritic hinges groan.

The ground is drying out in the warming air, the morning will be a furnace up here. I grind the earth beneath my feet as I stroll around the car and wander to the drop where the world plummets to oblivion. From here the water is still. The reflected clouds are vaporised by the sun before my eyes. Only the past remains.

A new year is born: I never noticed the old one die. Must have whimpered to its grave, but I remember the bang at the end. The door is open on the past. All my memories have returned, along with those of Wilson. Strange kid. Geek with so much knowledge in his head I'll need to enlarge my memory to fit everything in. Maybe it's why I have two brains, to give the boy room to grow. Much has happened; don't understand most things, I'm just a cop. Killed one bad guy, snared another.

Rickets knocked the whole damn wall down, brought Humpty Dumpty to his knees. No wonder he kept his plans to himself. If I'd known what he was going to do, I would've stopped him somehow. Right now, I'm trying to put all the pieces together: the bits I know together with all he knew and what it all means for tomorrow. He uploaded the entire shit show to the internet, assangebuttrue.com. My head spins at the thought. Wilson understands more than me. Jeez, the kid is smart, but I guess you have to be to be a forensic pathologist. I read a book once about some doctor in Britain who cut up over twenty-two thousand bodies in his time. Sure put ReSyk to shame. Speaking of shitholes, the green smoke is still intoxicating the city. Folks are getting sick; we're not immune to Pnu-90, not without the rain. Vetrurn are rolling out the vaccines, sticking pins in everyone passing by.

Shouldn't lose too many more.

Brompton sprawls along the valley basin, you can feel the beast gulping in the fresh air. With the sky clearing there'll be a sunset. The horizon fades to The Smoke in the south. Cosgrove, still in charge as she should be. ReGen won't be bothering her.

Sublime is how it is. The air is warm on the skin. The pink of the engine cooling chimes with the screech of buzzards. Didn't take them long to rise above it all. I'm sure there's a message for us all there.

Brompton looks good from here. The river shines like a string of pearls gathered around an ageing throat. Still some life in the old girl yet.

Datacorder chirps and chirps, a little bird with something to say. Can't stop the sigh escaping as I flip the screen open. The same blue streak. Those lips. I won't be the same anymore.

Think I'll sit awhile, light a stogie, keep an eye out.

Ends.

Thanks.

Thanks for getting this far. I hope you enjoyed Mind Cloud and would consider leaving a review wherever you bought it from.

Mathew.

Printed in Great Britain
by Amazon